Goner

A Novel

ann goethe

ISBN: 0999566806
ISBN 13: 9780999566800

for

Candy and Conrad

and the four little girls in the back seat

"Because this being here amounts to so much, because all this Here and Now, so fleeting, seems to require us and strangely concerns us. Us the most fleeting of all. Just once, everything only for once. Once and no more."

Rilke

"All that we see or seem
Is but a dream within a dream."

Edgar Allen Poe

Prologue

WE ARE THE caretakers of echoes. Our father is dying, blinking and bewildered as a newborn in these last days. Sometimes he is in his boyhood home in the sailor suited days of the early century. With all of life ahead, he cannot find his mother. She will not hear his ravished whispers. Daughters come instead. We too have lost a mother, are calling her. No mother comes. We are the lost children of lost parents passing ourselves in a hall of whispers.

In this story it is March 1980, already deep springtime in South Louisiana. The four sisters have returned home for their father's deathwatch. It is not burdensome work, as he asks little of them. He is ready to go. He is quietly resigned like a traveler whose flight has been slightly delayed, but who has been assured that the wait won't be long. After he is settled in for the night, the four of them sit around the kitchen table telling old stories over again, making one another laugh so hard that they choke on their cigarette smoke. The sisters grew up in a culture where the loudest laughter is heard at wakes and funerals, where sadness is threatening, a fire that must be stomped out before it spreads and becomes dangerous.

It is only when we are all together that we feel complete. There is no one in the world I know as well as I know the three women in this story. No lover, no child could ever be so close, so blood bonded. I create their words for them, just as each sister could write my lines for me. What intimacy would ever match this?

Kate, one of the two brown-eyed middle sisters, stands and ties our mother's apron around her slender hips. She reaches into the freezer for a small can of frozen lemonade. Her thick mass of curly brown hair is clamped at the back of her neck with a broad tortoise shell barrette. She opens the can and spoons out frozen lemonade, measures bourbon into the blender. Rebecca, Elizabeth and I have stopped talking to watch her. Kate wraps ice in a dishtowel and cracks it hard against the counter before shaking it into the blender. She lays the icy towel over the faucet.

They are carrying on. This had been their father's end-of-day ritual. Every evening he made one frozen whiskey sour for their mother. He served it to her in a fancy glass with a cherry. The maraschino juice made patterns through the citron slush: a red sun cooling into a lemony sea, a mother-of-pearl sunrise. Then he would mix a martini for himself, and sit across the coffee table from his wife, perfunctorily reading the newspaper, leaning forward in his chair ready to catch her gaze should she look up from her book. He was the lover and she was the lovee; he lived in their moments, she existed elsewhere. This one-sidedness may not be all that uncommon in marriages. Yet it would unduly influence the choices made by their daughters; it weighed who their lovers would be, and how they loved them. The daughters existed somewhere within the suspension of that parental imbalance.

Their parents were endlessly fascinating to them. They speculated about them and spied on them constantly. Kate was in the habit of hiding herself behind the living room sofa when their parents were expecting guests. She would lie still for hours, soaking in the adult conversation, breathlessly filling her sisters in after the company was gone and their parents in bed. It never occurred to their daughters that the parents might be interested in their lives, or even remotely curious about the daughters' friends, their aspirations. Their parents were the flame and the daughters were the moths. Now the four of them are gathered together to bear witness to the final fading of that light.

Elizabeth, our family's tall, sandy-haired, big-boned baby is here from France. Our mother's great fear had been that her daughters might settle for life in the slow South, marry local boys and move into ranch-style houses down the road from our parents. During her senior year at LSU, Elizabeth met a visiting professor from the University of Lyons. A week after her graduation they took a slow boat to Europe, giving Elizabeth the opportunity to pick up some French along the way. Six months after the boat docked our youngest sister married Jacques Deschenes in a small ceremony attended by Rebecca, the second born. Our budgets and children had bound Kate and me to the home front. We both loved the story of our other two sisters holding hands, walking down a cobblestone street in France singing "Going To The Chapel," on the way to the wedding. "*Ohhh, I really love you baby and we're gonna get married….*" Now her mother-in-law is back in Lyons caring for Elizabeth's one-year-old son, Gaston, and her three-year-old daughter, Alyce. Elizabeth manages an English immersion school catering to French business people.

From her small farm in the hills of Pennsylvania, Kate, the third born, is working on a natural foods cookbook. She also writes impassioned opinion pieces for left wing journals. Her attorney ex-husband has a practice in Lancaster, about twenty miles away from where Kate and her three children live. She and the kids grow all their own vegetables and keep goats and chickens. The weekends the children spend with their father they step into an entirely different world: a large ultra modern condo, complete with maid service. We joke that they'll grow up to be incredibly well rounded, or psychopaths with split personalities. Kate and Alfred met while working on the McCarthy campaign and got married when she was just nineteen, the two of them tumbling headlong in a sweaty heat of lust and politics. They couldn't keep their hands off each other, just as they were incapable of embracing any causes, other than the lost ones. To put her young husband through law school, Kate waited tables, was a secretary, and even worked briefly as a model. After Al graduated, they had the three kids: Martin, Emma, and Lenin, one after the other, barely a year between each of them. When, after five hardscrabble years, her husband was lured away from his public defender job by a high-powered law firm, Kate kicked him off the farm. Just like that. They were married, and then they weren't. Our sister doesn't believe in gray, only in black or white. She swears that Al voted for Reagan.

I can never decide which of my sisters is the prettiest, but most often I think it is Rebecca with her porcelain skin and her small hour glass figure, her delicate hands and feet. She has worn her helmet of shiny dark hair in almost the same style for most of her life. Two years ago Rebecca was living with Kate and teaching at Franklin

Marshal College in Lancaster. Before that, Rebecca was briefly married to a fellow graduate student at the University of Chicago. Omar was from Iran and I think they were both rebelling against their respective cultures when they got together, and re-embracing their own backgrounds when they separated ten months later. When our mother got sick, Rebecca immediately left her job and Kate's farm and returned to Louisiana to nurse her. The rest of us visited when we could, carrying the chaos of our children in and out with us. The second sister was steadfast. Our mother never went into a hospital. Rebecca accepted a teaching job in Vermont, just after our mother's death, and was ready to leave Louisiana when our father fell ill. She stayed on. Last week Rebecca called us back to make our farewells. Kate and I left our tender children with their indifferent fathers and rushed south. We met up with Elizabeth, who had flown in from France, at the New Orleans airport. No doctor has been able to pinpoint why our father is dying, only that he is.

While my three younger sisters took on our mother's intellectualism, her scorn for the South, and the grain of salt she always applied to any information, I chose to be like Daddy, an easy going and wide-eyed optimist. I don't strive, the way my sisters do, which might explain why I carry a bit more flesh. I'm not bone thin as they are, and not an exemplary feminist either. I married a much older man and set out to be the wife to him that I would have wished for our father. I chilled the martini glasses and kept our tykes from underfoot when their father was home. Our house was Stan's castle, his word the law. Chilling those glasses might have been a mistake. My husband was already an icy man. I remember him shaking free of my hand when I reached to hold his as we walked along the beach on our Caribbean honeymoon. Eventually, and late, the loneliness and isolation of my marriage became too much for me. The boys and I have been on our own for more than a year. We are poorer than church mice, but I eat dinner with my sons every night, go to their ball games and fall asleep hearing their breathing on the other side of the thin wall in our shoddy apartment. I'm the day manager at a popular local restaurant and leave work every weekday in time to drive Mark and Jason home from school.

Looking at these four lives so neatly tucked into a nutshell, I wonder if my story will be fair, reliable. And is it even relevant to ask that a *story* be reliable? What will be creation, invention, and what repetition? How would the story change if another one of 'the sisters' were telling it? How would the narrative transform if it were about two sisters? Or none? I have said that the sisters could write lines for one another. But each would fashion the lines, tell the story, differently. How might the storyteller better serve the story: by being within the narrative, or outside it? Family myths are created to instruct and preserve. They are eventually repeated, or altered, as acts of survival. I cannot say I am a trustworthy narrator, only that I am the one telling this particular story.

Part I

The Growneups

Chapter I

Margaret--1943

THE SWEATY FLUSH-FACED soldiers touched her with their bravado and noisy camaraderie, each of them thinking he was about to become inducted into the Sacred Club of Manhood. They couldn't possibly be following the news, and it would be hard to believe that anyone in the shouting, laughing crowd had ever read Wilfred Owen's poems or Dalton Trumbo's war novel. These eager soldiers were no different than her father had been when he left for the "war to end all wars." He had been one more bright, optimistic farm boy off to see the world and to defend innocent women and children from the evil Hun. He had returned home a different person, dark. Was Margaret's father really the only dad who talked to his children about the last war? His stories of a comrade's skull top sheared off, brains exposed like a bowl of cereal, and of another soldier trying to pack his own intestines back into his shattered torso were illustrations in Margaret's childhood nightmares. Didn't these boys waving to get her attention, extending their clammy hands for rum Cokes and beer know about the mud and gore, the boredom and horror? If they knew the stories, then they probably thought that *this* time would be different. Naturally, each generation thinks it is unique, and so the wheels keep turning. Boys go off to war, expecting to return as full men, brides ascend the altar sure they will be happier than their mothers—who had expected the same.

The band started playing again just as she stepped outside to cool off. The only destiny Margaret should be concerned with was her own and she had no intention of becoming part of the grind. Still, she couldn't help but feel sorry for the boys, their voices carrying above the music, even out here by the lake. They repelled her too, their raw damp eagerness to get her attention. But it was Margaret's sympathy for them that let her roommate talk her into volunteering on Friday nights at the Army canteen. She and Irene served drinks to boys who –unlike herself—had little idea of what awaited them.

Margaret had just turned nineteen and, instead of attending college in the same town where she had spent her entire life, she was a thousand miles away earning an actual salary, building a career. *I am a reporter for The Lake Charles Messenger*, she would say when asked what a northern girl was doing way down in Louisiana. The weight of the small notebook in her palm was like a medal of accomplishment, it validated her. Never mind that she never would have gotten the job if half the men in the newsroom had not been drafted. Writing came naturally to her; she could snatch phrases out of the air, pull words together like spinning sugar around a paper cone to make cotton candy. And she had never met a word she couldn't spell. Only a month at the newspaper and Margaret already had her own byline.

The dense warm April night was just one more affirmation that Burlington, Wisconsin was far behind her. Margaret lifted her chin defiantly; the endless arguments with her parents were over. She was an avid reader and had a sense of the larger world. She had always known that she would leave her hometown. As much as she loved her Burlington friends, she had not given a second thought to leaving them behind. She would go to an out-of-state college, or she wouldn't go to school at all. That was what she insisted when she turned down the scholarship to Burlington College. Her parents argued vehemently that their smart daughter was throwing opportunity out the window. They were wrong. She had opened the door to it. She would see the world and her profession would be her passport.

A Louisiana cousin, who was in Burlington visiting one of Margaret's friends, mentioned that she'd heard The Messenger was looking for reporters. Lake Charles was just the first stop for Margaret. Eventually she intended to end up in Manhattan. She went to the library every week, on the day The New Yorker arrived, and read the magazine cover-to-cover. Lake Charles was crowded with young men being trained to go to war, at the same time she was training herself for a move to New York. That city of skyscrapers, great newspapers, and publishing houses would be Margaret's 'front.'

A breeze rose from the lake and she ran her fingers through her pale hair, lifting it, letting the air cool her neck and shoulders. Margaret's Burlington friends would not believe there could be such balmy night air in the last week of April. April, not July! The lake breeze carried a strange perfumed aroma, so strong that it was dizzying. Stepping out into the warm scented evening was like entering a dream; something she might make up to put into one of the short stories she worked on every afternoon after the paper went to press. Margaret leaned on the railing of the gazebo and inhaled deeply; she tilted her face toward the colored lights reflected over the lake. *Scattered like small fires from unknown outposts*, she thought. *A Gypsy caravan reflected in the water.* Better. Already she was beginning to outline a new story. She took another deep breath of the fragrant air. She would use both phrases.

"Sweet Olive."

"Excuse me?" She hadn't heard footsteps. The soldier seemed to have just appeared. He was tall and broad shouldered, certainly not the apparition type.

"Sweet Olive, the scent. I asked about it. That's how I know. Not anything that blooms in Connecticut."

"Nor Wisconsin." She leaned her back against the railing. "The 'sweet' is perfect. But olive?"

"I swear." He raised his right hand. "Olive."

"My only guess is that Louisiana people like to eat so much that the highest compliment they can give to a flower is to name it after food."

He laughed, "I'll bet you're right. You can't walk into a house around here without being offered food in the first five minutes. "

"And it's considered bad manners to turn down second helpings."

"Food and music, local obsessions. Why don't we two Yankees try to blend in by taking a turn on the dance floor?" He held out his hand, reaching for hers. "It seems like bad manners to ignore that great band."

There were so many more men than women around Lake Charles that anyone wearing a skirt attracted a following. The attention had little to do with who was wearing the skirt. A girl could probably walk around with a bag over her head and still have boys trailing after her. Margaret had quickly become accustomed to dodging propositions from homesick boys wearing uniforms. She had even considered wearing a wedding ring as a deterrent. Now she blamed herself for not ducking out of this conversation earlier.

"I'd like to dance with you, of course, but I'm doing my bit for the war effort, making rum and Coke for the boys. I'm here to work." She ignored his outstretched hand. "I'm just finishing my break. Time to spell my roommate so she can have a break." She looked up at him and he was smiling as if she had agreed to dance with him. Maybe he hadn't heard her. "Really. I'm supposed to be working."

The unrelenting male attention buzzing around the female minority reminded her of flies hovering over a picnic. It made Margaret feel like some kind of leftover, maybe a watermelon rind, or a sandwich crust. Her roommate, on the other hand, was thrilled by the surplus of men. Irene had actually moved here from a small town in Mississippi because Lake Charles had an army air force base. She relished the male attention, invited it. She dressed in off-shoulder blouses and applied multiple layers of bright red lipstick on the nights they worked in the canteen. Whenever a soldier approached Margaret, she wished she could flick her hand out, like shooing away a fly. She didn't mind serving drinks over a crowded bar, but avoided making any conversation or eye contact. The wide wooden planks of the bar made a suitable divide, like a window screen.

The tall soldier slipped his arm around her shoulder, steering her back toward the dance hall. "Believe me, the war effort will be best served out on the dance floor."

Margaret had never spent time with a boy that she wouldn't have traded for an evening with a good book. She still felt that way, yet trailed along with her vivacious roommate on these Friday nights out of a sense of obligation to her friend and to the naïve young boys Margaret both pitied and avoided. She needed to get out of this situation.

"I'm really not much a dancer. On the other hand," she raised her voice to be heard above the music. "I can uncap a Coke-A-Cola at the speed of light."

"I don't think this beautiful song should go to waste." He was still smiling. He had large brown eyes and the thickest eyelashes she had ever seen on a man.

"My break is over," she protested. "Honestly."

He nodded and placed his left hand into the small of her back, guiding her into a slow fox trot. The band was playing "Sleepy Lagoon."

The soldier's name was Bruce Winthrop. He was a Captain charged with deployment training at the army base. He hung around for the rest of the night and then helped Irene and Margaret clean up. He drove them back to their boarding house and gallantly waited on the curb until he saw them both go through the front door.

The next day he sent her flowers with a funny note suggesting she invent a food name for roses. He was good looking and he laughed easily. He seemed to know about the history and geography of all the fronts and had turned small talk about the war into fascinating anecdotes. Bruce Winthrop wasn't like any other man she'd ever talked with, yet Margaret really wasn't interested. She didn't return his calls, didn't answer his notes. She had her own plans, a routine that kept her on track, and a career where she intended to excel. No distractions.

"Margaret, he's dreamy. What's the matter with you, girl?" Irene's Mississippi accent made everything she said sound honeyed and slow. "I would grab that boy up in a minute."

"Well, why don't you? The next time he calls here and you tell him that I'm not in, why don't you point out that you are?"

Bruce was undeterred; he began to show up at odd hours in the newsroom, ready to lead her off for a quick coffee, or a long late dinner. He seemed not to notice her reluctance to leave work. Each time he appeared to take her off she'd eventually agree, knowing that the next time—if there were a next time—she would be better prepared to turn him down. He charmed her, teased her, and persisted in appearing, with no notice, to take her out on the town.

"I thought there was a war going on. Aren't you needed at the base?"

"I'm just trying to keep the home fires burning, remind the lads what it is we're fighting for." He cut into his thick sirloin steak.

"Which is," she raised her left eyebrow. Her friends had called it her 'Margaret O'Hara brow,' after Scarlet from Gone with The Wind who lifted her left brow when perplexed.

"The pursuit of happiness," he smiled at her and pretended to sharpen his knife on his fork. "There's nothing more American."

"We're supposed to be rationing." She gestured at her full plate.

"We are. We're rational, Meg, more rational than most. If we don't eat this fine meal, I can assure you the troops won't be eating it instead."

Bruce's unfailing charm and gift for conversation gradually lured her away from the straight and narrow path she had so tenaciously set for herself. She had worked so hard for so long, taking time out to have a bit of enjoyment really would not matter much in the long run. Margaret discovered that eating out in good restaurants with no regard for the menu prices delighted her and that going to movies and nightclubs made the unwritten stories in her head worth postponing. Bruce was so sophisticated that he was almost intimidating.

He had graduated from Brown University eighteen months before Pearl Harbor, and was expected to follow his father as president of their family's small electrical parts factory. He volunteered for the army on December tenth, three days after the bombing. The war had opened doors for him, given him a chance to use his education in ways that interested him. Apparently Bruce had been restless, bored by the same work routine that seemed to invigorate his father. He had been to Europe several times and was fluent in French. She did not know much more about him. Unlike her dates in the past, Bruce seldom talked about himself; he said he preferred listening to Margaret talk. He wanted to know everything about her and had even asked to see every single article she had written since arriving at the paper. He seemed fascinated by her job and encouraging of her ambitions. He swore she wrote as well as Scott Fitzgerald or Jane Austin. They discovered that they had read many of the same books, and they would argue for hours about writers and writing. For all of her life Margaret's thirst for books had been a private pursuit, solitary. Finding someone who shared her passion for reading completely enthralled her.

"Sleepy Lagoon" became their song. Whenever they went out dancing, Bruce would slip the bandleader two dollars, asking him repeat the song, or extend it. "*A sleepy lagoon, a tropical moon and two on an island/A sleepy lagoon and two hearts in tune in some lullaby land*," he recited the words in her ear, deepening his voice, making fun of himself, while he pulled her closer. Nothing Margaret had ever known or read prepared her for the way she found herself waiting for Bruce, marking off the hours until they were able to be together. Even the smallest event experienced away from him became a story she would embellish for him. On the nights he couldn't leave the base he would call her. She would answer the hall phone at her boarding house and begin to color in her day for him.

"When I walked into the newsroom this morning, everyone was huddled over a big table. They had a map spread out and I could hear them arguing. Charlie saying something like, 'That's where they made their mistake. They should have dug in there. Right there!' Then Ben interrupts him to say. 'They couldn't, they were outflanked. It would have been impossible.' Back and forth, all the guys were really animated, interrupting one another and jabbing their fingers on the map." Margaret wrapped the phone cord around her wrist and leaned out into the hallway, assuring that no one was waiting for a turn to use the phone.

"The radio had been on in the coffee shop. I couldn't believe there had been a major battle and it wasn't on the news, and that the paper had no prior word of a build up for an offensive. So, there I was, the only woman in the newsroom, a reporter missing out on the big story of the day. I felt like an idiot and elbowed my way in to get a glance at the map. Which turned out to be a map of Hardin County, Tennessee."

"The battle of Shiloh?" Bruce was incredulous.

"Exactly," Margaret laughed. "The Nazis are leveling London, advancing on Russia, the Japanese have taken over most of Asia, and the people down here are still fighting, and refighting, the Civil War. Every day hundreds of America boys are shipping out and these crazy southerners are still more concerned with their Confederate troops. It's unbelievable!"

"If only Stonewall hadn't died," Bruce said, putting on a fairly good southern accent.

"I'm not positive that my colleagues even know about the Munich Agreement. If they do, it is vastly overshadowed by Appomattox."

"The South will rise again," Bruce drawled.

If none of the other boarders appeared to claim the hall phone, they would talk for hours. Margaret telling Bruce about stories she was working for the paper, spinning them out, exaggerating. Or she'd tell him about funny mishaps with her gang of friends back home, parties gone wrong, flat tires and missed curfews.

If she went to lunch with a friend from the newsroom, she kept looking over her friend's shoulder, expecting to see Bruce walk in, willing him to. She was distracted and preoccupied.

"I feel like a brainless teenager," she told him.

"You are a teenager," he laughed. "Pretty brainy, but still a teenager."

One late Sunday afternoon he picked her up at the boarding house saying that he had planned a surprise for her. They drove past the grand old houses sprawling on the outskirts of Lake Charles and then smaller houses, an occasional grocery store. The asphalt soon gave way to gravel roads where small weathered cabins leaned at the edges of watery rice fields.

"Bruce, I followed up on a really unbelievable story yesterday." Margaret raised her voice to be heard. It was hot and they had both rolled down their windows. "This white woman had taken the train all the way down from Michigan to visit a woman in colored town whose son had saved the life of the white woman's son over in Guam. The way I heard it, second hand, is that the mother from Michigan had been inside the colored woman's house less than five minutes when the police showed up and arrested her!"

"What?"

"Yes, really. They gave her a choice, saying she could wait four hours in the train station for the next train north, or she could spend the night in jail."

"I'm missing part of this story. What did she do wrong? I mean, what was the charge?"

"Apparently. . ." she rolled up her window, so she wasn't shouting. "Apparently, there is a law, a Louisiana law, against the races mixing socially."

"A real law," Bruce reached over and tucked a wave of Margaret's hair behind her ear. "Or a Jim Crow law?"

"The Jim Crow laws are the law. My understanding was that the two women were visiting in a private home." She took a cigarette from the pack of Camels on the dashboard. "Those laws are supposed to just apply to the races mixing in public places. But who pays attention to subtleties?"

"Are you going to write about it?" He flicked open his cigarette lighter.

"Oh, right." She leaned into him to light her cigarette. "That's the whole point. No, I'm not." She turned her head and blew out a long stream of smoke.

"No? You could write that up so brilliantly, like one of your short stories, except it wouldn't be made up."

"The editor said no one could write the story. That we'd just be asking for trouble. Having a way with words, Mr. Bennet went on to brilliantly coin the phrase, 'Let sleeping dogs lie.'"

"That's outrageous."

"Listen to yourself, Captain Winthrop. I don't see any colored soldiers at the canteen." She tapped her cigarette over the ashtray, "and I surely bet none of them sit at the table with you and your fellow officers."

"Well, Meg, the Army happens to be segregated, I don't ---"

"Just like the South, so let's ---"

"OK, point taken!" He lifted his hands off the steering wheel, surrendering. "I suggest we just 'let sleeping dogs lie.' I know I can't out argue you. Anyway, we have almost reached our mystery destination."

The Daughters—1980

"Remember when Mama left the church?" Elizabeth puts two hands around her whiskey sour, as if to warm it. "In a hurry?" We all laugh.

"That's a good one. *Left*," I say.

We love this story. Whoever tells it has to stand, arms flailing for emphasis. The story of the rainy morning our northern mother was fast walking her way out of Mass just behind a flock of nuns. Her high heels slipped on the wet top stone step and she went spinning downward, a whirling dervish sending the nuns tumbling like so many black and white bowling pins. The Sisters of Charity's bulky habits had mercifully slowed and buffered her decent. Our mother hit the ground, got up on her feet and ran to her car. She did not look back.

"It, not so coincidently, was the last time she ever went to Holy Savior Church," Elizabeth says. "We started attending the black church after that."

The reason the sisters loved this story so much was that their mother would tell it on herself. She was brainy and reserved, not at all like the irreverent storytellers of their small town. Those disrespectful, hilarious storytellers were a dime a dozen in South Louisiana. Yet their mother told her humiliating story with gusto, almost like a native. For the sisters, the thought of their mother's dignity getting such a beating was similar to imagining Grace Kelly on a pogo stick, or Jackie Kennedy blowing her nose in public.

"Wrong. She was in the white church for Mark's Baptism." Rebecca gives me one of her dark-eyed looks and swirls her whiskey sour around her glass. "Emily, ten years later it still makes no sense that you hauled your perfect little newborn to have the devil cast from him in a Catholic church."

"It was a Baptism, not an exorcism," I say. "I did it for Daddy." Second-born Rebecca tends to be a bit critical of me. A trait she picked up as she entered adulthood.

"But it wasn't really humiliation that kept her away, it was righteous indignation" says Elizabeth reaching for the drink topper Kate offers. "She heard about the Monsignor refusing to serve communion to a black man, from out of town. The poor man ---"

"A *black* man who had mistakenly attended the *white* church." Kate adds.

"That infuriated Mama and we all started going to St. Catherine's. We ---"

"To the black church," Kate interrupts, as if the rest of us didn't know.

"Mama left," Elizabeth, the youngest, continues, unfazed. Kate interrupts all the time. "Mama left because of the Holy Savior Church's backward position on civil rights."

"'Backward?' Cowardly. Non-existent. Racist!" Kate bangs the blender into the sink. "Remember when Catholic High was *forced* to integrate and then the homecoming dance suddenly became an invitation-only event?" She leans against the kitchen counter, her wide brown eyes bright with outrage.

"And guess who wasn't invited?" Elizabeth and I say in unison.

"The hypocrisy drove Mama crazy." Kate refastens the barrette holding back her mass of curly hair.

"And she was so proud of you, Elizabeth, for writing that letter to the bishop, tattling on the Monsignor." Rebecca says wistfully. "The baby of the family speaking out and all."

"Remember she told us we needed to correct our friends, to insist they call us '*Negro* lovers' rather than 'nigger-lovers?'" says Elizabeth. "Our friends, our real and actual friends, accepted our activism as an endearing character flaw. Joking about us, rather than burning crosses on our lawn."

"Illuminating the difference between the Bible Belt South and South Louisiana," I say. "I wonder how courageous we would have been if we had lived in Georgia?"

"'Negro.'" Elizabeth shakes her blonde head. "It was so radical, back then, so revealing, to say Negro, rather than Colored, or the 'N word.' It made you a suspected Communist, at best."

"Stokely Carmichael would have made mincemeat of our 'radical' mother."

"She kept up, Kate. Maybe she began a few steps behind, but she caught up to speed." Rebecca lights her cigarette and tilts her head to blow out the match, her shiny cap of dark hair shadows her cheekbones. "It wasn't her fault she was trapped in the backwards south. Our generation created 'political correctness.' She was down here on her own."

"Mama wasn't particularly brave, but her moral compass was never off," Elizabeth says.

The sisters came of age in the age of Civil Rights and, from the very beginning, race struck a cord with all of them. Their northern mother had never worn the mantle of white entitlement comfortably. Her difference helped make the family story partially a morality tale. Their mother was their reference for style and taste and right and wrong, a touchstone for all of them. She took that reference when she died. Their house was hollow with her absence and their sleeping father was dying of it.

Margaret—1943

The low sun lingered above a flat horizon, illuminating untold miles of rice fields, and laying shimmering trails of light over the shallow water ditches irrigating the fields. Bruce turned the dark green military sedan away from the sun, off the gravel, into a shadowy stand of woods and onto a road that was little more than a pair of wheel ruts.

"Bruce, it's going to be dark in less than an hour. Where in the world--"

"You'll see. We're just about there." He looked over and grinned at her. "I told you, it's a surprise. Just for you."

He pulled off the rutted road, steered the car carefully under the low hanging branches of an oak tree and parked. Water glimmered just past the screen of leaves. "Yonder is English Bayou, our very own '*Sleepy Lagoon*,'" Bruce said. He walked around and opened her car door. "Here," he said taking her hand. "There's a path along the edge."

"It is so beautiful and so quiet." She looked both ways over the water. "And isolated. Where, exactly, are we?"

"Just wait."

They walked, following a curve in the bayou, neither of them talking. Bruce held her hand, leading her single file. The slow moving swampy water was so different from the rushing streams of the Wisconsin hill country. Margaret realized, now, that the evening wasn't at all quiet. There were bird calls echoing back and forth, none of them familiar, and then the chirping of crickets, or maybe frogs; the rustling of small creatures in the underbrush. The woods were filled with life preparing to settle in as darkness encroached;

the hum of mosquitoes that she waved away with her free hand. She could see a faint sprinkling of stars above the broad waterway, and felt the woods begin to cool down, shedding light.

"OK, hold just here. Close your eyes." He stepped behind her, placed his hands on her shoulders and gently turned her and pushed her forward. "Keep them closed. Promise."

He left her then. She kept her eyes closed, hoarding the mystery of this early June twilight in a place as different from the land of her childhood as any place could possibly be. Her heart was so full that her chest almost ached. Love, she knew this was love: the anticipation, the trust, and the unimagined joy. She held her breath waiting for Bruce to call for her.

"This way, Margaret. Open your eyes and look over here."

She could see the flickering of lights through a scrim of leaves and walked towards them and into a small clearing ringed in flaming oil lamps. A picnic basket, with a bottle of wine leaned against it, sat on the edge of a multi-colored quilt encircled by the lamps.

"Lamps for illumination and also as insect repellant," he bowed at the waist and gestured. "And a feast poached from the officer's club for your pleasure, my lady."

"How did you ever find this place?" Margaret turned, trying to take in the columns of massive trees: knotted cypress, moss-draped oaks, the small opening to the darkening sky.

"I stumbled on it. Literally." Bruce smiled. "A couple weeks ago a few officers and I came down the bayou with a guide. We happened to choose the bank, over there, as a place to pull up the boat. I climbed the ridge to stretch my legs, and here it was."

"And how did you get the basket and the lamps here?"

"The same way I will get them out." He knelt on the quilt and reached his hand toward hers. "I hired that same guide and he got a colored boy to help him. Five dollars go a long way with these locals." He laughed and shook his head. "It's shameful. But I couldn't think of another way to surprise you. And the minute I saw this enchanted little clearing I thought of you, Meg, of course. I wanted you to see it too."

Margaret sat next to him and folded his hand between hers. "It's the loveliest place I've ever seen. Like something out of a painting by. . . by Maxfield Parrish. Any minute now we'll sprout gossamer wings."

"My first thought when I found this place was that maybe a hundred years ago someone who was very much in love transplanted those trees, created this mossy dell as a place to bring his true love. When it was exactly the way he wanted it, he led her here one midsummer night."

Margaret leaned her head against his shoulder. "Little dreaming that the two of us would intrude here a century later with a basket filled with stolen goods."

"He would approve. I know he would."

"You are a fan of situational ethics?" Margaret teased.

"No, an incurable romantic." Bruce took her face between his hands and kissed her eyebrows, her cheekbones; he ran his forefinger over the bridge of her nose. "The other thing I know is that his lady could not possibly have been so beautiful as the thief's lady. And I doubt he loved her as much as I love you."

Margaret didn't know how to respond. She realized she had been waiting to hear him say that he loved her, that she had been afraid her feelings were stronger than his.

"Look, Bruce, over the bayou, like the lines in our song, *'The fireflies' gleam reflects in the stream.'* There they are, fireflies!"

"Of course," he kissed her. "All part of the plan, my darling."

Margaret lay back on the quilt and pulled him to her. "I think I'm crying."

"I think you are," Bruce whispered. "Delicious, delicate and salty. "He touched the corner of her eyes with the tip of his tongue.

"Whip-poor-will. Maybe that's the bird call we hear?" She turned her face away, embarrassed. "I've read about them, and now we're hearing one, and the sound is even more--"

"It's all right Margaret," he pressed his fingers to her lips. "I love that you are crying, and I love you. I do. I want to say it out loud. And I want you. I want you so much. And I want our first time to make love to be momentous, unforgettable. Like our song." He pushed himself up on his elbow and, with his free hand, loosened the top button on her dress. "My love," he said, leaning down to kiss her, and then lifting her head to halo her hair around her, combing it out with his fingers. "My bright and beautiful love," he kissed her throat, and then kissed the opening in her dress. He slowly unbuttoned the front of her dress, moving his lips over her bare skin.

Margaret tried to catch her breath. She didn't trust herself to look at Bruce; instead she gazed overhead at the stars, trying to center herself with the sky, trying not to breathe so hard and fast. She had stopped crying. She wasn't herself. She wasn't anyone she had ever been; someone she had never imagined was taking her over. All that she felt was desire, she was trembling with it; she wanted this man, she wanted to be naked; she wanted his lips on hers, his lips on her bare skin. She arched her back, reaching for all of him.

Without even knowing how, she was helping him to undress her, impatient to have nothing between them.

Later, when the almost full moon was directly over the clearing, Bruce served her French bread with slabs of bitter, soft cheese. He finger-fed her slices of ripe peach and pound cake. The two of them sat naked, sharing food in the leaf-speckled moonlight, encircled by lamp glow. He uncorked the wine bottle and poured out brimming glasses of warm red wine. They knelt and clinked their glasses together.

"To this moment."

"To love," she rejoined. Her voice broke and she was crying again. At the same time she was laughing and wiping at her eyes.

"You amaze me." Bruce pulled her close into his chest, spilling wine over her pale forearm and his back.

"I'm amazing myself," she said, leaning away to take a deep sip of the wine. "For instance, now. This is my first ever glass of wine."

"Momentous, Margaret" he said. "Like our song."

Then he sang to her, really sang, not mocking at all. His voice was low and pleasant. "*We're deep in a spell as nightingales tell. Of roses and dew. The memory of this moment of love/ will haunt me forever....*"

"Bruce! You can sing! I never guessed."

"Lead alto in St. Matthew's Episcopal choir. "He lifted his glass to her.

They dressed one another slowly and carefully as clouds began to skitter before the moon and the clearing darkened. Bruce crossed over to the picnic basket and pulled out a flashlight. He walked around the clearing blowing out the oil lamps while Margaret began packing up the glasses and picnic remnants. A sudden wind swirled the leaves and bent the trees and they could hear rolling peals of advancing thunder.

"Leave that, Meg. The boys will get it all tomorrow. Here, give me your hand and keep your eye on the flashlight beam. Let's try to run!"

They had almost made it back to the car when the sky ripped apart and a heavy rain poured down, drenching them both. She grabbed onto his sleeve and raced blindly for the car. Bruce opened the door on her side and quickly closed it after her. The rain was so dense that she lost sight of him and the flashlight as he ran around the front of the car. He flung himself onto the front seat, pulled the door quickly shut, and they sat listening to the heavy drum of rain beating over them. Margaret tucked her wet self as close into Bruce as possible and she was still shivering.

"Here," he reached over the backseat. "Wrap up in my jacket. That should help." He adjusted his leather flight jacket over her shoulders like a snug cape.

"You aren't cold?" Her teeth were chattering.

"I don't imagine I'll ever feel cold again." He laughed, half shouting, to be heard. He lifted her chin and kissed her. They kissed and she ran her hands over him as Bruce pulled his jacket like a cocoon over her, bringing her even closer into him. The rain pounded so loudly on the car roof that they could not have possibly heard one another, even if they had been talking.

When the rain began to quiet down, Bruce turned on the motor and cautiously backed the car from beneath the rain-weighted oak branches. He eased out into a broad circle and straddled the tires over the flooded road ruts. He drove slowly, skillfully turning the steering wheel whenever the car began to skid in the mud. They both relaxed when they turned onto the more stable gravel road. By the time they had reached the asphalt road, the rhythm of the windshield wipers and her first half bottle of wine had lulled Margaret into a sound sleep.

"Sleeping beauty, wake up." He was kissing her forehead and cheeks, lifting the damp mass of her hair to kiss her neck. She woke up smiling. They were parked in front of the boarding house.

"I had the most amazing dream." She stretched. "Wondrous."

"Did you, by any chance, kiss a donkey, Tatiana?"

"I think I may have," Margaret laughed. "And I think I'd like to never stop, even though I'm awake. But I have to be at the paper before sun up." She reached to slip his jacket off her shoulders. "I'm sorry to say."

"No, no, Meg, your hands are icy. Keep the jacket, I'll drop by and pick it up tomorrow." He rubbed her cold hands between his warm ones. "We want you bright and fresh, Miss Reporter. I won't detain you." But then he kept her hands between his, looking into her face. Finally, he let go and opened his car door, still looking only at her.

He got out of the car, walked around and opened her door. She stepped out onto the sidewalk and laced her fingers together behind Bruce's neck.

"There will never, ever be such a beautiful night. It was perfect, even the rain." She pushed her forehead against his chest. "And I love you. I love you so much."

"Don't say 'never,' Margaret. We have an entire season of summer nights ahead." He took hold of her hands again and held them tightly, as though he had no plans to let her go.

"I really have to be at work in less than five hours," she laughed. "I do, I do." She backed up the stairs, kissing him, as she reached behind herself for the front door handle.

"Tomorrow," he whispered, nipping lightly at her earlobe.

She opened the door, tugging her hand from his, and closed the door, not looking at Bruce, afraid she wouldn't be able to leave him. She leaned with her back against the thick wooden door until she heard him start the car and drive away.

Who was she now? What had happened? She wanted to take the night apart into infinitesimal pieces and slowly reassemble it. She needed to see herself in a mirror. She couldn't possibly look the same way she had looked this afternoon, just a handful of hours, and a different world, ago. She climbed the stairs, felt her way along the wall and into the small hall bathroom. Margaret pulled the dangling string to turn on the light above the mirror.

She looked the same. It was unbelievable that she could feel so transformed and look exactly as she had when she brushed her hair, in this very room, just before Bruce arrived to whisk her off into the forest. Her hair was tangled and dark with rainwater; otherwise, she appeared to be the same Margaret: fair skin, grey green eyes. Maybe her lips were slightly swollen, maybe that was different. She turned her head from side to side, staring into the mirror. Then she lifted the jacket off her shoulders and slid her arms into the sleeves, crossed them in front, hugging herself with Bruce's leather sleeves. She was smiling, almost laughing, at her own reflection. She dropped her arms down and slid her hands into the jacket's deep pockets, raising her shoulders and lowering her head to the scent of leather and Bruce; the smell of cigarette smoke and Louisiana rain. Her right fingers closed over a ring, deep in a seam of the pocket. She lifted out a broad gold band, turned it between her fingers, held it up to the bare light bulb above the mirror. Inside the ring, there was a miniature inscription: *BWW & JMJ*.

She dropped the ring--as if she had pulled it glowing hot from a fire--and was instantly sick, gagging, vomiting and sobbing, trying to shrug out of the jacket as she leaned over the sink. When there was nothing left in her stomach, she huddled on the floor in the corner of the stuffy little bathroom, shuddering, and taking deep breaths.

A mistake? Could it be a mistake? Maybe there were initials and a wedding band but the wedding had never happened? Then why would Bruce still be carrying the ring with him? No, she had been a fool, an easy mark. The night they met, he must have slipped the ring off his finger as he approached her beside the lake. Slid it off, but kept it close, every time they were together. Margaret could smell him; smell their sex. She gagged. She had willfully missed the blank places in his history because she wanted him, needed him to be who he said he was. How had she let this happen? He had become her entire world. Now it was the end of the world, the dead end. She had fallen off.

Finally, she made herself stand, leaning against the wall for support. She felt infinitely tired, too tired to ever leave this room. But she had to get clean. Though she was paralyzed with fatigue, she made herself move. She pressed the rubber stopper into the tub and turned on the hot water, full stream. As Margaret undressed she saw that her thighs and underclothing were stained the color of wine. She would never drink wine again. Never.

The hall phone began ringing, the caller seemingly heedless of the late hour. The phone kept ringing and ringing. No one, sleeping in the house, woke to answer it.

The Daughters—1980

Rebecca walks back into the kitchen carrying her empty whiskey sour glass. She had gone to check on our father.

"I know he's not going to wake up, or get out of bed. But before he got sick he would wander the house at night, for all the world like a little lost boy in his too big pajamas." Her voice broke. "One night I had just had it. I got up, stepped out into the hall and told him to go to bed. Like he really was a child breaking the rules. And he said..." She takes a deep breath. "He said, 'I just miss her so much. I don't know what to do, Rebecca.' And I said, bitch that I am, I said 'Well, we all miss her.' And I stepped back in my room and slammed the door."

My sister begins crying and I put my arm around her. "You had too much to carry all by yourself, Rebecca," I say. "You had your own grief."

"We're all grieving," Elizabeth says. "And we all loved her and she got sick so suddenly. But think of Daddy, so sure she would outlive him. The shock, and then the sorrow."

"And now he's dying of it," Kate says. "God he loved her."

"I think his love was a burden to her," I say.

"What are you talking about?" Rebecca wipes her dark eyes with the back of her hand. "Who wouldn't want to be loved like that?"

"Unconditional love. Like a dog?"

"Emily!"

"I think Daddy saw her his way, the way he believed her to be. Not like she really was. That had to be hard on Mama." I reach into the sink, pull out the blender and set it in front of Kate. The night will be long and there is a half-gallon of bourbon on the kitchen counter. "Don't you think we all have a longing to be known, truly known? Isn't that longing for the 'other' what drives relationships? That elusive hope that another person can understand you, that desire to be truly known."

"He knew her," Elizabeth says, with all the wisdom of the youngest child. "He just chose to overlook the hard parts, all those shadowy places in his sunny view. Sure, Mama was always raining on his parade. But realize it wasn't the parade Daddy loved, it was the rain."

"There was no one like her," Rebecca says, her shiny straight hair catching the light from the kitchen lamp. "No one."

We all nod in agreement. Our mother was a woman of strong and informed opinions, stranded in a time and place that noticed her good looks and dismissed her good mind. When she walked down the street, people turned to watch her. But when she talked, it seemed that only her husband and daughters were listening. Margaret Sobral was witty, ethical, and the smartest person we knew. She had difficulty displaying affection, and that flaw made us feel protective of her, perhaps inordinately loyal.

She is six months dead. The house she lived in for thirty years is going empty. Her daughters are all adults. But we miss our mother. We linger in the kitchen of our childhood waiting for Kate to mix up the next batch of whiskey sours.

Later the sisters will blame their mother for almost everything wrong about them, or their lives. The mothers are the easiest to blame: too dominate, too meek, too cloying or--in the case of

Margaret Sobral--too remote. The mother tends to be the 'sitting duck' for the family shooting gallery.

Well, actually, three of the sisters will blame their mother for everything. Not Rebecca. In the story, Rebecca--bless her--will remain ever steadfast, fiercely holding her ticket to *Margaret Sobral, The Greatest Show on Earth.* Standing in line, waiting her turn long after the show had folded its tents and left town. The field where it had once performed would become overgrown, indistinguishable from any other flat grassy place. Yet Rebecca would continue to clutch her ticket to the show. Her blinders were as firmly fixed as her father's.

As time and experience eroded their versions of their mother, the seal that bonded the sisterhood seemed to wear down. One or two of the sisters might not speak to another for months at a time. There would be arguments, shifting loyalties, duplicities, contradictions, and held grudges; a breaking apart where once there had been an immutable covenant.

But--returning to the story of the year their parents died—the four sisters, like their father, still thought their mother had hung the moon. No, that she *was* the moon. The sisters were minor constellations, hardly deserving of her proximity; each of them knew her self to be an insignificant reflection of her mother's brilliance. Their father was the enraptured astronomer who mapped their sky and interpreted it. While they knew they were the stars in his blue heaven, the sisters only came to light when the moon was elsewhere. Mother moon, daughter stars, and earth bound sky guide: The subsequent reordering of the heavens cracked their galaxy apart.

If the story continued, past their disenchantment and the resulting dissolution of their bond, eventually one of them would die and the surviving sisters would gather in memory and sorrow. Most likely they would be dressed to the nines and sitting around a table in the house of the deceased. The three of them drinking good wine and telling the old stories. For a while it would feel like all the years they were so close, back when each one sister was the compass for the others. Back when not one of their personal decisions, heartbreaks, or triumphs went unconsidered by council, all of them weighed upon the scale of sisters. But then, going again far into the future, maybe that night after the sister's funeral, while sitting around the table, one of them would interrupt at the wrong time, or insist on a different story sequence. Elizabeth: *That crazed cow chased me through the fence, Rebecca, not you. I was the one all sliced up by barbed wire. You weren't anywhere around!* Rebecca: *Mother's dress was blue. She never wore yellow. It was my graduation, I ought to remember. She didn't even like yellow.* Kate: *No, it was Kennedy's Catholicism, not his liberalism, that attracted Daddy. He could have been a right wing nut case and Daddy would've still voted for him!!* Memory, like luck, is never 'a lady.' Memory always flirts around the room playing with some other girl's dice. Voices would rise, interruptions intersect, a hurtful verbal jab would be aimed just right and the fissures would reopen. Maybe it would be better if they had never even gotten started, if the story had remained only Margaret's story.

Chapter 2

Margaret—1943

"Hot enough for you?" The woman across the aisle was fanning herself with her hat.

Margaret nodded in agreement, and then returned to reading her notes as the bus picked up speed, rattling toward the city's edge.

The heat was all anyone talked about. It was nearly Halloween and Lake Charles was as hot and humid as it had been in July. She relished the heat, though, wished she could rub it into her dry, icy skin like Ponds hand cream. Margaret had lost so much weight in the last five months, become so thin that maybe her bones were taking on the cold. She often slept under a blanket and never turned on the fan in the room she shared with Irene, unless her roommate was home. Irene worked nights now, so the two seldom saw one another. Margaret was cold all the time, and tired. Given the chance, she would have slept twenty hours a day. She had been a light sleeper for all of her life and an early riser; she had never had need for an alarm clock. Now it was only the clock that got her to work on time, saved her job. The clock waking her in the morning and the uncounted cups of coffee were what kept her on her feet during the workday, coffee and cigarettes. Food repelled Margaret. She forced herself to eat a bit of the supper served up every night at the boarding house. The food all seemed greasy, difficult to chew, and more difficult to swallow. Yet, it was included in the rent and Margaret had no money to waste. She was saving every penny to buy her way out of Lake Charles where every day threatened to snare her with some glimpse of Bruce. When she had enough money set aside, she would take the train to New York. She would not go back to Wisconsin, not ever; that would be far too humiliating. She would stick to her original plan, no matter that she had lost her zest for it. Moving to a big city and starting over would revive her and allow her to focus. Margaret would become a real journalist again, instead of someone barely going through the motions of holding onto a job.

She was on her way to interview the headmaster at a boy's boarding school. He had instigated a mildly controversial program for the school's upper classmen. Opinion was divided on whether the extended fifth year might be a form of draft dodging. Or, since it included military courses, the extra year might be considered as officer readiness training. In truth, this interview was a token assignment on a slow news day.

Last week her editor had taken Margaret off the courtroom beat. He told her it was temporary, but she knew she'd been doing an inadequate job. Her lack of initiative and last month's foul up with the judge made the demotion seem a kindness. The judge story was still a newsroom joke.

It had all happened so fast, the gunshots were so loud. There had been no time to think, to take in the whole picture. Margaret had been walking outside the courthouse with Judge Elkins. She was interviewing him because a man he'd sent to prison, a man who had sworn revenge upon the judge, had escaped the day before. The portly old judge had just begun a detailed explanation of the escapee's trial, when he abruptly turned away from her and pulled a pistol out of his suit coat pocket. Margaret looked up to see a man standing a couple yards away aiming a shotgun right at her. There was a loud pop and the man with the shotgun fell to the ground in a splatter of blood. She dropped her notebook and ran as fast as she could back to the courthouse, grabbed the first phone she saw, and dialed the newspaper.

"Someone's been shot. Send a reporter!" she had shouted into the phone. She had been shaky from drinking too much coffee, and then deeply rattled realizing, again, how everything could change in a second. Happiness could become unbearable sorrow; you could be alive, and then dead, in one beat of the heart. Of course, she came to her senses as soon as she heard a voice at the other end of the phone. But it was too late. She knew the people she worked with meant no harm, but "Send a reporter!" had become the standing joke in the newsroom. Once she would have cringed at every reminder, now she merely wondered when the joke would get old. She had no energy for self-defense, just getting through the workday was demand enough.

The ante bellum school building was set back in a towering stand of pine trees and surrounded by gardens sectioned off by white stone paths. It looked so peaceful, a world away from the sprawl of new industries and roadways the bus had just driven through. As Margaret followed a path winding though hedges and bushes toward the school's broad front porch, the traffic noises faded behind her. A polished wooden bench, nestled in the shade under an arch of pine boughs, tempted her to pause. If she could rest there, maybe close her eyes for a couple minutes, she might be able ease away her cloying fatigue. She forced herself to walk faster, to climb the porch steps and ring the doorbell beside the ornate double doors. A colored woman, wearing a dark dress and starched white apron, answered the door and led her into a formal front parlor. Margaret waited, perched on the edge of a deep purple loveseat, rubbing her arms against the chill of the shadowy room.

"This way, mam," a uniformed boy, with a ruddy complexion, led her down a short hallway. He opened a door for her and then stepped back into the hall.

The headmaster stood up from behind his desk as she walked in. He was slightly taller than Margaret and slender; he had longish dark hair, a streak of gray at his temples.

"When the Messenger said they were sending over a reporter, I guess I just didn't expect, didn't think---"

"I'd be a woman," she finished his sentence for him.

"A lady. Now Dorothy Thompson is a fine newspaper writer, but for the Lake Charles Messenger to have a lady reporter is quite a step up for the paper. I wouldn't have expected it." He gestured for her to sit in the cushioned straight back chair facing his desk.

"I think it is a war time exception, Mr. Sobral. More a scraping the bottom of the barrel than a step up." She said, sitting and crossing her legs.

"Well, nevertheless, I intend to renew the school's subscription. I canceled it right after I arrived." He sat facing her and folded his hands on the desk. His fingers were long and blunt, like a pianist's.

"And when was that?" Margaret took a pencil out of her purse and opened her small notebook. "How long have you been here?"

"I arrived a year ago in August." He leaned forward. "You are from the North. 'There's no mistaking that.'"

"A Yankee, I think is the term applied locally for anyone from above the Mason Dixon." She tapped her pencil on her wrist. "And before you came to Lake Charles?"

"It is wonderful listening to you talk," he smiled.

"And before here?" She looked down at her notebook. The sooner this interview was over, the sooner she could get back to her room and try to nap before the tedious boarding house supper.

"I was almost eight years a teacher, and then assistant headmaster at a school in St. Louis. Same type of school, you know, boys from good families. Before that I taught at a Catholic boarding school for Indians out in Oklahoma."

"Really?" She looked up. "That's unexpected. You are from the Deep South. There's no mistaking that.'"

"A small town about an hour up river from New Orleans," he smiled, acknowledging her jab. "I joined the Brothers of St. Francis, a religious order, when I was very young. My first teaching assignment, after I graduated from Loyola, was that school in the middle of a forsaken landscape with no decent food within a day's journey."

"A sentence worse than death for someone from Louisiana."

"Yes, but it wasn't the uninspired cuisine, or the boys. I liked teaching them. I had qualms about trying to erase Indian customs, the boys' own religion." He brushed his hands back and forth over the desktop, as if it were a blackboard. "That is what they were instructing us to do. We stole the Indian's land, and then we were supposed to also steal their history. So I left the Order."

"You left the Catholic Church?"

"No Miss. . . . Here I am going on and on, and I don't even know your name. Excuse my manners."

"Margaret Peterson."

"I could never do that, Miss Peterson. I would never leave the Church. I merely left the brotherhood. I still go to Mass every morning. Rain or shine."

Margaret had just joined the group of silent women gathered around the boarding house supper table, when the doorbell rang. Mrs. Benson, the landlady, stood up with an exaggerated sigh of annoyance.

"Is anyone expecting a caller?" She gazed accusingly at her boarders, before she left the dining room to answer the door.

"You think there's a rule against unannounced callers?" asked Maxine, a round-faced country girl. "Like smoking in our rooms?"

"Or opening the Frigidaire without asking?" Added Maxine's roommate Louise, her eyes wide in mock horror. The two girls had arrived together from a small Texas town an hour's bus ride from Lake Charles. At the table, they only spoke to one another. Margaret, Irene and Connie, a stern older woman who was a secretary at the munitions plant, could have been invisible.

"The boy at the door said I was to make sure you got this." Mrs. Benson placed a tureen, wrapped in a white linen cloth, next to

Margaret's plate. "And this note." She pulled a small pale gray envelope from her apron pocket. "A chauffer drove that boy over from Jefferson Academy." The landlady seemed impressed. "I reckon you need a spoon," she added, with a small touch of resentment.

Margaret opened the envelope and pulled out a translucent square of note paper:

"Dear Miss Peterson,
Someone so thin as yourself is an affront to Southern hospitality and to our aforementioned Louisiana cuisine. Della makes the best chicken gumbo this side of New Orleans. I hope you enjoy it nearly so much as I enjoyed this afternoon's conversation with you.

Sincerely,
Matthew Sobral"

Even before she lifted the heavy china cover, the spicy scent of the soup was wafting over the table. Margaret suggested going to the kitchen for bowls so that she could share her bounty.

"We are quite satisfied with the supper we was interrupted in starting on." Mrs. Benson spoke up, daring the other women to contradict her.

The next evening, as Margaret and her fellow boarders gathered around the table, the doorbell rang again. This time the boy delivered pork chops smothered in a rich tomato sauce, green beans and a mound of rice and gravy. The next night he appeared with a dark beef stew. Margaret felt almost ashamed of herself, of her profound sadness, sorry for all the weight she had lost. She was so thin that she had elicited the pity of that kindly man. She labored over the wording of a thank you letter to Mr. Sobral, an assurance of the suitability of Mrs. Benson's flavorless fare, a promise to take better care of herself.

He called and invited her to join him for supper at the Academy. He would send a car. Three weeks after she first met him, when she still thought of herself as his personal charity cause, an object of mercy, Matthew Sobral asked Margaret to marry him.

The Daughters---1963

"'I'm a goner,'" said Rebecca, who was fifteen and the family actress. She crossed her hands over her heart and fluttered her eyelashes.

"'I'm a goner,'" echoed Kate, two years younger and still shy.

"What daddy said to himself when mama walked in his office," continued Rebecca.

The sisters have heard the story about the day their parents met uncounted times. That day is the unshakable base of all their family myths. Imagine the four girls as teenagers sitting on their parents' bed in their shadowy bedroom. It was the coolest room in the house and both parents were at work. Kate was holding a framed picture of their mother she had just lifted from the dressing table. It was a black and white photograph of a young woman with pale shoulder length hair, curly, with short bangs on her forehead, in 1940's style. Margaret stares intently at the camera, almost as if she were daring the photographer to take her picture. She is wearing a simple white blouse and a flared plaid skirt, saddle shoes and socks. Her elbow is propped on the top of a mailbox, the kind that sits on corner curbs; her right ankle is crossed over her left. Their mother's legs were beautiful, long and slender. The mother in the story is beautiful: classically chiseled cheekbones, smooth skin, arched brows over light, serious eyes.

"'If you girls grow up to be half as pretty as your mother, half as smart,'" Emily deepened her voice, drawing the words out slowly like their daddy did. "'You'll be damned lucky.'" She slipped off the high bed and walked over to the mirror in the wardrobe. "I do have her eyes." She leaned closer, looking for something else.

"Me too," Elizabeth chimed in. The blonde youngest sister had just started seventh grade. Emily's eyes were truly grey green like their mother's. Elizabeth's were paler; an arresting blue that changed shades depending on the light and the color of her clothes.

"Us middle ones have dark ones. Latin eyes, like daddy," Rebecca sounded wistful.

"You and Kate have great eyes, like Audrey Hepburn. Both of you," Emily said, encouragingly. Though it was Kate who had the really large eyes and great eyelashes. Rebecca's eyes were deep and thoughtful, almost ebony. Her straight, shiny hair accentuated their darkness. Kate once heard their maid, Loretta, describe Rebecca's hairstyle as being "Like that boy upside the shoe with the dawg." "*Buster Brown?*" Kate had asked.

Tomorrow, Sunday, their father would be driving Emily to New Orleans to catch the train. She was going off to college in the north. It was the last day, for a very long time, that the sisters would be alone together. They haven't said it out loud, but it was what they were all thinking about. They spent the day together in a tight little bunch, inseparable. Who would they be when the set was broken up?

Kate flopped back on the bed, her curly hair haloed behind her, pressing the photograph to her chest. "Do you think they have sex?"

"No! No! No!" Rebecca stuck her fingers in her ears.

"Of course they do." Elizabeth opened her arms expansively. "Here we are!"

"'A little bit of knowledge is a dangerous thing.'" Emily quoted. The older sisters had only recently told Elizabeth *the facts of life*. She was thrilled, heady with information. "That only proves they did, did have sex. Once upon a time. Well, four times."

"Right, I'm talking about now." Kate patted the bed. "Do they do *it*?"

"I am positive they don't," Rebecca insisted. "Think about how mama goes limp like a rag doll and rolls her eyes when daddy is giving her a hug." She tilted her head as if her neck were made of cotton. "Think about how she leans her head away from his kisses."

"Which doesn't discourage him in the least," Emily noted.

Chapter 3

Margaret and Matthew—1943

When the kindly headmaster asked her to marry him, they had just finished Sunday dinner at a restaurant that served only chicken and duck, both cooked in heavy spices and served with "dirty rice" and okra. Margaret was trying to imagine her parents and her little brother, who had the same roast beef and potatoes, sliced bread and pickled beets dinner every Sunday, sitting at such a meal. She was pouring cream into her coffee when Matthew leaned across the table.

"Margaret, I'd very much like to marry you. If you'd have me."

He spoke quietly, what he was saying was very personal, only for her to hear. Yet Margaret wasn't quite sure that he had been speaking to her, or that she had heard him correctly.

"I'm sorry, Matthew. My mind was hundreds of miles away. I missed what you said."

"You are such a dreamer, that is one of the things I love about you. One of the thousand things." He took the cream pitcher from her, placed it beside her cup, and folded her hand between his. "Will you be my wife? Will you marry me?"

"Matthew, you don't even know me. How can you be asking me to marry you?" She was incredulous.

"The first time I ever saw you, you marked me in a way I had never been touched before. Before God, that is the truth." He pressed her hand between his, as if trying to wring out her disbelief. "I have listened closely to every word you've ever said to me, or to anyone else nearby. I do know you, Margaret. I know you to be intelligent and humane and, to make you even more irresistible, you are witty like no other woman I have ever known."

"A dinner companion is not the same thing as a wife, not someone who ---"

"I know you, Margaret. And I love you. My heart is set on marrying you." He released her hand and leaned back in his chair, keeping his eyes on her. "Tomorrow, if you'll have me, or as long as it takes for me to convince you."

This would have been the time for Margaret to point out that she felt affection and gratitude, but surely not love for the nice-looking, brown-eyed gentleman facing her with such hope. There was nothing, absolutely nothing about him that stirred deep feelings within her. Bruce had taken that capacity away and left numbness in its place. It made no sense to her why this genial older man, who had never so much as tried to kiss her, was proposing marriage. Not once had she thought she was being courted, or considered that she was anything but an object of compassion for him. When he took her hand, just now, they had changed places.

More than her sense of astonishment, she suddenly felt sympathy, pity, for Matthew. How could someone, with traces of silver already in his hair, have so little life experience that he would consider his nutrition campaign a romance? He was eighteen years older than she, a lifetime older, but Margaret now seemed his world weary elder. His earnest hopefulness disarmed her. Matthew Sobral was a generous and good man, with a zest for life. All she really felt was tired and still so sad that she couldn't imagine rising to any occasion, much less trying to become the person he imagined her to be. Matthew had called her a dreamer. As if he had met her former self, the girl who had arrived in Lake Charles a year ago. Back when Margaret had been even more naïve than he.

"I am a fallen away Catholic, Matthew, aren't you worried about your soul?"

"Only about yours," he joked. "You've found me out, I'd do anything to bring you back into the Church." He reached across the table and took her hand, serious again. "Besides, what good is a soul if it has no heart? And I have lost my heart to you."

When he kept up his pursuit, in the face of her pragmatism, she found herself relenting, and agreeing to marry a man she had known for less than two months. Matthew could easily have been a kindly older relative or a generous neighbor, given her feelings for him. Though she had other incentives—her life needed to change--her main reason for accepting his persistent proposal was that she just did not know how to turn him down; she couldn't bear to hurt that good man's feelings. Matthew Sobral was like a cook offering a feast to someone with no appetite for food and no aptitude for refusal.

Margaret's only stipulation was that they move from Lake Charles. She did not want to continue her mediocre newspaper work, nor did she want to keep living with the fear that she might turn a corner in the street and see Bruce. Being married would offer a new start, an escape. Not what she had ever imagined for herself, but something solid to fill the void left by her imagination.

Matthew sent out inquiries and easily found a position teaching history in a Baton Rouge public school. He needed a couple of weeks to transfer his Jefferson Academy duties over to the assistant headmaster. He would begin his new job after Christmas. Margaret would go to Wisconsin a few days before Thanksgiving and Matthew would meet her there. They would get married the Friday after Thanksgiving and honeymoon in Chicago. Margaret turned twenty on the first day of November.

"What could you be thinking, Margaret?" Her father was still in his mailman's uniform. His snow boots were in the mudroom, he had leather slippers on his feet. "He's practically my age. You don't even know him."

"I know he's a kind man. And sweet tempered," she added pointedly.

Margaret wondered how well her mother had known her father when they got married. She couldn't recall ever seeing them even holding hands. They had separate bedrooms. She has seen her mother cower during her father's infrequent, but terrifying, rages. Afterwards, she heard her excuse him, say how the war had changed him. Though her mother had not known her father before the war. Margaret had never heard her father talk about her mother, either in a good way or a bad one. They lived quiet and separate lives in the same house. She had never before considered that. Now it frightened her.

"He is changing his life for me." She folded her arms and looked across the living room toward her mother, who had an open book, face down, on her lap. "I asked him to and he didn't ask me why. He just did it."

"No one has ever been able to tell you anything." Her father turned abruptly and went downstairs.

Then she heard him shoveling coal into the basement furnace. Her mother picked up her book and began reading again. Margaret realized neither of her parents would ask her why she had made such a request of Matthew. She looked out the window at the lifeless landscape, the bare trees, and the crusty ledges of old snow along the driveway. She thought of Louisiana where, even in winter, sweet olive bloomed; it had been blooming when she left Lake Charles.

The bellman placed their suitcases inside the bedroom, accepted his generous tip with a broad smile and firmly closed the door as he left. Matthew had reserved the bridal suite at the Palmer House Hotel. He led her proudly into the sitting room and opened the drapes to a view of Lake Michigan.

"Look at that, Margaret. It stretches out just like the Gulf of Mexico. You can't see the other shore!" He was thrilled.

The dappled reflection of winter sun over water played over the thick blue carpet. Margaret sat down in the middle of a curved pale gray sofa; her eyes closed against the light, and she began to cry.

"You know, I have no idea how wide Lake Michigan is. I never even thought to find out." He turned to her. "Isn't that …? Oh, my god, darling. What's wrong?"

She tried to catch her breath, stop herself from crying. The reception in the church hall had been so sad and such a small gathering. Her friends were confused by the change in Margaret and they were shy and awkward around her gracious and gentlemanly husband. Everyone was startled when Matthew opened champagne and began pouring it into coffee cups. No one in the Midwest openly drank alcohol at ten in the morning. There were a few feeble attempts at ceremonial toasts. Her mother and father stood with their empty hands at their sides, their faces grim and unsmiling. Her fourteen-year-old brother switched his weight from foot-to-foot, uncomfortable in a borrowed suit, awkwardly holding an inappropriate cup of champagne. The priest and guests hustled out of the church hall as soon as they possibly could, leaving Matthew, Margaret and her family to clear the coffee cups of champagne and throw away the uneaten cinnamon buns. Her parents drove them to the train station, but didn't even stand on the platform to wave off their daughter and her groom. Margaret knew how people celebrated, even for the smallest occasion, in Louisiana. Before he entered the brotherhood, Matthew had been the son of a wealthy man. He had told her of the banquets and receptions where, as a motherless boy, he would fall asleep with his small head resting on heavily-laden tables, his father's guests laughing and drinking, the tinkle of crystal and silver all around him as he slept. Matthew had to be horrified at their pathetic little event, yet he kept offering refused drinks and smiling broadly, looking over at Margaret as if she were the shining belle of a magnificent ball. It was all so incredibly sad.

"Margaret, what's wrong? Please honey, please don't cry."

"I'm sorry, Matthew," she sobbed. "Sorry everyone was so rude. And my parents, they ---"

"No one was rude, Margaret. Everybody celebrates differently. I surely learned that in Oklahoma. The boys' families would come in from the reservations for a party and clear out all the food and drink without saying a single word." He sat beside her. "I mean eat everything in sight in a matter of minutes." He snapped his fingers to show how fast. "And then they were gone." He put his arm around her shoulder. "Now that took getting used to. And your parents? Well, you're their only daughter. You can't expect them to be happy about losing their little girl." He pulled her close and pressed his lips against her forehead.

It startled Margaret. They had kissed before, careful, tentative kisses, held hands in the parlor at his school, and had lightly embraced on the front steps of the boarding house. But now they were alone, and it was their wedding night. And she had made a mistake, a terrible, terrible mistake. She couldn't go to bed with someone just because he was kind. What had she been thinking? Margaret moaned and pushed away from Matthew, ran into the bedroom and threw herself, sobbing, onto the rough brocade covering on the over-sized bed.

"Shhhh---" He stood in the doorway shushing her, as though she were talking too loudly in a library. "Shhhh, Margaret, honey. Please, please don't cry. Shhhh…."

She cried harder. He backed out of the doorway and paced the sitting room, fiddling with the drapes, shading the room and then filling it with light. Margaret was still weeping when she heard him leave the suite, carefully closing the door after himself. There was only one person she would ever want to go to bed with, but he was a liar and a cheat. The woman who had so willingly made love with Bruce was gone. The shell left behind had just become a wife to someone else.

Her life was over, ruined. It was nothing like what she had supposed it would be. She was not going to have a life of mystery and excitement, a life where she wrote about adventures as she experienced them, and wrote about the world as she traveled it. Margaret was a married woman now, a wife and a nobody. She would become as invisible as her own mother. She thought of her friends and how far they were from her now. Everything that would ever happen to them lay ahead. She was here, alone in a strange city, expected to have sex, a wedding night, with a man who had lived like a priest for most of his life.

How had she gotten here? What was the heavy dark thing inside her that had given up? Her heart had been broken and she had lacked the energy to even step away from the heartbreak and examine it. She knew she had once been strong and vibrant. And hopeful. Margaret could almost remember the feel of that. Almost. Now she was a fester, a mold; she lacked resistance. Whatever had come along, offering a life change, she would have followed. She had once been so willful, and now she had no will at all. And she was always tired, too tired to think.

"Margaret, honey?"

She had fallen asleep and now Matthew was again standing in the doorway of the bedroom, his arms filled with roses. She sat up on the side of the bed and watched him arrange the flowers in a vase on the dresser. He went into the bathroom and came out carrying a full glass of water.

"These were the sweetest smelling flowers in the entire shop," he said as he poured the water into the vase. "Two dozen, Margaret. I watched the lady count them out. Twenty-four red roses!" He set down the empty glass. "And here, I know you love these."

He reached into his coat pocket and pulled out a bundle of Hersey bars. Not the war rationed ones, thin bars wrapped in waxed paper; but thick slabs wrapped in foil. Where could he possibly have found them? He sat beside her and fanned the candy bars over the bed. He was so proud, eagerly spreading out his treasure for her. It just broke her heart. She buried her face in her hands and began crying again.

"There, there," he patted her back, being careful not to sit too closely. "I didn't mean any harm. I know you love chocolate. Did I do something wrong, Margaret?"

"It's not that. It's just …"

She moved her hands away and turned to face him. His look of bewilderment made her cry harder; she covered her face with her hands again. When he understood that he was of no comfort to her, Matthew stood, smoothed the place where he had been sitting, and then walked quietly out of the room. Margaret heard the outside door close again.

After he left she took a long hot bath in the hotel's deep tub and gradually stopped crying. When the water became lukewarm, she got out of the tub, dried off and dressed in the green satin nightgown Irene had given her as a wedding gift. She ate two of the candy bars, unpacked the suitcases and folded their clothes into the dresser drawers. She brushed her teeth and then stood in front of the mirror brushing her hair for a very long time. She was a bride.

This was her wedding night. Margaret turned on the small lamp beside the bed and opened the window curtain. She slipped under the covers and lay on her back watching the halo of city lights beyond the window.

She heard the outside door slowly open. By the bedside clock, Matthew had been gone for over two hours. He had been out all alone on his wedding night, in windy, cold Chicago. When he paused in the open doorway of the bedroom, Margaret sat up in bed.

"I'm sorry. The flowers are beautiful," she gestured toward the vase on the dresser. "They really are."

"There's nothing to be sorry for. You're frightened." He was unbuttoning and slipping out of his coat, cautiously, as if a sudden movement would startle her. "That's to be expected. And don't you worry, we have all the time in the world."

"No, you don't understand. This isn't…."

"We're going to have a wonderful life, Margaret." He sat carefully on the edge of the bed, folding his dark overcoat over his lap. "I promise I'll make you happy."

It had been an endless and hard day. Twelve hours ago Matthew was opening champagne, joyously celebrating in a void. He was such a hopeful person, so guileless and good. She took a deep breath and pulled back the covers, making a place in the bed for her husband.

The Daughters—1980

"'Twenty-four roses!'" says Elizabeth. We are well into Kate's second batch of whiskey sours. We have checked on our sleeping father and now are retelling the story of him trying to cheer up our weepy mother on their wedding night. It was a story our parents often told on themselves.

"Such a sad wedding night." I say. "Poor daddy."

"'Poor daddy?'" Kate joins us at the kitchen table, wiping her hands on our mother's apron. "He got exactly what he asked for. Mama married him. I don't think the terms mattered."

"Him wandering alone, a Southern gentleman among all those Yankees, down on the streets of the city that never sleeps; and a scary bride crying her eyes out in the bridal suite?" I light up a Salem. "Surely, as spellbound as he was, even Daddy deserved better terms."

"The mystery to me," says Rebecca, pulling a cigarette from my pack. "Is that the same woman who felt like such a failure for getting married, never once tried to slow down any of our marriages. "

"My impression is that she wanted us to make our own decisions," I say.

"No, it was something else," Rebecca insists. "When I was twenty-three, and still single, I felt like a spinster." She widens her dark eyes for emphasis. "There I was, the second born, sandwiched between two married sisters."

"So you quickly got married. Figuring a couple months would do the trick."

"Funny, Elizabeth. Hysterical." Rebecca picks up my lighter and continues. "I'm serious. There I was in graduate school. Which

I paid for myself, I might add." When she bends to light her cigarette her straight hair curtains her face. She leans back and her hair falls perfectly back in place. "And on the rare occasions I called here and tried to talk about some of my courses, or my professors, Mama would interrupt to tell me Mark was learning to ride a bike. Or that little Emma had gotten her first tooth. The fact--"

"Bullshit!" Kate interrupts. The two middle children have a long history of interrupting one another. "She pushed us to get out into the world, she ---"

"Maybe into the world, but not alone," Rebecca insists. "Think about it. You and Emily were both married before you were old enough to vote. Can either of you remember her objecting, cautioning you to wait a while?"

"Your point, Rebecca?"

"My point, Emily, is that she had this weird double standard. Probably because she came from the time when a woman could have a family *or* a career. She loved us enough to not want any of us to be alone in the world."

These sisters were raised as middle class children of the post war boom, a brief, quirky time when the husbands went off to work and the wives had time on their hands. There was no churning of butter, or boiling of laundry water; the women didn't garden or can, bake their own bread, or scrub floors on their hands and knees. Sometimes they visited with other women and, if they were mothers, they looked after their children. Then all of them—the women and the children --waited for the men to come home. There was waiting and there was working; there were the bread servers and the bread winners. Back then, when little boys were asked what they were going to be when they grew up, the question had an element of seriousness. When the same question was asked of little girls, there was whimsy implied. Of course it would all change. It would change hard and sudden and catch many of those grown up little girls by surprise. But, in those days, a woman with a career was just filling in time until she became a wife. Depending on your point of view, a woman's real story began, or ended, at the altar. Then, if the woman became a mother, she disappeared altogether, or loomed larger than life. It all hinges upon how the story is told and who is telling it.

"So you married Omar for your mother?" Elizabeth asks. "Is that what you're saying?"

"The first time I made love with Omar was the very opposite of Mama's first night with daddy. I couldn't wait to have sex with him." Rebecca shakes her head, smiling at the memory, pointedly ignoring her youngest sister. "He had about a zillion candles burning all over his bedroom; cheeses and dates, crusty bread and two chilled bottles of beer set on this copper tray right in the center of the bed. And rose petals scattered over the bed and over the floor leading from the bed to the bedroom door. We undressed ---"

"That's where Daddy made his mistake," I say. "He should have ripped the petals from his two dozen roses! Tore them lose. Set them --"

"Three months later we were on a plane heading here to get married. It was my first airplane ride."

"We were all here for the ceremony." I remind her, raising my glass in a salute. "All of us knee jerk liberals so proud that you were marrying a dark-skinned foreigner," I continue. "It set the BelleBend gossips in a spin. And Daddy was very brave about you getting married in a Unitarian Church."

"Face it, as short as that marriage was, Daddy never saw it as such." Elizabeth runs her hand over her wavy short blonde hair. "Since, as a baptized Catholic, you had not actually been married in the eyes of the Church. So, in Daddy's heart your marriage to a non-Catholic made you not really married."

"I never thought of it that way. Rebecca, you're still a spinster, having *married*---" I pause to make quotation marks in the air. "...A man that was not Catholic. You were never married."

"*Who*," Kate says. "Emily, you have to say 'a man *who* was not Catholic.' Bad grammar to say '*that* was not Catholic.'"

I extend my middle finger in Kate's direction. We four are a security force ever on the look out for grammatical errors, interrupting any conversation to arrest the offender.

"You all know that Omar gave me my nice new Volkswagen, right? Seven years later and he's still showering rose petals."

"If only you'd allowed him to have a few more wives to share the tent with you."

"You're such a xenophobe, Emily," Rebecca says affectionately.

"No. What I am is jealous. The only thing I've ever gotten from Stan is child support. A 'car?' Ha! I was lucky to get out of that house with a set of Corning Ware."

"Look at us," Kate reaches for my cigarettes. "Not a one of us has seen a tenth wedding anniversary."

"Six years and still counting. Time yet for me."

"You know the main secret to your on-going marriage, Elizabeth?" I say. "I mean besides the fact that, as the youngest, you had the benefits of our mistakes. I think the secret is that--very early on--Jacques realized he could never compete with us for your attention. He yielded the floor to your sisters."

"And the secret to Mama and Daddy's long marriage?" asks Rebecca.

"The times," I say without having to think. "It was the curse of their own decades that kept them mismatched and together."

Chapter 4

Margaret and Matthew—1943-1945

HE HAD NEVER paid rent, or an electric bill. Neither one of them had ever hung curtains or set up a bookshelf. Margaret didn't know how to cook and Matthew didn't know how to replace a fuse. She had gone from her parent's house, to Mrs. Benson's boarding house, to this squat cinder block house on Stanford Avenue in Baton Rouge. They had spent a week in the bridal suite at the Palmer House. Which basically decimated the trust fund that was intended to last Matthew a lifetime, had he remained a Brother of Saint Francis. He had never balanced a checkbook and artlessly, and forever, wrote bad checks. The notices from the bank sent Margaret into fits of weeping, or of rage. Matthew always believed that he would be more careful the next month. But the truth was that money was not interesting to him. Just in the way that some people don't care about sports, or opera. Matthew didn't care about money. It was his blind spot.

"We're going to the poor house. A wagon is coming to take us all away!" Margaret would stand clutching the latest bank statement. "The poorhouse," she'd repeat, her voice heavy with doom. The little girls clustered anxiously in their room, weathering the storm. Their parents had read The Children Of Dickens to them. The Sobral girls knew what a poorhouse was, and gruel and having to sleep on dirty straw thrown on cold stone floors. They didn't want to be sent out into the streets to beg. They wanted their father to save them all. They needed desperately to believe, with him, that he would do better next month. Margaret told her daughters, with disgusted resignation, that their father had been raised with a silver spoon in his mouth. A terrible thing, that silver spoon, thought the daughters.

But before the daughters enter the story and before there was a history of books and banks between them, Margaret and Matthew moved into their first home. A soldier, off fighting in the Pacific, owned it and all the furniture in the modest Baton Rouge house. There was a tiny entry hall that opened onto a living room holding a faded blue and orange polka dotted sofa, one wooden rocking chair, a strangely ornate sideboard, and a tall forked lamp with two lampshades. The double bed and matching veneered dresser took up most of the space in the one bedroom. The kitchen was in the back of the house and contained a small marble top table, three wire-backed chairs, a gas stove and a shoulder high Westinghouse refrigerator. The bathroom was across the hall from the kitchen, and there was a screened porch at the end of the hall, facing a large back yard dominated by a massive oak tree. The front of the house was set close to a street of heavy traffic, so that it was almost never quiet.

On their first Christmas together, Matthew gave Margaret a leather-bound anthology of nineteenth century poets, and a diamond and pearl brooch. The heavy brooch was the only memento he had of his mother who had died before Matthew's third birthday. He was just sixteen, and a novice in the brotherhood, when his father also died, leaving the brooch and a modest trust fund to the only surviving child of his first marriage. Margaret gave Matthew a double volume of Sandburg's Abraham Lincoln. Her parents had sent them a cautiously packed and wrapped box of dishes. They sat on the floor in front of the small gas heater in the living room to open their gifts. Afterwards, Margaret carefully smoothed and folded the wrapping paper, as she had seen her mother do.

That afternoon they walked the half block from their house to the bus stop and caught the downtown bus. They ate their Christmas dinner at a small French restaurant. Matthew was effusive and talkative, so happy to be a married man on Christmas Day.

"The oysters from the Gulf are the freshest and biggest in the world, Margaret. If you would only try one, I know you'd just love it." He waved the miniature fork over the wide rumpled gray shell. "On second thought, maybe if you closed your eyes, and tried one," he laughed. "I never quite noticed, before this very moment, that a raw oyster lacks certain aesthetic refinements."

"Even dressed like the Queen of Sheba, I wouldn't look at it. Much less eat it." Margaret sliced into her roasted quail. "Oysters, or any seafood for that matter." She felt homesick for her family's traditional Christmas dinner, the turkey and dressing, the cranberry sauce still holding the shape of its can. She was disappointed with herself for missing anything about Wisconsin.

"To live in Louisiana and not like seafood is like living in Alaska and hating to bundle up."

"Or being a violinist with an aversion to music," Margaret added gamely.

"You'll come around, honey. I know you will." He raised his wine glass to her. "And you'll learn to appreciate wine."

"Never," she said with certainty. Wine would forever recall the feel of cold bathroom tiles on her knees, nausea.

Each morning Matthew got up at four forty-five, dressed, and walked three blocks to attend Mass. He returned home a little after six and brewed a pot of coffee and chicory. He then carried two cups of dark coffee and a newspaper into the bedroom on a tray, waking Margaret with strong Louisiana coffee and the news of the day. For thirty-five years that would be how their days began.

Margaret made breakfast while Matthew looked over his class notes. After breakfast, he caught the bus and spent the day teaching history at Baton Rouge Eastern High School. Margaret filled the shallow kitchen sink with water and soap suds, washed the two cups and saucers, the two plates, and then scrubbed the burned bits of eggs from the small frying pan. She dried and put the dishes away; she made the bed and smoothed down the chenille bedspread. Then she would take whatever book she was reading and curl up on the ugly sofa and read until noon. For lunch, every day, she had a glass of milk and a slice of bread smeared with wartime margarine and sprinkled with sugar. After lunch she took her patent leather pocketbook and walked to the neighborhood grocery store. At the store she wandered among the three aisles trying to match her ration cards to her limited cooking skills. The chubby, smiling woman behind the counter gave her suggestions and was soon passing on simple recipes to the young bride. Margaret eventually realized that the woman enjoyed talking to her and looked forward to her daily shopping trip. So Margaret tried to always arrive at the store at about the same time. Mrs. Gimbroni and Matthew were the only people she talked to.

"They are smart as they can be. It keeps surprising me." Matthew had just arrived home and Margaret was sliding a lopsided meatloaf into the oven.

"Who? Who's so smart?"

"They are, the girls. The girls are as smart as the boys!" Matthew pulled a Jax beer from the refrigerator. "In fact, I'd say some of them are a lot smarter."

"Are you joking?" She ran water over the pair of potatoes in the sink.

"No I'm not. I got the first tests graded today and the top four papers were all girls!" He got a glass from the cupboard and carefully poured the cold beer down its tilted side.

Of course he was surprised. Margaret suddenly understood that Matthew had never been around girls. Never. Maybe he knew a few women who answered phones, took dictation, or cleaned house. He had never had a woman friend. And he had certainly never been around young girls. It wasn't at all a matter of male arrogance. It was genuine awe. No wonder he had been so smitten by Margaret. The weight of the realization took her breath away.

Once a week she walked the seven blocks to a small library and checked out four or five books. By the end of the week she would have read them all. She reread the Victorians, Hawthorn, Melville and all of Willa Cather's novels. She read Hemingway, Steinbeck and Faulkner. Margaret had originally found Faulkner difficult, obtuse, and then she found herself drawn to his long sentences, the constricted perimeters of Yoknapatawpha County.

"Matthew, did you read The Sound and The Fury?"

"I did. I thought it was quite good. Perhaps my favorite Faulkner."

Margaret had just finished washing the supper dishes and dried her hands on a red checked dishcloth as she sat across the table from Matthew. He had been grading student papers.

"It is almost as though Faulkner is drawing back a curtain, letting me observe bits and pieces of the things you and Irene and the people at the newspaper take for granted. Odd as his characters are." She folded the cloth over the back of the spare chair. "Those people living back in those woods are people you already have a sense about. They are native to you. Even just reading about them makes me feel like a clumsy archeologist, or an alien."

"Well, I can see how that might be, Margaret." He put down his red pen, eager for conversation. Most evenings she left the kitchen as soon as the dishes were done and was still reading in the living room when he went to bed. "You didn't grow up around colored people and plantations and share croppers. I get the feeling there wasn't so much inbreeding in Wisconsin," he joked. "More fresh blood and sassiness."

"That's not what I ---"

"Now Faulkner is from an old Mississippi family." Matthew pushed his chair back. "Southern aristocracy is altogether different from upper classes elsewhere. Bloodlines matter and wealth does not, lost wealth is respected more than held wealth. But keep in mind, Margaret, that Mississippi is also very different from Louisiana.

Some might say the difference between the Scottish influence and that of the Spanish. Mississippi people don't seem to have a sense of...of, for want of a better word, *munificence.* They draw their shutters, rather than sitting out on the porch. And the ground is harder. I had an old aunt who always said that Louisiana was God's masterpiece, that ..." He could see that he was not holding her interest. So he stopped talking and waited for her to say more. She had taken a Chesterfield from the pack next to his notebook.

"I still have problems with the dialect." She leaned forward while he struck a match to light her cigarette. She had hoped for a conversation, a back and forth, rather than a lecture. She had wanted to talk about her sense of isolation. Margaret stood up and walked out into the living room.

February was endless. It had begun with a string of warm days, as warm as Wisconsin in June, and was abruptly followed by an extended cold snap, days of monotonous drizzle. Though the temperature stayed above freezing, the damp chill crept into her bones in a place where buildings were not designed for cold weather. Margaret was cold at the library, cold at Mrs. Gimbroni's grocery, but most of all she was cold in their little block house. She went back to bed after Matthew left for school and stayed huddled under blankets to read. When she got up, she stood as closely as she could to one of the house's three small gas heaters. The blue flames flickered like the ends of lit matchsticks, giving out barely enough heat to cast a glow. She had scorched a nightgown and once had almost caught her coat on fire by standing too closely to the house's only source of warmth. She returned to bed in the afternoons and read and stared at the water patterns on the windows and listened to the groan of traffic just past the front door. She tried to be on time for her grocery shopping. She tried to be interested in cooking. She tried to look forward to Matthew's homecomings. The days were endless.

But February did end, and by late March all of Baton Rouge was in bloom: azaleas, gardenias, camellias, and roses; ruby colored flowers and pale gold ones, riots of pink in every possible shade. The air was heady with thick rich scents, sweet olive among them. Matthew and Margaret began taking walks after supper. Sometimes she would leave her hand in his as they walked under the glistening domes of massive oak branches and past front yard gardens gone almost wild with bloom. She learned to not be so impatient with him, to slow her fast northern pace and stroll, to listen to his stories of growing up along the Mississippi, and of the characters from his boyhood town. He was a good storyteller, though most times his stories took far too long to tell. She would edit them in her head, pare them down and make them concise, like stories for a newspaper.

She kept the windows open all day and warm scented breezes blew through the house, along with noise from the traffic. Her cooking improved and she had almost worked her way through all the novels on the shelves of the neighborhood library. Yet the long days still seemed too long, each day exactly like the day before. Margaret was bored and restless, weary of her own company.

"Matthew, I wonder why I'm not pregnant yet."

"Pregnant?" He almost dropped the bucket he was carrying, sending a splash of warm water and ammonia over the linoleum floor. It was a Saturday and they were washing windows together. "Margaret, why would you be pregnant, I mean …" His voice trailed off, confused.

"Surely you know how women become pregnant?"

"Yes, of course I do. But we haven't talked about it and, and so it hadn't occurred to me. That you, that you and I might have a, a baby."

"Really?" Margaret turned away from the windowpane she had been drying with one of Matthew's discarded undershirts. "It didn't occur to you? What were you expecting to happen?"

"I don't know." He carefully set the bucket down and crossed the living room to sit in the rocking chair, as if he had just realized he had worn himself out washing windows and needed to rest. "I guess I thought we would go on the way we are. I've already gotten that position running the summer school. Which will be nice for us."

"But you hadn't considered that we might start a family?" She sat across from him on the sofa, thinking of the weight of the long voiceless days when Matthew was teaching, the different weight when he was home. When it was just the two of them in the little house rattled by passing traffic, two such different people. A baby would change all of that. Margaret thought that she might be better at mothering than at being a wife.

"That would be wonderful, Margaret. I mean, if it is something you want. If we had talked about it, I would have been considering it all along. But we haven't."

"I took it for granted. After all, you're such a good Catholic. We don't do anything to not have babies."

"Margaret, honey," Matthew winced. The conversation was difficult for him. It had taken him by surprise. There was so much they hadn't talked about. So much he wanted to talk about, and also so much he wasn't comfortable discussing. On the occasional nights they made love they kept the lights off in the bedroom. In the mornings it was as if nothing had happened between them. If she had spoken of it, he might have had an idea of what to say back. Their lovemaking was a wonder to him. He was so grateful. At first it disturbed him that the morning afterwards seemed like any other morning to Margaret. But he came to accept that, along with her extended silences. She was a dreamer.

"The thing is, maybe there's a problem. A medical problem. I wanted to suggest that you go to see your doctor." She leaned over and patted his knee. "The one who gave you the school physical? You liked him, didn't you? Ask him to see if he can find a reason that I'm not pregnant yet."

So Matthew did as she asked and went to see a doctor, who could find nothing wrong with him. Six weeks later Margaret went to the same doctor, with a loss of appetite, an inability to sleep, and was told that she was almost three months pregnant.

There would be a change, a break in the monotony. She had something to plan for, to anticipate. At the library she checked out children's books, she rediscovered A Child's Garden of Verses and set about memorizing all of the poems. She would be a mother, her hands and days full. *And does it seem quite fair to you/ when all the sky is clear and blue/ and I would like so much to play/ to have to go to bed by day?*

When she was five months pregnant, and had known Matthew for almost a year, they received a letter from the sergeant who owned their house. The hastily written letter said that he would be arriving in Baton Rouge before Christmas, ready to move back into his house. Several weeks later Matthew's principal told him, with great regret, that three former teachers were returning from the war and the school was obliged to make room for them on the faculty. There weren't enough students, or money, to make it possible for the school to retain its highly qualified new history teacher. Margaret assumed that Matthew would begin working on new arrangements. He filed the soldier's letter away; the forfeited house and vanishing job were bridges that they would cross when they came to them.

Her labor pains began on a Saturday in the first week of December. Matthew was beside himself, pacing the perimeters of the small house, brewing coffee, which she refused, sweeping and re-sweeping the kitchen floor. He filled a basin with cool water, swirled a washcloth into the water, wrung it out and carefully placed the damp cloth on her forehead.

"Matthew, this house is cold enough. Please stop," she handed the washcloth back to him. "Dr. Ball said when the pains were six minutes apart it would be time. I've watched the clock. It's time to go to the store. Please tell Mrs. Gimbroni the baby is coming."

Mr. Gimbroni drove them to the hospital in the van he used for delivering groceries. The boxes of meats and produce slid precariously around in the back of the van as he sped through the streets, squealing into curves, and shedding precious war era rubber in his nervous haste. He parked the van, and left its motor running, in front of the tall hospital building overlooking a small lake. He and Matthew both grappled with the suitcase, neither willing to relinquish his hold on the handle, as Margaret walked alone into the hospital. Mr. Gimbroni stayed with the couple while they filled out paperwork and until a nurse arrived to order Margaret into a wheel chair. Margaret watched the kindly old man walk out of the hospital and fought the urge to call him back. She felt as though Mr. Gimbroni carried with him her very last chance to change her mind, to call off the impending birth, the entire absurd idea of a baby.

"She's a genius, Margaret. Really! Her eyes are already opened, I swear. Wide open."

Matthew was standing in the doorway of the hospital room. His hands were crossed over his heart, his hair was rumpled and his shirt wrinkled. Margaret wanted only to go back to sleep. She could think of nothing to say to her husband. She had been trying to pull herself above the thick molasses of leftover ether. Now she wanted back in.

The nurse, who was setting a pitcher of water on the table next to Margaret's bed, laughed. "Babies aren't puppies, Mr. Sobral! Their eyes open right away. They don't see very much at first." She fluffed the pillow behind Margaret's head. "But they are born with their little eyes open."

"We'll name her Emily," her voice was slurry. After Emily Dickinson, she thought, who wrote beautiful poems and never married. *The soul selects her own society, then shuts the door...* Margaret slept.

It was hospital policy to keep new mothers for ten days. On the second day Matthew arrived for the early morning visiting hours looking as though he had slept in his clothes. Which, apparently, he had.

"Sergeant Raymond LeBlanc was at the house when I got there last night, Margaret. He said he'd sent a telegram." Matthew stood by the bed, "Which never arrived." He was careful not to step too closely. He was still struggling with the idea that a fully formed baby, a complete human being, had come from his wife's body. He was awestricken by Margaret, her power and resiliency. "I will get someone from the school to drive over with me this afternoon. It won't take long to pack up our things."

"Where did you spend the night"? She pushed herself into a sitting position.

"Here."

"In the hospital? The lobby?"

"I caught the last bus. I couldn't think where else to go."

"Here?" Her voice cracked, shattered.

"Please, Margaret. Please don't cry." When he reached for her hand, she slid it under the covers. He took a step away from the bed. "It's going to be all right. It will work out, Margaret. Wait and see, don't worry honey. It will all work out. We'll be fine." When he left to catch the city bus for school she was still sitting up in the bed, shuddering with soundless sobs. Tears were streaming down her face, over her chin, wetting the front of her hospital gown.

She had finally calmed herself, was taking deep breaths and looking out the window at the lake when the nurse brought the baby in for her feeding. "I don't think I can hold her right now, Ernestine. Maybe later." Margaret turned her face to the wall.

What had she done? Christmas was almost here and they had no home and no money. No future. It seemed that Matthew was incapable of taking care of the two of them, and now there was this baby. What could she possibly have been thinking when she wanted a baby? She knew no more about babies than she knew about sailing yachts. What would become of them, and poor little homeless Emily? And why had Margaret married Matthew? She could not, for the life of her, remember why. As miserable as her life had become in Lake Charles, she had known how to navigate it. Here she was helpless. Sliding down in the bed, Margaret covered her face with her pillow and howled into it.

The Daughters—1963

"When Mama was a teenager, do you think she talked about sex?" Kate was still flopped back on their parents' bed, her curly hair haloed around her head. Rebecca had returned the photograph of their mother to the dresser top.

"Or *had* sex," Emily added, just to get a rise from Rebecca, their mother's second born and staunchest supporter.

"That is pure dee disgusting, Emily," Rebecca almost shouted. "Daddy would wash your mouth out with soap if he heard you!"

"But first he'd have to wash out his own ears." Elizabeth had a point, their father was quite squeamish about open discussions of human reproduction.

"Well, she wasn't a Catholic," Emily said.

"Number one she was a Baptized Catholic, she just didn't go to church." Rebecca pushed one forefinger against the other. "And number two, do you think non- Catholic teenagers go around having sex here, there and all over the place?"

"Things are different in the north," said Elizabeth. "We don't have any idea of what those teenagers are like." Her blonde hair was teased into a puffy bouffant. She imagined that she looked like Petula Clark.

"As a recent high school graduate," Emily said, "I have to admit that I don't know a single girl who has ever had sex." There was no need to spend their last afternoon together getting Rebecca mad at her.

"What about Denise Denoux?"

"Kate, she was in eighth grade and she was a Protestant and she got married long before she had that baby. Denise's own mama got married when she was thirteen too."

Sex was the Bermuda Triangle, the Loch Ness Monster, and Area 51 to those Deep South Catholic girls. Their most explicit, yet vague, reproductive information came from a line in the Hail Mary, "Blessed is the fruit of thy womb---" Everything *down there* was *womb.* The sisters did know that babies came because of sex, but they knew nothing of their own sexual organs, never mind having even a clue about male anatomy. Not a one of the girls in this story had ever heard the words: *vagina*, *sperm*, or *gonads*. There was something huge and unknown that happened between heavy kissing and the womb, but what that was remained a mystery to them. The sisters were like Nancy Drew, and Trixie Belden trying to solve the mystery of sexual intercourse. The only thing more unsolvable was the bind between their parents.

"Do all Protestants commit birth control?" asked Elizabeth.

"If Mama and Daddy had, then maybe they would have waited to have Emily until after they got their feet on the ground." Rebecca tapped the framed photograph. "If they hadn't been so poor maybe Mama wouldn't be such a nervous wreck, always worrying about money."

"She worries about money because of the Depression," said Elizabeth.

"Well, it's not as if she's the only one her age who grew up in the Depression," Emily said. "I just don't think our friends' mothers go around slamming doors and crying their eyes out every time a letter comes from the bank. Daddy is good friends with Mr. Sam and those other people at the bank. They're looking out for us."

"A year after I was born Mama was still wearing maternity dresses, with belts cinched around her waist," said Rebecca. "And then daddy got you that gigantic tricycle for Christmas. You were three years old and still couldn't reach the pedals two years later."

"Hey! I remember that tricycle!" Elizabeth delighted in finding ways to include herself in the distant past of family history. "I never did learn to ride it. That thing was gigantic."

"And he bought the Oldsmobile, without even asking Mama." Kate sat up on the bed and wrapped her arms around her skinny knees. "He worships the ground she walks on, yet spends money we don't have without thinking for a minute that it will break Mama's heart."

"Daddy gets carried away. He's a dreamer," Emily said. "'If you don't have a dream, and you don't ever dream…'" She made her fingers do happy talk, like in South Pacific, which they all saw together at BelleBend's Grand Theater.

"Now, despite everything, all of Mama's objections, you are going off to a college that there is no way on earth we can afford." Rebecca looked at Emily as if she had just run over a puppy, or knocked down somebody's great grandmother. "Why couldn't you just go to LSU like everybody else?"

"Something will work out," Emily said. "It always does."

Chapter 5

Margaret and Matthew----1945-1946

THAT EVENING MATTHEW brought Margaret a box of chocolates and the good news that a colleague had agreed to store their two cartons of household goods in his family's attic.

"I found a hotel room, right off State Street." He lifted the lid of the candy box as if he were unveiling a rare treasure. Margaret turned away from him and stared at the lake through the window. "It rents rooms by the week. A lot of the Louisiana troops are coming back just now. "Matthew replaced the lid on the candy box. "Finding a place was a lucky break." He stood quietly at the foot of her bed, holding the box with both hands. Margaret closed her eyes and tried to fall asleep.

The next afternoon Margaret woke up from a nap to the sight of Matthew extending his arms to take their daughter from the nurse. His face was pale and reverent; he looked as though he might cry.

"She's not made of glass, it's just that head you have to be careful of," the nurse was saying. "Support it in the crook of your arm, like this. Now sit down and I'll hand her to you real easy."

Margaret could see that Matthew was holding his breath, and that he kept holding it as Ernestine settled the small bundle into his arms.

"Now that's the way, hold her good with your left arm and I'll hand the bottle over to you in your right. You're doing just fine."

Margaret's milk had not come in. She was sure it was because she had cried so hard and long that she was withered inside, dry and used up. She hadn't wanted to hold the baby because the sight of all that helplessness broke her heart; made her begin crying all over again. And she was so unbearably tired. She fell back to sleep and dreamed that Matthew was telling her one of his unending stories. They were walking on a winding path that, in the dream, Margaret understood led to nowhere. As they wandered, her husband droned on and on.

"If that isn't the sweetest thing."

The nurse's voice woke her. Evening had come, the room was dusky and in the shadows she saw Matthew, still in the chair, still holding Emily; his voice a low murmur, as he talked to his daughter.

One early afternoon she woke up to the scent of lilacs. A small plump woman, her hair a crown of tight silver curls, was sitting next to Margaret's bed crocheting.

"Well, there you are, awake at last. And still pretty as a picture after all you've been through."

Margaret pushed herself into a sitting position. "Do you work here?" She suspected that she might still be asleep. "Have I---"

"Heavens no, honey!" The woman put her needlework down and rocked forward leaning on her knees and laughing, as if the bewildered young woman in the bed had just told a wonderful joke. "I am your cousin Irma. Well, Matthew's father's cousin by marriage, which makes me your cousin by marriage. Once removed. You see?"

"But where did you come from?"

"Bayou Goula, Mrs. Matthew Sobral, which is exactly where you are going just as soon as we can get you and little Emily away from this place with its elevators and institutional fare. We are going to get you your strength back with some good country cooking and fresh air and more rest than you'll ever know what to do with."

When Margaret was finally released from the hospital, she, Matthew, and their baby went to live with Irma and Pierre Richard on their Bayou Goula farm, a few miles outside the town of Plaquemine and an hour's drive from Baton Rouge. Pierre was a soft-spoken man, broad shouldered and bulky, with large work worn hands. He cautiously drove his old black Buick, loaded with all the Sobrals' earthly possessions, along the dirt roads and did not even try to inject a word into his wife's happy chatter.

"Oh, Pierre can coax anything from the ground. We have the best greens, all winter long. You will be as strong as an ox, Margaret, before you even know it. Take my word!" The baby began to fuss and Irma leaned over and took her from Margaret. "And eggs? My heavens. Our egg yolks are just as gold as if Midas, himself, touched them. We only have the one cow, but she gives the sweetest milk!"

The Richard home was the center of a small settlement, a suspended island of trees bordered by the meandering bayou and surrounded by a flat sea of sugar cane fields. The two-story house was set within a grove of massive oak trees and overlooked Bayou

Goula. It had a large screened-in front porch and a wide central hall that ran the length of the house. Past the back yard, the garden and the chicken yard, there was a scattering of inhabited cabins that had once been the slave quarters for a long-gone plantation. Pierre owned and farmed about a hundred acres of land where he raised hogs, corn for the hogs and eighty acres of sugar cane. The men who helped him work his farm all lived in the cabins of 'the quarters.'

"This is as far away from the kitchen as possible, nice and quiet for you, "Irma said. She opened the door to a high-ceilinged bedroom that held a large black walnut bed with matching dresser. "That crib has been in the Richard family for over a hundred years." She pointed to a miniature rosewood spindle bed, a pale blue satin quilt tucked into its corners.

The room had two ceiling-to-floor windows overlooking the bayou, which was fringed by moss-draped oak and cypress trees. Margaret walked to the window and saw that, past the bayou, fallow sugar cane fields stretched as far as the eye could see. "A lovely room, Irma. Thank you." She was thinking that most of their Baton Rouge house would fit into this one room.

"We have the indoor bathroom at the end of the hall, and a temperamental hot water system."

It was soon obvious that, though his heart was in it, Matthew was ill suited for farm work. In his first week of trying to help Pierre and his small crew, Matthew parked the tractor at an angle, forgot to set the brake and it had eased slowly into the side of the barn. A day later he nicked the edge of his shoe with a pick ax, a bare fraction away from amputating his little toe. The following day Pierre drove into town and returned a few hours later to say that, if he wanted it, Matthew had a job at Plaquemine's newly opened appliance store.

Country people were beginning to abandon their wooden iceboxes in favor of refrigerators. Business at Nelson's Tool and Appliances was thriving. Pierre assured Matthew that the owner was desperate for help, for someone who could read and write, who had experience talking to the public. Matthew took the job and borrowed Pierre's dusty black Buick for his commute; solemnly keeping the tank topped with gas, stopping at the two-pump station on the highway each afternoon before turning onto the dirt road to Bayou Goula.

Rose, the young woman who cooked and cleaned for the Richards, had given birth to a little girl, Josephine, a week before Emily was born. In the early mornings Matthew lifted Emily from her crib and carried her down to the kitchen, letting Margaret sleep in. Before he left for work he would place his daughter beside Josephine, in a wooden cradle on the brick kitchen floor so that Rose could keep an eye on the two infants. Margaret wandered downstairs sometime in the mid morning. Often she and Rose sat across from one another in rocking chairs, Margaret giving Emily her bottle while Rose nursed little Josephine. Margaret tried to make conversation, but found that the slender black woman was very shy and uncomfortable when pressed to talk. Irma refused to let Margaret help with house cleaning, insisting that she rest. Every day, near noon, Rose placed a plate of chicken livers and collard greens at Margaret's place at the dining room table, and then set about serving up the Richard's main meal. Irma watched over Margaret as she ate.

"You need to build up your blood, honey. Childbirth robs you of your natural iron," she insisted. "It will be at least another month before you feel like yourself." The sweet natured woman seemed oblivious to the other new mother, the one in the kitchen holding a baby on her hip as she scraped flour into bacon drippings in the bottom of the cast iron pot.

In the evenings the Richards always retired to bed right after supper. On the warmer nights Margaret sat on the porch reading and smoking while Matthew carried Emily outside. He walked along the sluggish bayou, with his daughter cocooned in blankets in his arms, and told Emily stories. The thick moist air was noisy with the sounds of night birds, frogs and crickets; still Margaret could hear the slow murmur of Matthew's voice.

"See the moon, Emily, that curved shape? It is a very young, or a very old moon and is called a *crescent* moon. The Mississippi makes a crescent around the city of New Orleans, the river forms that very same shape you see in the sky now. That's why they call New Orleans 'The Crescent City.' We'll go there one day, you and your mother and I. It's a magical place once frequented by pirates. Now pirates are usually unsavory characters, robbers and crooks. But there was once a very noble pirate, Jean Lafitte, who …"

Matthew liked to keep Margaret, haloed by her reading lamp, in view; so he didn't stray very far on the path beside the water, it was more a walking back and forth, the baby cradled in his arms. He returned to the porch once Emily was asleep. Then he would carry the baby upstairs while Margaret trailed behind them, turning off the house lights as she went.

"It's a criminal thing, Margaret. Plain evil. James sold a refrigerator today to coloreds he knew don't have electricity at their place." Matthew had just turned off his bedside lamp but was still sitting up. "Those poor people came in and put down their money, so proud of themselves for being able to afford a down payment."

"He really knew for a fact that they had no electricity, nothing to hook it to?" Matthew nodded. She placed her hand on her open book to hold her place. "What will happen when they get the refrigerator and realize it doesn't work?"

"I asked him that and he said that when we delivered the Frigidaire, to leave it out on the porch." Then he imitated his boss's countrified accent. "'They would want to have it setting out like some kind of trophy for them other niggers to see.'" Matthew shook his head, as though he couldn't believe what he was saying. "James told me that he already knew they couldn't afford the payments. It would make it easier for us when we went to repossess." He had raised his voice, and looked over to see if it had disturbed the baby. "To have the Frigidaire left out front," he whispered. "He told me he always keeps the down payments. He bragged that he has sold that same refrigerator to coloreds a number of times already."

"He really said that?" She closed her book.

"Like he was showing off a straight flush hand in a poker game."

"That is about the most mean-spirited thing I have ever heard."

"I tried to argue with him, but ---"

"Matthew, you can't risk losing your job." She put her hand on his arm. "At the same time, you have to find some way to protect those people. Maybe if you just innocently ---"

"Oh, don't worry, Margaret. I didn't make James angry at me. He thought it was funny, a joke." Matthew slid down into the bed. Margaret lifted her hand from his arm. He turned on his side, away from his wife, and faced the wall. "Like I was some kind of rube at the country fair, his pockets turned inside out."

Margaret began to work with Rose in the kitchen, nothing strenuous enough to earn Irma's censure. She wanted to learn to cook. She would chop onions or help punch out biscuits while the babies napped in their shared cradle. The two women eventually began talking to one another about small things: recipes, the spring plantings, or the babies' sleep schedule. As the weather warmed, Margaret began carrying the little girls outside. She would spread a quilt over the grass under a wide branched oak and read while the babies lay on their backs watching the patterns of leaves and clouds. Both infants learned to sit up on their own and began crawling at about the same time. If either one of the babies started crying, Rose or Irma would always seem to hear it and rush outside to scoop up the unhappy baby while Margaret returned to her reading. She had no notion of how to comfort a crying child.

In late April a letter arrived for Matthew from the school board of a district in Northern Louisiana. The letter said that the local high school was looking for a new assistant principal for the next school year, someone who was qualified to teach history.

With the warm weather Margaret began waking earlier. Though Matthew had no newspaper to carry up to her, he resumed the ritual of serving morning coffee to his wife in bed. He would have already dressed for his work day and taken Emily downstairs and handed her over to Rose for a diaper change. While Rose was setting out breakfast for Pierre and Irma and feeding the two babies, Matthew carried a tray up the stairs to his wife.

He would sit, dressed in suit and tie, on the bed beside Margaret. The two of them sipped their coffee, speculating about his new job and commiserating about his present one. It was the best part of Matthew's day: the eastern light slipping like a cat over the bedcovers; bird song and muted barnyard clatter wafting through the open windows; his beautiful wife, sitting up in bed, her hair sleep tousled and her pale eyes looking directly at him. Seeing her hopeful and present was like turning the first page of a brand new book.

After Matthew left for town, Margaret dressed and went downstairs. Rose had shown her how to distract the chickens from their nests and gather their eggs. The chicken yard had become Margaret's special territory. She collected fresh eggs, fed the chickens, and refreshed their nests with new straw. Inside she helped Irma and Rose with light housework. And so the mornings passed. She still occasionally took the babies out into the yard, but was finding it more difficult to concentrate on reading now that the babies were really crawling. One late morning she had looked up from Katherine Anne Porter's Ship of Fools just in time to glimpse two diapered rear ends disappearing over the ridge above the bayou. She threw down her book and made a dash for the babies, lifting them both just as their little dimpled hands dipped into the mud along the water's edge.

At noon Margaret joined Irma and Pierre in the dark cool dining room. Now that Irma felt her blood was sufficiently iron-infused, she had released her from her liver diet. Margaret found herself looking forward to the rich mid day meal: the gumbos and stews, roasted chicken with dressing, or a glimmering baked ham, bowls of overcooked vegetables, flaky biscuits and always a fresh-baked pie. In the afternoons, Rose placed Emily and Josephine on a quilt under the ceiling fan out on the screened porch floor. She sat beside them, patting and singing the little girls to sleep. Then she set up her ironing board by the living room window facing the porch and ironed clothes, watching over the babies until they woke from their naps.

Margaret and Irma went upstairs to their bedrooms for their own afternoon naps. Sometimes Margaret actually slept, drowsy and sluggish, overcome by the rich meal. Other times she wrote long amusing letters to her friends, detailing life on the farm, exaggerating her barnyard skills. She wrote of Bubba the bloodthirsty rooster and of the rotten egg she once dropped on her foot, the stunning stench of it. After the first few weeks at Bayou Goula Margaret had found the energy to reconnect with her Wisconsin friends, once she had something to say. But for most of the afternoons Margaret sat in bed reading from the stack of books and magazines Matthew carried home for her from the Plaquemine library. When the heaviest heat of the day had passed, Margaret would walk down the hall, run a cool bath and soak. After she dressed she would go downstairs and take over the babies from Rose. She sat out on the porch and read poetry to them: "*When I was sick and lay abed I had two pillows at my head---*" If the babies were restless, and in no mood for poems, she jingled a bundle of metal measuring spoons, or rolled a bright bed rubber ball covered with yellow stars across the boards of the porch floor. "Whee!" she'd exclaim, checking her watch to see how much longer it would be until Matthew arrived and took over the childcare. "Catch the ball!"

While Margaret watched the babies and kept glancing toward the road for the Buick to come into view, Irma and Rose set out supper: a cool pitcher of butter milk, cold biscuits, jars of jam, slabs of ham, leftover pie. The door to the Buick slammed shut and Matthew would rush up the front steps, swing open the screen door and scoop Emily into his arms. About the same time they would hear Pierre washing his hands at the pump outside the kitchen door, his heavy step on the backstairs. The return of the men marked Rose's departure time. She would gather up her daughter, and a flour sack packed with dinner leftovers and a Ball jar of buttermilk. She closed the kitchen door quietly behind herself, and walked quickly through the back yard toward her little house in the quarters.

The hot long days were almost seamless, sporadically cooled and shaken by a heavy thunderstorm; but other than the times of wind and drenching rain, they were the same. The green blades of sugar cane were ankle high, and then waist high, tall enough to bend and rise with any wind that touched the fields. By late July a large man could take three steps into the cane and disappear. The nights resounded with a cacophony of frogs and crickets, whip-poor-wills called from the trees along the bayou and around the house, the paddles of the ceiling fans churned the slow dense air, mosquitoes hummed at the window screens. The summer was passing.

One August Monday Matthew took the day off and he and Margaret drove to Bunkie, Louisiana. They were to look at a house a school board member had offered to rent to them at a low price. They left right after breakfast when the roads were still cool, the asphalt not yet softening and sending up wavering lines of heat. Within an hour of leaving Bayou Goula, they were driving through cotton country, miles of cotton fields with rows of parched, narrow bushes as far as the eye could see, the stiff, spindly crops so different from the lush sugar cane fields they had just left behind. They were driving north, yet the landscape was becoming hotter. Shortly before noon they passed by the town limit sign for Bunkie, a scattering of weathered building and a small grocery store dwarfed by a tin R.C. Cola sign. After driving through the deserted town center--a railroad station, a cluster of stores, and a small church set back on the only green lawn in sight--they found Lee Street. The two-bedroom house was the smallest in a row of houses on a quiet, almost treeless street. They had yet to glimpse a single soul, the dusty, shade-less neighborhood was deserted.

"Dr. Monroe said the door would be unlocked. For us just to make ourselves at home, "Matthew said as he turned the knob on the front door of 205 Lee Street.

"It's certainly quiet around here," he added, pushing the door open.

"Only mad dogs and Englishmen."

"I beg your pardon?" He was holding the door for her.

"A Noel Coward song: 'Only mad dogs and Englishmen go out in the mid day sun.'"

"Well, I'd feel enlivened by the sight of either," Matthew stepped aside to let Margaret walk into the house ahead of him.

The inside was clean and appeared to be almost new; the house had probably been built shortly before the war. There was a spacious front room, a sunny kitchen and two bedrooms: a very small one and a larger one divided by a bright pink bathroom. A narrow back porch opened onto a fenced in back yard that was not much larger than the front porch at the Richards' house.

"Our own place," Matthew exclaimed, as though he planned on signing a bill of sale, rather than a one-year lease.

"Yes," Margaret said, looking out the window and wondering if she could ever adjust to the absence of trees.

Daughters—1980

"Remember 'Devil in the Ditch,'" I ask. It is late; we've probably had too much to drink. We should go off to bed, in pairs, as we did for all our years in this house. Rebecca and I, the older ones, off to our double bed in the back with its wide windows overlooking a grove of pecan trees, our neighbor's pasture, and the distant watery fields of rice; the bedroom next to the kitchen. Then Kate and Elizabeth heading to their double bed in the front room facing the River Road, the levee and the Mississippi.

"What was the thing with all those ditches in Bunkie," asks Elizabeth, who is the only one of us who never actually lived there. "That's what I remember most about our trips back to Bunkie, playing 'Devil in The Ditch.' It was so scary, the scariest game I ever played."

"Because the devil was alive to us," I say. "Whatever kid was in the ditch trying to catch us, drag us down, while we jumped back and forth across the ditch, whatever kid that was, truly became the devil."

"Exactly. Scary."

"I never believed in the devil," Kate insists. She has unfastened her barrette; her Botticelli hair reaches past her shoulders. "I just didn't want to get hurt. I stayed on one side of the ditch. None of that back and forth shit for me."

"Kate, did you ever even believe in God," asks Rebecca. "Believing in the devil is the easy one. God is the conundrum."

"Not for Daddy." Elizabeth gestures toward the hall that leads to the bedroom our parents once shared. That room, at the end of the house, where our father is waiting for God to come to get him and carry him away for his reunion with our mother.

"We were talking about Bunkie," I say. "All those flat straight streets, all those ditches."

"When I think of Bunkie, I think of it as the place where our parents had fun, back before I was born." Elizabeth turns to face us. "*Fun.* I can't imagine."

"They did. I remember," I say.

"I think there's one more can of frozen lemonade." Kate abruptly stands up.

"One more for the road," Rebecca raises her glass and sips the lukewarm dregs of her whiskey sour.

Of us all, Rebecca drinks the least. She is abandoning her habitual sobriety in favor of the company of sisters, the last hurrah before we are orphaned. Kate opens the freezer and our father's frosted pewter beer mug falls out, as if on cue. It lands on the floor, makes a weighted bounce, swivels, and stops next to Kate's foot. All four of us look at it, speechless.

Daddy's mid-morning ritual: while his colleagues were taking their coffee breaks, he would come back to the house and fix a plate of crackers and a chunk of hogshead cheese. He would open a beer, take his frosty mug from the freezer, carefully tilt it, so as not to raise too high a head of foam, and fill it with beer. Within fifteen minutes he was on his way back to the office. Yet, every mid morning, there was that same ritual and the same pride in the beer's icy vessel, the simple pleasure he never, ever failed to relish. Not a one of his daughters is a beer drinker, and not a one of us wants to reach down and claim that beer mug. It seems, though, that grief is asking after us, demanding the homage of daughters.

Chapter 6

Margaret and Matthew---1946—1948

THE LAST DAY of August and the pavement in front of the little house was so hot that Matthew and Pierre gingerly stepped over it as they unloaded furniture from the farm truck. On days like this there was always talk of frying eggs on the pavement. Margaret didn't doubt it could be done and envisioned dropping a spoonful of lard and a couple of farm eggs to sizzle on the concrete, an impromptu lunch for the movers. In addition to the spindle-railed baby bed and the battered high chair, Irma had rounded up the smaller sofa from her front parlor, and from the attic a brass double bed, a maple dresser, several lamps, a sturdy card table and four wooden folding chairs.

While the men put the bed together in the back bedroom, Margaret unpacked the ice chest. Emily had just about learned to walk and was staggering from chair to chair in the kitchen, catching hold of her mother's hem for balance.

"Emily, the ice is all melted, I've got to get these things in the Frigidaire before they spoil," Margaret unfastened her daughter's fingers from her flared black and white checked skirt and patted both little hands onto the seat of the nearest chair.

"This is the house that Jack built. This is the malt that lay in the house that Jack built. . . ." Margaret started reciting the long poem that always enthralled the little girl, kept her still with listening. She put a metal tray of deviled eggs, several waxed paper packages of fried chicken, a peach pie, a basket of eggs and a jar of buttermilk into the refrigerator. She unpacked a fruit crate of jars filled with the summer's bounty: green beans, snap peas, butterbeans, cucumber pickles, and round red globes of tomatoes that Irma and Rose had canned in the big Bayou Goula kitchen.

". . .This is the maiden all forlorn, who milked the cow with the crumpled horn . . ."

The late morning sunlight filtered through the window and caught the glassy colors of the vegetables as Margaret placed them on the kitchen shelf. She had seen the greens and red of this summer harvest ripen on their vines, and had helped to pick and sort them. She had watched over the babies while the other two women scalded the vegetables, spooned them into jars and rushed back and forth moving deep cauldrons of boiling water over the big gas range. Now the Sobrals had two shelves filled with preserved Bayou Goula mornings. Would they think of the Richard's farm with each jar they opened?

". . .This is the cock that crowed in the morn. . ." Margaret scooped her little girl into her arms and looked out at the small barren back yard. *"And woke the preacher all shaven and shorn."* She had not cried, though Irma and Rose were both sobbing as they hugged goodbye on the porch this early morning. What had broken Margaret's heart was the sight of the two little girls—dark and light--crawling over the vivid greens of a shady clover patch, the babies pulling up and

holding onto one another like two miniature drunks, falling and laughing, in their last moments of company.

Emily had finally fallen asleep. Matthew and Margaret were at the kitchen table making a list of missing household items, things they would have to buy, when there was a knock on their front door.

"Hello? Ya'll home?" The door opened, with Matthew halfway through the living room to answer it. "Beg my pardon for disturbing you. I meant to make it earlier." A tall man, with thinning blond hair, a tanned face, and steel rimmed glasses over a pair of lively blue eyes, reached out to shake Matthew's hand. He put his other hand in the middle of Matthew's back, steering him back toward the kitchen. The tall man walked with a slight limp. "I meant to be a help, to lend a hand."

"Margaret, honey, this is Dr. Monroe. Our landlord."

"Lord no," the man laughed. "David, call me 'David of the good intentions'. I intended to be here to welcome you and help you move in." He stood in the doorway of the small kitchen, looking around, seeing there were no boxes to unpack, nothing to put away. "Then there was an emergency, a field worker fell into a piece of running machinery. I had to drive out there to try to patch him up, and am just getting back."

"Can we offer you a beer?"

"That would be wonderful, Matthew. Thanks." He turned to Margaret and put both hands on her shoulders as though they were having a reunion, instead of meeting for the first time. "My wife, Mable Glen, is just dying to meet you. I don't think anyone new has moved to Bunkie since we got here from Birmingham, seven years ago." He pulled out a chair and sat down heavily. "You're a sight to behold. Pretty as a lady in a Flemish painting and a Yankee to boot!"

"Don't say I didn't warn you." Matthew shook a cigarette from his pack of Chesterfields, offering it to David, and proudly smiling as if his tired young wife were a form of validation. Proof that he would be a good assistant principal, worthy of the school board's faith in his leadership. "And there's not a book in the English language she hasn't read."

"The Boy Scout Handbook, Matthew. I don't think I've read that." Margaret stood to get a beer from the brown bag Pierre had slipped into the refrigerator just before he drove off in the empty truck.

"I happen to have a copy back home, Mrs. Sobral." David leaned over to light his cigarette on the match Matthew offered. "And would be honored to loan it in order to fill the appalling void in your education," he laughed.

"See, Margaret. Even though there isn't a Bunkie library," Matthew took the beer from her hand. "It seems we can rely on the libraries of our neighbors." He popped off the bottle cap with the beer opener he had pulled from the kitchen drawer. "Town living."

"I believe you will find the chapter on fire building particularly riveting." The tall friendly man kept his blue eyes on her as he closed his hand around the beer Matthew handed him.

"It sounds very much like something I read by Jack London," Margaret laughed.

"A warmer outcome, I promise you."

"Town living," Matthew repeated, delighted with their first visitor.

The next morning, after taking coffee into Margaret, changing Emily's diaper and putting her in the bed beside her mother, Matthew went off to begin his new job. He walked the five blocks to Bunkie High School and left Margaret completely alone with her daughter for the very first time in the more than nine months she had been a mother. Margaret had not realized before that she had never been alone with her daughter. This would be nice. Just the two of them. She put Emily in the high chair and set about scrambling eggs for her. "Remember Nettie, Emily? She laid the biggest eggs of all. We will miss her eggs, won't we?"

After she cleared away the baby's breakfast, she put a set of measuring spoons on the high chair tray and headed for the bedroom to make the bed. As she walked out of the kitchen, the spoons dropped to the floor.

"Oh Ohhh," said Emily.

"'Oh Ohhh,' indeed." Margaret picked up the spoons and put them back on the tray. As she walked in the bedroom she heard the spoons hit the linoleum floor again, and Emily's "Oh Ohhh." She would ignore her until she got the bed made. Emily's "Oh Ohhhs" became louder; Margaret could hear her slamming her little palms on the wooden tray. By the time Margaret had run back into the kitchen, Emily was already crying.

"I was just in the next room, Emily. Somebody has to make the bed and Rose is gone bye-bye."

Emily immediately stopped crying and looked at her mother with interest. It was definitely the 'bye bye' that had gotten her attention. She clapped her dimpled hands together.

"Yes, honey. '*Patty cake patty cake, baker's man, Make me a cake as fast as you can*." Margaret put the frying pan, plates and coffee cups in the sink and began running water over them. "*Pat it and roll it and mark it with a B and put it in the oven for baby and me*!"

They had no soap; she would have to scrub the pan extra hard. Thank goodness Irma had thought to pack a scrub brush. *Irma*. How would they ever be able to repay that sweet natured, lilac scented little woman? What would have become of them without her? There had been no alternatives. None. It made her so anxious that she had to take a deep breath. Emily was slapping the tray and fussing, not crying, but ready to cry.

"*Pat it and roll it an mark it with a B*! Let me just finish these dishes, Emily and we'll go see your new yard." The crying was starting up again. "Just one minute."

Now Emily was really crying, rocking in her high chair, which was threatening to tip over. Margaret slammed the pan down hard into the sink, wiped her hands on her skirt, and reached to pull Emily out of the high chair. The loud slam had startled the baby and now she was howling.

"Don't cry, don't cry. *Ride a cock horse to Baneberry Cross to see a fine lady upon a white horse*." She jiggled Emily up and down. "*With rings on her fingers and bells on her toes, she shall make music wherever she goes*. There, there, horsy. Remember Pierre's horsy Emily? Wasn't that fun? Wasn't that nice?"

The little girl had stopped crying and now stretched around in Margaret's arms so that she could see her face. She patted her mother's cheek, smiling and bouncing in her arms.

"Right, honey, horsy. Emily is a fine lady upon a white horse." Margaret headed back to the bedroom to finish making the bed. As soon as she put the little girl on the floor she began crying again. Margaret let her cry. It would just take a minute to finish the bed, pull up the spread, and tuck it into a ridge under the pillows.

"Yahoo. Anybody home?"

Obviously it was local custom to walk into the home of strangers with no fanfare, no previous notice. Margaret grabbed up her screaming baby and almost bumped into a busty woman wearing a pale blue housedress; the woman's hair was fastened up in pin curls.

"Here, hand me that little fire engine." She lifted Emily out of Margaret's arms and slung her expertly on her hip. Emily instantly quit crying; perhaps out of surprise, or maybe the softness of those large breasts made her think Irma was holding her again. "I'm Caroline," the woman smiled, while swishing her hips, keeping the baby quiet. "Caroline Robacheaux. We live two doors down. Mable Glen called me early this morning and told me all about you. She swears David is in love with you. And they're both having fits about you here in this house with no telephone. Mabel Glen has already called the phone company. You can expect a knock on the door any minute now. It'll be the boys from the phone company. There is no foot dragging if you get a call from Mabel Glen. That woman has authority with a capital A, I swear!"

"Can, can I offer you some coffee, Caroline?" Margaret could really think of nothing else to say.

"Honey, I'd love some. But you come on over to my house and get a good cup. I know you're from the north and their coffee is legendary. I hear it is the same color as iced tea." She switched Emily to her other hip. "Besides you're just moving in here and you don't have your help yet. Now don't you worry, my Sally already knows about someone, back of town, who is looking for work for her daughter. Sally says the girl is fifteen and a hard worker, used to keeping up her mama's house and looking after a passel of brothers."

"'Help?' We just don't have that kind of money," Margaret looked around. She thought that, considering they'd just moved in, the house was in good order. "And besides ---"

"There's hardly any money to it, honey. Whatever you can pay is more money than she'd have otherwise. And I don't know who'd expect you to manage this bad baby all by yourself." Caroline reached over, still swishing her hips for Emily's sake, and tucked a strand of Margaret's hair behind her ear. "You know, you may be the first Yankee I've ever met. Ya'll all so quiet?"

"That's Emily on your hip and I've only known her to be a good baby." Margaret sat down on the bed. "But I've never had her all by myself and I guess---" She was about to cry, in front of a stranger. "And I guess …"

"Why bless your heart!" Caroline sat on the bed beside Margaret, and stood Emily up between her knees. "Of course this is all hard for you and new and you must just be beside yourself, honey." She put her arm around Margaret and pulled her close. "We are all just happy as can be to have someone new show up in town. If you count Lucille, who spends half of every week in bed with headaches, there's four of us girls with little ones all about the same ages. We play cards and grocery shop together. We pile all the kids in Mabel Glen's Buick and Renee's Cadillac and go on out to the country club; there's a swimming pool there. Honey, we have fun!"

That afternoon the other three women, Lucille, Renee and Mable Glen, went by Caroline's to meet the newcomer. They gathered around the Robacheaux's big kitchen table where Sally had set out glasses and pitchers of iced tea and lemonade. They had arrived with children of varying ages and dropped then off in the family room for Sally to watch, along with little Emily and Caroline's three children.

"You're my first Yankee," said Lucille, a pale stoop shouldered woman. "I just want to sit here and listen to you talk."

"Shame on you, Lucille. You make Margaret sound like a Martian!"

"Caroline, I'm just saying what's on my mind. Ya'll are all thinking just about the same thing." Lucille put her hand on Margaret's wrist. "You don't mind do you, honey?"

"I hear you used to be a newspaper reporter. That's a lot more interesting than your place of origin." Mable Glen Monroe had dark shiny hair pulled away from her face by bobby pins. She was tall like her husband, and thin; compared to Lucille, she stood straight as a ramrod. "Try not to pay attention to all our hen clucking, Margaret. Bunkie is dull as dishwater. We're thrilled to have some new blood. As I'm sure you've already heard."

"And I haven't clucked once." Renee had dyed blonde hair and bright red fingernails. She reminded Margaret of Irene. "Horace and I went to New York City for our honeymoon and met about a million Yankees."

"A newspaper reporter? You got *paid*?" asked Lucille, with disbelief.

"Caroline, you got any gin to go in this lemonade?"

"Renee, it's not even three o'clock. You're just trying to shock Margaret. If I'd known ya'll would be coming in here giving her the third degree and showing your behinds, I would have locked my front door. I swear I would have. This girl hasn't even been in Bunkie twenty-four hours!"

"I haven't been around anyone remotely my same age in almost two years." Margaret reached for her Chesterfields. "I'm the one who's thrilled. I feel like Judy Garland when the movie went from black and white to Technicolor."

Maybelle arrived at the house every weekday morning just as Matthew was leaving to walk to the high school. She was short and round faced and wore her hair in a multitude of small tight knots tied with brightly colored bits of yarn. She was always either barefooted or had on a pair of oversized bedroom slippers that slapped against the dried rinds of her heels as she dashed around the little house, cleaning with one arm, balancing Emily on her hip with the other. Maybelle's voice sounded more like a grown man's than the voice of a fifteen-year-old girl. Caroline thought the way she talked was hilarious and called the Sobrals' maid "Froggy," whenever Maybelle was not around.

But then Caroline seemed to think most things were hilarious, especially her big bellied husband, Ernest. Until she met Caroline, Margaret couldn't remember ever knowing someone who could accurately be called a *devoted wife*. Ernest would extend his arm with his hand opened and Caroline would actually race to get a beer to slide into his waiting palm. He was a great fan of The Life of Riley and never missed the opportunity to say, like Riley did on every show: "'What a revolting development this is!'" Even if Ernest said, "'What a revolting development this is!' five times in the same night, Caroline laughed as if it were the first time she'd ever heard it. *Love*, Margaret thought. *That's what love can do for you, let you laugh at the same joke a thousand times.*

Except for David Monroe, none of the husbands were as interesting as their wives. Ernest smoked fat cigars, owned a tractor business and had an electric train set running through a little wooden village and a forest of two-inch trees that the children were not allowed to touch. Renee's lawyer husband, Horace, was handsome, with dark wavy hair and a flirtatious manner that made Margaret uncomfortable. Lucille's husband was Ernest's first cousin and as quiet as Ernest was boisterous. Ed owned the car dealership across Main Street from his cousin's tractor store. When the five couples went out to a restaurant together, it was always Matthew who fought for the check. Though he was the only one of the five men who couldn't afford it. Most often David would insist the check be divided among them. Matthew considered split checks to be inhospitable and mercenary; they disheartened him.

Several evenings a week the couples played cards together, sometimes four of the women at one table playing bridge and Renee and the men at another playing poker. They would gather in the Monroe's sprawling living room and listen to "The Bell Telephone Hour," "The Philip Morris Playhouse," and "Truth or Consequences" on a big Philco Radio that dominated the room.

"We need to figure how to get Margaret on one of the quiz programs. I bet, whether she admits it or not, that girl can answer any question thrown at her," said Horace. He leaned forward to pat her knee.

"Hardly." Margaret moved away from Horace's hand to flick her cigarette ash. "The category Sports, for instance. I think the only athlete's name I know is Baby Ruth, and that's because of the candy bar."

"Margaret has an impressive sweet tooth," said Matthew, as if that were additional proof of her intelligence.

"Not that you'd know it to look at you," Renee patted her own ample waist.

"Chocolate gives me a headache."

"Hell, Lucille everything gives you a head ache!" Ernest relit his cigar. "A god damned leaf falling off a tree gives you a headache."

"A 'leaf'!" Caroline shrieked. "I swear, the things you come up ---"

"I think there is a connection between chocolate and migraines." Mable Glen had been a nurse before she married David. "A lot of things can start migraines, but nothing much takes them away."

"So, Margaret, you honestly can't say who Joe Louis is?" David laughed. "Admit that you're holding out on us."

"A band leader?" She pinched a fleck of tobacco from her tongue, using her ring finger and thumb. "A ballet dancer?"

David and Matthew stood out from the other three men. Neither of them laughed at tasteless jokes about colored people, and they looked after their wives, rather than the other way around.

They didn't expect to be waited on. Margaret liked that David seemed casually solicitous of her. Not in the blindly loyal trip-over-his- own-feet way Matthew was, but in an understated way, watchful and smart.

"I just don't want the new baby's christening to be like Emily's." Matthew put his card hand down on the table. The Sobrals had been living in Bunkie for a year and Margaret was five months pregnant. "A priest we didn't know, that empty church, Pierre and Irma as godparents, then us. And, of course, little Emily. The five of us and that bored priest the only people there." The Monroes and Sobrals were playing bridge at the little Lee Street house. "A Baptism ought to be a celebration." He picked up his hand, but didn't look at his cards. "Afterwards we went back to the farm and had cold fried chicken and iced tea. And that was that. Pierre and Irma were good to us, God knows, yet ---"

"Yet," David leaned forward. "This new baby will be heralded in like royalty. As the godparents, Mabel Glen and I will contribute a case of champagne." He slammed his cards down. "Let's invite everyone we know. Get Lucille's girl, Agnes, over here making those little pies she made for their anniversary party."

"And I'll buy some gallon jugs of bourbon and gin, and a case of beer." Matthew turned happily to face Margaret, as if announcing that all their hard times were behind them. "It will be a day to remember!"

Margaret forced herself to keep quiet. They could hardly afford their low rent and here Matthew was, trying to outspend his generous landlord. Her husband was a poor man, with no notion of poverty. He didn't even realize that the Monroes were covering the Sobrals' phone bill. He had let David convince him that the phone was included with the house, like the kitchen sink and the Frigidaire.

Less than a month after Emily's second birthday, Dr. Monroe delivered her little sister, Rebecca, in the predawn hours of a January morning. A week and a half later, on a bitter cold and cloudy Sunday, the Sobrals' friends and neighbors attended noon Mass at St. Joseph's. Afterwards, they all crowded into the nave to watch Father Guilery touch salt and oil to baby Rebecca's lips and forehead. He poured a small silver cup of holy water over her little head as Mabel Glen held her suspended above the fluted marble Baptismal font. The baby blinked, startled by the cold water, but didn't cry. She stared into Mable Glen's face, as if holding her godmother responsible for the sudden discomfort, or perhaps asking for rescue. The christening party stepped out of church and into a land transformed.

Snow was falling. Already a thin layer of white covered the automobiles, the streets, trees and bushes. Shouts and laughter greeted the miracle; members of the congregation were standing in front of the church with their heads tilted, feeling the strange soft sting of snow on their faces. Matthew held tightly to Margaret's arm and turned to watch that the Monroes, who were holding Rebecca, were taking care on the slick steps. Several people had already slipped. Children raced down the snowy sidewalk in front of the church, sliding on purpose, falling and rolling in their Sunday best, covering themselves in snow. They tried to make snowballs from the fluffy wet snow, scraping it from car hoods and the grass; as if they were play actors in a movie starring northern children. The flat featureless town looked like the Christmas window of a big department store. The adults were turning in slow circles, shouting and pointing, calling out to their children who were deafened by the muffled silvery spell of snow. Margaret and Matthew were probably the only people in the exultant crowd who had ever witnessed a real snowfall. Matthew was laughing and proud, as though the snow were part of his plan for the celebration of his new daughter. Margaret watched the impromptu carnival and imagined describing it to her Wisconsin friends, such delirium over snow.

Back at the little house on Lee Street, Agnes was instructing Renee's maid, Loretta, having her pull trays from the oven and pile platters with miniature pies and bread slices cut in quarters and spread with pimento cheese. Maybelle was in the small bedroom watching the snow through the window while Caroline's one month old son, Tommy, slept in the crib next to Emily's little bed. Maybelle was waiting for Rebecca's return from the church. She would be in charge of the newborns. Sally was in the backyard keeping an eye on Emily, Caroline's three older children, Renee's two daughters, Lucille's two sons and the Monroe's daughter and son as they ran around in the foreign land of snow. All of the children had been fed an early lunch at the Robacheaux's. Now Sally's only task was to keep them from underfoot during the party.

Matthew and David made a production of setting beer and champagne out into the snow to chill. The Robacheauxs had brought over their Victrola and Rene carried in her stack of Perry Como records. Soon Sally herded the shivering children through the crowded living room and into the back bedroom. Champagne corks popped; there were toasts, shouts, and laughter. Even Margaret had a glass of champagne. David had urged her on, looking her in the eye and gallantly quoting Emily Dickinson: "*'I taste a liquor never brewed/from tankards scooped in pearl/not all the vats upon the Rhine/yield such an alcohol*!'" He poured a glass and handed it to Margaret. "To the mother!"

The living room furniture was stacked and pushed against the wall and they jitterbugged. *Oh no, no, no hubba-hubba/yes, yes, yes hubba-hubba/Bop, bop...* Those who knew the silly lyrics sang along. *Dig you later A Hubba-Hubba...* The room was so hot that someone opened a window. It grew dark outside while the music played on and the guests kept dancing. Agnes dodged through the twirling couples with platters of finger food for the partiers, or carrying sandwiches back to the children. Matthew mixed drinks and proudly watched his young wife, less than two weeks away from childbirth, now the life of the party.

The party went on and on, the music carrying out into the dark January street of melting snow. After the champagne supply went dry, Matthew's drinks took center stage. Some time, around ten, Sally walked the little Robacheauxs home while the other children remained sleeping in a jumble of sweaty small bodies over Matthew and Margaret's bed. Matthew danced with Margaret. *They say that falling in love is wonderful, so they say...* He was a good slow dancer and, when he pulled her closer, she pressed her forehead into his neck. *It's wonderful, so they say....*

Rene indulged in so many of Matthew's hi-balls that she had to be carried out to the car. Horace tucked a blanket around her and returned to the party. Near midnight Lucille drove the remaining maids home and then returned for the very intoxicated Ed and her sleepwalking children. Matthew carried Emily back to her own bed. A deeply exhausted Margaret finally went off to bed, making room for herself between the two sleeping Monroe children. Matthew turned the music down and fixed more drinks. The last guests left around two, staggering out into the rain. When the new baby woke up crying, no one heard her, not even Emily.

It turned out that Matthew had depleted their bank account to pay for the Baptism extravaganza.

"I'll write my parents. They wanted to do something for Rebecca, I'll ask them to send money, that ---"

"Are you god damned crazy?" Matthew almost never raised his voice. Emily, who was sitting in her highchair, began to cry.

"We have to eat." Margaret was sitting at the kitchen table giving Rebecca a bottle. "We have rent to pay."

"And I'm getting paid again in two weeks! Shhhh, Emily, Shhhh." He took her out of her highchair. The little girl kept crying. "It will work out, Margaret. You can't go to those people asking ---"

"But you said we have nothing in the bank. Nothing!" Now the baby was crying too.

"We have credit at the grocery store and David won't mind if we're a little late with the rent." He talked while he danced, turning in circles to quiet Emily. "Everything will be fine."

"I can't stand this, Matthew." She slammed the baby bottle down on the table. "I really can't. It's humiliating and hopeless." Margaret lifted Rebecca and lowered her face into her crying infant's stomach; afraid she would begin screaming and wouldn't be able to stop. The cries of her children resounding in the small kitchen were noise and misery enough. If she began screaming out loud, they would all be hauled away.

"It is going to work out," Matthew turned round and round. "Fly Emily, fly like a bird." He lifted his daughter overhead and her crying turned to gurgled laughter. "Fly, fly, over the rainbow. Emily is a blue bird. Birds fly over the rainbow. "

Chapter 7

Margaret and Matthew---1948—1951

MAYBELLE DIDN'T COME on Saturdays and Emily wouldn't nap. Rebecca was a solemn little baby and, even if she were awake, she was likely to lie on her back and quietly gaze around herself with her deep dark eyes. Emily chattered constantly and asked to be read to, played with. It was impossible for Margaret--who always seemed to be tired on weekends--to get any rest with Emily in the house. So Matthew took his older daughter off on Saturday afternoons. He would hold her hand and tell her stories as they walked the straight flat streets of Bunkie. They would wander into the church where he repeated for her the stories of the statues, the lives of the saints. In the cemetery he would read aloud from the gravestones, "*'There was a band of angels that was not quite complete, so God took our darling baby to fill the vacant seat.*' Isn't that the saddest thing, honey?"

"Tay it da den Daddy."

"Their little baby didn't live to be a year old, Emily. I can't even imagine."

"Tay da angels da den."

Before heading back to the house on Lee Street, they would stop in at the dark smoky front room of the Lamp Light Tavern. If it were football season, the men sitting there would ask Matthew questions about the high school team. Otherwise there would be talk of sports games they had heard on the radio, or complaints about the weather. Matthew would sit his daughter up on the bar, buy a round of drinks and get a Regal Beer for himself.

When Margaret became pregnant again, she hoped fervently for a boy, while Matthew claimed that all he wanted was another daughter. She had watched the sons of her friends and thought they were more interesting than little girls, not so needy. She would be a better mother to a son. She was sure of it. At her seventh month check up David encouraged Margaret.

"Based on the baby's heart rate, Meg, I can almost promise you it will be a boy." He moved the stethoscope around on her stomach, keeping his eyes on her face. "Of course, that's not always a sure thing. I've seen exceptions."

"I've already decided that we'll name him Mark."

"That will go very nicely with Matthew." David turned from her to put the stethoscope away.

"Yes, I guess it does." She sat up on the examining table, pressing the top of the sheet against her collarbone. "Though I was thinking of Twain."

"Whose real name was Samuel." David stepped close to Margaret and reached for her hand.

"Exactly. His real name will be Samuel, but we'll call him Mark," she laughed. "That way he can work undercover for the FBI."

"Always thinking ahead, you Yankees." He took her pulse, and then kept her slender wrist between his fingers. "*Sweet olive,*" he murmured.

"David, what did you say?" Margaret's heart began racing, she thought she might lose her breath.

"Eat more, Meg, you're too thin." He tapped the edge of the sheet where it met her collarbone. "You are too pretty to waste away."

"I do eat. I'm hungry all the time."

"I don't think it's food you're hungry for," he said thoughtfully, not looking at her. "You're trying, Meg, but you are just having a difficult time domesticating. Sometimes I think of all your smartness as some kind of wild animal forced into a cage. All that pacing back and forth in confinement, no wonder you can't hold weight."

"Seems like all of us, but Mabel Glen, are pregnant again," she said, abruptly changing the subject, looking away from David, bunching the sheet in her fist.

"Two children are enough." He patted her sheet-covered knee. "I mean, enough for us. For Mabel Glen and me." He rested his hand on Margaret's knee for a moment; both of them were silent, thoughtful.

Margaret's water broke in the middle of the night and then her contractions began close and hard. She phoned the Monroe house while Matthew woke Emily and Rebecca. He slipped untied shoes onto their little feet and practically ran with them to the Robacheaux's. When he got back to the house, David was already helping Margaret into his car. The three of them sped through the deserted streets to the Bunkie clinic.

"You're doing just fine, Meg. But this little guy is in a hurry." David tied on his surgical mask.

The nurse bent over and covered Margaret's face with the stiff ether mask. It was like a concave fly swatter. Margaret wanted to say something while there was still time. Her voice swirled into a bubble and floated away. Pale blue eyes, the color of imagined oceans, framed behind the reflection of bright light on glass hovered over her. David's kind eyes were all she saw as the operating room dimmed into nothing.

When she woke up David was sitting on the side of her hospital bed, holding her hand watching her. His face was serious, troubled.

"Is the ..." Margaret couldn't sit up. "What happened? What happened to the baby? Oh no! Is something wrong? Please ..."

"No, Meg, she's fine." He took off his glasses and cleaned then with the edge of the bedspread. "Your little girl arrived quick and easy." He forced a smile. "She couldn't wait to get here."

"You mean my little boy," she corrected him. Though, groggy as she was, Margaret already knew he had not misspoken. David stroked her hand, running his fingers over hers.

A few minutes later, when Matthew arrived at the hospital, he could hear his wife sobbing from all the way down the hall. Along with the legend of Rebecca's spectacular Baptism party, there would be the story of Kate's heartbreaking birth.

One day, in the late winter of 1951, a letter arrived from BelleBend, Louisiana. Matthew had been offered a job as principal of the public schools in the little Mississippi River town where he'd grown up. Though his salary would be markedly higher, both he and Margaret were reluctant to leave Bunkie. They were inclined to stay and hope that, after this offer, the school board might give him a pay increase. Kate was almost two years old, and Margaret was three months pregnant.

A traveling rodeo arrived in Bunkie and was performing at the high school football stadium. Matthew took Emily and Rebecca off to see the show and Margaret stayed home with Kate. The phone rang and it was Ernest, shouting and almost incoherent, he had to talk to Matthew. He had gotten a call from Dr. Monroe's nurse. She had just discovered David slumped over his desk, dead. Earnest needed to find Matthew to take him over to break the news to Mabel Glen. Matthew would know how to talk to her.

Daughters-----1980

"Probably the most fun, of all the fun they had, was Rebecca's baptism party," I say. "The apex of Bunkie fun."

Our father's house felt airless and too full of sorrow. We have taken fresh drinks and cigarettes outside and are sitting on the back porch steps. There is a waxing half moon slung low in the partly cloudy sky; a warm breeze ripples light and shadow through the leaves of the pecan trees. On the far rim of the rice fields, we can just make out a scattering of lit train windows going by and hear the low whistle as the train approaches BelleBend. It is a Hank Williams night, lacking only the whip-poor-will. *I've never seen a night so long...*

"The Bunkie people were even talking about Rebecca's baptism party at Mama's funeral," says Elizabeth. Our tall baby sister has settled on the highest step.

We are staggered down the plank porch steps in reverse chronological order: The middle sisters are on the middle steps. Wild haired Kate sits a step above Rebecca with her sedate Buster Brown haircut. I sit three planks down from Rebecca, on the bottom step, my ankles crossed and legs extended over the crushed oyster shell stoop.

"I have heard about that party all of my life. I'm not kidding. It's as though I, personally, started with a bang and faded to a whimper. 'Oh, Rebecca, that was such a wild party. Everyone had so much fun and here you are all grown up and so boring.' The Bunkie people make me feel like a thirty year long anti-climax."

"Now I remember what happens when you drink," Kate reaches down as though she is going to take Rebecca's whiskey sour out of her hand. "Maudlin, poor Little Match Girl, Rebecca."

"Well, it's the---"

"I was barely two years old, yet I can really remember that party," I say. The snow? Startling and senseless and magic. The awe of that all mixed together with being squashed in with a mass of other children, crammed into a small hot bedroom. Not allowed out. And hearing the loud noise of grownups raising cane? It was scary. No-one-in-charge scary."

"The maids were in charge." The voice from the top step sounds ghostly in the sudden darkness. Clouds have covered the moon. *The moon just went behind a cloud to hide its head…*

"Yeah, Elizabeth, they were so in charge," says Kate. "Real Black Power. They got to change the white babies' diapers, rinse the shit out of them in the white people's toilets, in real running water. Those bossy maids got to leave their own little children without their mamas, until whatever time the white ladies decided to let them off work."

"You know what I mean."

"Anyone recall ever being alone with Mama when we were little?" asks Rebecca, abruptly changing the subject.

"You mean *when she was little*?" Kate pulls her mass of curls over one shoulder.

"Kate, what in the hell are you talking about?"

"If you say any*one*, Rebecca, then it's *she*, for the one. It can't be *we*. When *she* was little. It can't be *we*." Kate begins weaving her hair into a single braid.

"Don't you mean it can't be *us*?" Elizabeth adds slyly.

"I remember tramping around Bunkie with Daddy, to 'get out of Mama's hair'," I say, raising my voice for attention. Our grammatical quibbles have waylaid many a conversation. "I don't think Maybelle came to the house on Saturdays. Since we didn't have a car, Daddy and I walked everywhere. The downtown had one bar. We'd go in there and Daddy would lift me up on the bar and buy a round of drinks for everyone. The patrons liked to ask questions to make me jabber with my cute, funny lisp. I'd be swinging my little legs back and forth, lisping away. I loved being the center of attention."

"A trait you completely outgrew."

"Fuck you, Elizabeth."

"I always liked your story about the peanuts," says Kate. "About how you went to all the Bunkie High football games with Daddy and he bought you peanuts. Which you hated."

"But I ate them all, every peanut, because I didn't want to hurt Daddy's feelings."

"Then one time you noticed the people sitting next to you peeling their peanuts, and throwing way the shells, which you had been painstakingly chewing up and swallowing."

"Daddy oblivious the whole time," says Rebecca from her middle step.

"We weren't watched over." I put my empty glass down carefully. "Right now I can still see Miss Mable Glen speeding down the road, laughing and talking with Mama in the front seat of that big Buick. God knows how many kids were jammed in the back. I was leaning on the car door when it flew open. John Monroe grabbed my dress and pulled me back in. I don't even think Mabel Glen slowed the car down. Another time everybody was at a basketball game, up in the bleachers, and I crawled under the feet of the grownups so I could see. I pushed past the edge and John caught me by my ankles, just as I plunged, headfirst, toward the gym floor."

"We've heard both those stories before." Elizabeth leans down and pulls a cigarette from the pack next to Kate. "I still think you dreamed them. Wasn't John Monroe just two years older than you?"

"Yeah, but he was watchful."

"And fatherless before he was eight years old," says Rebecca with tipsy sadness.

"I swear I never hear the word *rodeo* that I don't think of the world going all wrong the night Dr. Monroe died. It was like the whole town got thrown from a bucking bronco. An epoch hit the dirt," I say.

"Not that people tend to speak ill of the dead, anyway," says Kate, "But to hear it, he was tall, handsome, witty and wise, deeply beloved by all." She unbraids her hair, tugs her fingers through the mass of it.

"And kind to children," I add. "I loved Dr. Monroe so much that one of my happiest memories is of waking up after my tonsillectomy. My throat was killing me, I couldn't swallow, my head was woozy from ether, but Dr. Monroe was sitting on my bed, sitting there waiting for me to wake up. And I had him all to myself."

"Sometimes I think that if Dr. Monroe had lived, we would have all grown up in Bunkie. We would have stayed there." The clouds have skittered away and I can see Elizabeth clearly, her chin in her palm, her elbow on her knee.

"He was like King Arthur and Bunkie was Camelot," says Rebecca mournfully.

"Bunkie?" Kate is incredulous. "Flat, treeless, racist?"

"And waterless," I add, with a sense of the Mississippi at our backs. "When Daddy said we would be able to cross the river on a ferry at BelleBend, I remember being enchanted. I had visions of gossamer wings. Though I worried how one fairy could manage to carry us all."

"Now Daddy's waiting for a band of angels to carry him back over the river." Rebecca's voice breaks.

"Did you really just say that?" Kate is, again, incredulous.

"We've been out here too long," says Elizabeth. "Let's go check on him."

"He's so lonesome he could die," I murmur.

"Cry."

"What are you saying, Kate? Are you telling Rebecca to cry?"

"The song, Emily. It's not *so lonesome I could die*. It's *so lonesome I could cry*."

The moon is a tilted, swollen D fixed to a mother-of-pearl sky the night our father dies. It is near midnight, with the moon three quarters full. I know because I watch it through the window with my hand resting on my father's cheek, feeling his skin grow cool and become something else.

Earlier tonight our father had begun repeating the names of our children. He rubbed the fingers of his right hand, thumb to fore and middle fingers, as if he were reciting the rosary, running his grandchildren through his fingers like beads. Rather than *Hail Marys*, strung one after the other, he mumbled and rasped: *"Mark, Jason, Martin, Emma, Lenin, Alyce, Gaston."* The priest had come the day before and given our father The Last Rites. We all understood that Daddy was done with dying and was arriving at death; the process part was about over. He had eaten nothing for days and kept slipping in and out of consciousness. With so little time left, his daughters expected him to call out for our mother, or even to ask again for his own. We thought that, if he talked at all, he might have advice to offer, or some favor to ask. But, no, just the string of names over and over. Perhaps he was rehearsing for his reunion with our mother? Maybe he was making sure to remember the names of all of their descendants, in case she had forgotten. *"Mark, Jason, Martin, Emma, Lenin, Alyce, Gaston."* We wanted him to stop, his breathing was labored and the recitation obviously torturous for him. Then, suddenly, he did stop. He silently fingered the invisible beads a few more minutes and then began to tap his chest with the slender, blunt fingers of his left hand. *Tap, tap, tap....* slower and slower as though he were damping down his own heart. *Tap... tap... tap....* We were there, my sisters and I, all of us tearful and watching his face when the tapping stopped. Our father folded his hands, one on top of the other, over his chest like the saints pictured on the gilt-edged holy cards he used as bookmarks in his Missal. Then he was dead.

We now knew what to do. We are no longer amateurs. We are awash in redundancy, a déjà vu of coroner, funeral home, church and cemetery. The Sobral daughters have already cried, "wolf." And both times the Big Bad Wolf had actually slunk in to get us. The people of our past and the past of our parents arrive armed and dressed for mourning. The second time within a year that death has come to this house, everyone surely knows the protocol.

Our county was in the midst of an ice storm when the phone call came from Louisiana telling that Mama had terminal cancer. Afterwards, I remember a feeling of almost satisfaction as I walked through the devastated landscape, seeing nature metaphor my grief. Stunned homeowners wandered among their shattered hedges and severed trees. The roads were impassable, traffic and commerce at a standstill. Entire forests were flattened and all the ruin was sheathed in brief and fragile glass.

Within a week, the nestlings had re-gathered at the nest. Our own children clustered around us, we began the long good-bye. Mama never went into a hospital. Her daughters nursed her and, in the nursing, discovered more than we'd ever suspected about pain and passage. We took cancer on like a wrestling partner. And lost. We struggled for the privilege of sitting beside our mother all night, listening for her dreams. One baby learned to walk, trying his beginning steps beside the sick bed. We mothers became confused as the illness made our own mother turn child-like. The magnolia tree outside her window grew glossy new leaves; the white blooms came and turned brown. Six months, winter turning slowly to summer, and our mother died, encircled by the generations she had begun; we had supposed her here forever and, suddenly, she was gone. She was Mother, and we never knew her secrets.

She would have known what we needed to wear to the funeral. We motherless ones fumbled through our wardrobes, unsure, becoming aware of the long time ahead without that final reference. Actors without scripts, we greeted the mourners. Uncertain of etiquette, we stumbled through with her memory as our example. The limousine ride to the cemetery was unreal in the bright summer day. People watered their lawns, children raced tricycles over the sidewalks, dogs barked, traffic lights changed. All the while our mother was dead.

Part II

The Daughters

Chapter 8

BelleBend----1951

A NEW LIFE, a new town: On a late Wednesday morning in August, Matthew met his wife and daughters at the BelleBend train station. He had parked their first car, a second-hand green Chevrolet, out front. The Sobral family walked out of the station and paused on the top step leading down to the graveled parking lot.

"Daddy, it looks like a rocket." Emily was delighted.

"Who knows? Maybe it really is a rocket, and we'll zoom right up to the moon."

"Let's just make it to the house." Margaret's voice was tired and dry. "I would like a little quiet. Emily didn't stop talking for a minute and Kate refused to get off my lap."

For the past few months in Bunkie, Margaret and Caroline had loaded their seven children into Caroline's Studebaker and driven over to spend their weekday mornings at Mabel Glen's sad house. The older children played on the Monroe's sloping green lawn, Sally watched over the toddlers, and the widow and her friends drank coffee and smoked cigarettes around Mabel Glen's scarred old oak kitchen table. In the afternoons, back at the Lee Street house, Margaret closed herself in her bedroom, leaving the children to Maybelle and, on weekends, to Matthew. She was tired, exhausted, all the time. Sometimes the children thought they heard their mother crying.

"Right out there is Railroad Avenue. It runs from here, at the train station, all the way straight to the river. See that girls?" Matthew had little Kate balanced on his right hip, and his left hand hooked in Margaret's arm. Emily was holding onto the corner of her father's coat jacket, and Rebecca's small hand gripped her mother's wrist. "This is it, the main street of BelleBend. The clothing stores, the Grand Theatre, the Five & Dime, The Elks Club, Town Hall, you name it. The heartbeat of BelleBend runs right along this one wide street. We can see the entire length of it from up here. Down at the end, there, in front of the levee? That's the Welcome Bar and Restaurant. And here, to the left, right by the train station, is The First and Last Chance Bar and Restaurant. They have you coming and going, you never want for a cold beer and a platter of fried shrimp in BelleBend!"

You would think that Matthew Sobral had personally put the town together, built it himself for his young family. The same way Ernest had put together a small wooden village to go with his electric train set back in Bunkie. Except for the fact that no children were allowed near Mr. Ernest's village. Matthew sounded like the proprietor of BelleBend, rather than someone who had only arrived back in town a week earlier, after more than thirty years away.

"The church, Matthew? I thought you said the big Catholic Church was the heartbeat of BelleBend?" Margaret was almost eight months pregnant and, except for her large stomach, she was too thin, skinny and wan. "You told me that everyone, even the Jews, are Catholic here."

"Now Holy Savior Parish Church is the size of a cathedral, you'll see. The church is on Mississippi Avenue, which runs, as you might guess, along the path of the river. It curves, like the river curves. He let go of his wife's arm and gestured a bow into the air. "Whatever important that is not on Railroad Avenue is on Mississippi Avenue. BelleBend is set inside a great curve of the river, a bend. Which is how the town got its name. Then the bayou circles behind it. The town lays almost like an island."

"And the fairy, Daddy? Where's the fairy," asked Emily.

"We'll have a tour," Matthew laughed. "I'll show you everything. Then we'll come back and eat lunch at The First and Last Chance Restaurant. It'll be a celebration."

"A restaurant?" Emily asked. So many new things at once!

"All of us?" Rebecca echoed. They had their own automobile and they were going to be eating in a restaurant! Their Mama had cried on the train. Now she would be happy.

"Matthew, we have that car to pay for and ---"

"And nothing to worry about, Margaret." He squeezed her arm lightly. "It's a happy day, honey. Our little girls will be growing up in the same town where I grew up." He let go of her arm again and spread his hand out toward the sun drenched main street. "There are people here who knew me as a little boy. People waiting to meet you and welcome you and our daughters here."

"Shrimps, Daddy?"

"Yes, Kate. Crunchy fried shrimp." Matthew laughed again, and pulled his youngest daughter into a tight hug. "All the shrimps you want!"

He drove them straight down Rail Road Avenue. The little girls were hanging out the back windows, giddy to be in their own car, fascinated with everything their father pointed out to them. He turned left where the main street ran into Mississippi Avenue. "B. Mayer's, the biggest store in town. And there's Crescent Park. When I was a boy that was where the market was. Every day fresh produce and all matter of merchandise were carried off the riverboats and set out here. Now it's a park. And over there is the house where I was born and lived until I went off to join the Brotherhood."

He slowed the Chevrolet by a tall dark brick house encircled with graceful wrought iron balconies. He pulled to the curb and sat with the car's motor running.

"Back there, see how the wall reaches to the end of the block? That's where my Papa kept his menagerie. He loved animals and had a little monkey and a couple deer back there, a pony for me. The yard was the size of a small park. He had an aviary too. He even had an eagle. Over there, by the levee? That's where his soda pop factory was." Matthew turned to look into the shiny little faces of his daughters, all three of them leaning on the back of the front seat, Emily and Rebecca standing on the car floor, Kate balanced with her feet on the edge of the back seat. "Can you imagine? Your grandfather owned a soda pop factory, an icehouse, and was the beer distributer for Anheuser Busch in a five-state region! I remember the night the soda pop factory burned down. I was just a little boy, standing out on that balcony there. I saw my papa pacing back and forth with that big ole eagle perched on his arm, watching the firemen trying to save his factory. I'll see that sight all the days of my life, the flames, those big wings spread out, the--."

"Matthew, the girls are hungry."

"The house is cut into apartments now." He pulled away from the curb. "My stepmother sold it years before she died."

When Matthew left BelleBend, two years after his father remarried, the town had been a bustling center. There had been a synagogue, a brisk river trade, and even an opera house. The Depression, and then the creation of bridge and highway systems during the Huey Long years--transportation systems inconvenient to the town--had isolated BelleBend.

It was the first time the little girls had ever eaten in a restaurant and they were reluctant to leave. They had finished their lunches, but a jukebox was playing music and there were people to watch at the other tables. Emily and Rebecca were sipping root beer through a straw, pinching the straw to make the sweet fuzzy drink last. When, in the midst of a story about his boyhood, he noticed that Margaret was teary-eyed with fatigue, Matthew quickly hustled his daughters out of The First and Last Chance. He opened the back car door for the little girls and helped Margaret into the front seat.

They drove down Mississippi Ave, past the big church, a grocery store and a gas station; at the edge of town, Mississippi Avenue became the River Road. A mile later they turned into the pecan tree lined driveway of a large white house, raised on brick pillars high above the ground, facing the levee and the river.

The Sobrals were eating their first breakfast in their new house when a black woman, well over six feet tall, walked into their kitchen. She stood, with her hands on her hips, shaking her head and smiling as if she'd just heard a joke.

"Ya'll don't look like no hicks, even though I hear ya'll come straight from the cotton fields." She spread a big hand over Kate's curls and patted them. "No sign of hook worms I can see!" She laughed.

"Tee!" Matthew pushed back his chair, wiping his mouth with the back of his hand. "Margaret, this is Tee, she ---"

"Theresa Ophelia Landry. I goes by Tee and Mr. Matthew say you be needing my help six mornings a week. No Sundays. I sing in the choir at St. Catherine's. No afternoons when I be working at Miss Elaine's in town." She took her hand off Kate's head and extended it to shake Margaret's. Margaret was so startled that she stayed seated while her arm was vigorously pumped.

"Matthew mentioned you'd be coming by, I didn't think---"

"Nice meeting you. But don't you look jus like somebody tied a watermelon upside a beanpole! You the skinniest white woman I ever seen. And pregnant!" She took a step back to get a better view. "You don't eat?" She turned to Matthew. "Mr. Matthew you got to bring in some groceries. Women in the family way supposed to have some meat on they bones!"

"Tee, it's not for lack of trying. Almost this entire …" He cleared his throat, still not comfortable with what he called *female terminology*. "This, this entire pregnancy she doesn't seem to have an appetite. She just picks at her food. I'm at a loss of what to do with her. Try as I--"

"I'm right here, you know," said Margaret, standing and reaching to clear away the breakfast dishes. "Not a third party."

"What is a hick?" Emily asked.

"Somebody be from north Louisiana, or the state of Mississippi."

It would turn out that, in addition to Protestants from northern Louisiana and anybody from Mississippi, Tee was also prejudiced against Italians: *they nothing but ignorant immigrants think they're better then the coloreds,* and converts to Catholism: *I won't take communion next to no convert. Fake Catholics.* She would watch over the girls, do the laundry, and keep the house reasonably clean for the next two years.

"Are you a giant?" Rebecca asked in a hushed tone, her dark eyes wide.

Mathew's promise of a warm welcome never quite materialized. That first week, the wives of the school board members had trooped over for a coffee klatch. Thanks to a generous farewell gift from Caroline, Margaret had the right number of cups and saucers. She was just slicing the pound cake when Tee walked into the living room carrying Margaret's dripping wet, very padded, bra.

"Miss Margaret, you want I should hang these little titties out on the line?" Tee asked, with disbelief. She couldn't imagine that Margaret would want such flagrant proof of her flat chest flapping free on the clothesline. She assumed the ladies of the school board to be Margaret's friends and that they would back up Tee's righteous defense of her. No need for the neighbors to know that, even pregnant, the new principal's wife was flat as a board.

The story circulated throughout BelleBend for months. There were also the rumors that the new principal's pretty Yankee wife refused alcoholic drinks, just like a Baptist, and that she spurned seafood. People had seen her at gatherings sipping coffee when everyone else was enjoying hi-balls or beer; they had also seen Margaret eating only bread and sliced tomatoes at a crab boil. She held herself apart. She was a book reader and a teetotaler, too brainy and standoffish to fit into BelleBend society.

There were no kindergartens in rural south Louisiana, so, when the school year began, five-year-old Emily started first grade. Matthew was principal of both the elementary and the high school. Emily was the *Principal's Daughter*, a position of great power in an area where many of the children had parents who had never attended high school. Education had arrived slowly to the people in the backwaters of Louisiana. Some of the children had at least one parent who had never been to school at all. Even the teachers at BelleBend Elementary were somewhat intimidated by the presence of the new principal's daughter. Emily sensed her specialness and, like a power-crazed traffic cop at a busy intersection, seized the opportunity to test her limits. One day, in the first week of school, she cleared the entire play yard at morning recess.

"Stop everybody," she shouted from the top of the sliding board. "Get off my daddy's merry-go-round! Get off my daddy's swings!" She raised her skinny arms overhead, making sure she had the attention of all the other children. "Get off!"

It was so outrageous, and yet so possible, that the children listened. Who knew what the new principal was like? Thirty-five pound Emily Sobral climbed down the ladder of the sliding board and strutted the perimeters of the playground, patrolling it, keeping a schoolhouse full of children backed into an anxious circle. The swings and merry-go-round stood still, the sliding board was empty. The schoolyard was silent.

"Emily Sobral, just who do you think you are?" Miss Zacary, who taught fourth grade, shattered the silence when she marched out and faced Emily with her hands on her hips. Then she turned to the stunned circle of children. "Ya'll don't pay her any mind. This is ridiculous!" She stomped her high heel in the playground dust. "This is everybody's playground. Ya'll get back on those swings!"

The braver of the older children tentatively headed back to play. And soon the rest of the school followed them. There were people who, thirty years later, still recalled the principal's daughter kicking them off the taxpayer's playground and never quite forgave Emily her failed experiment. Her sisters would later claim that that one event had gone on to disproportionately shape their own BelleBend social interactions at school. The three younger daughters had all felt a need to keep their heads low, not make waves, the way the firstborn had. They were forced to go to extremes to display their lack of entitlement, their humility, the very 'ordinariness' of being the *principal's daughter*.

Two weeks after school began Matthew put Margaret, Rebecca and Kate on the train back to Bunkie. They would stay with the Robacheauxs, and David Monroe's replacement, Dr. Folse, would deliver the fourth Sobral baby. Emily would always recall that period alone with her father "those two weeks as an only child" with profound nostalgia. One night they ate out at the First and Last Chance and the next night at the Welcome, every night they had supper in a restaurant. People would come up to their table and introduce themselves, buy Emily a Coke-A-Cola and her daddy another beer. It reminded her of the times in Bunkie when her Daddy had lifted her up to sit on the bar downtown and she'd been the center of attention, *cute as a bug.*

The two of them drove all over BelleBend and she got to sit in the front seat and hear stories about the 'olden days.' After her father dressed Emily in the morning, he would return to the kitchen to smoke and have another cup of coffee. Emily would go into her parents' bedroom, open her mother's dressing table drawer and stand on her tiptoes to look in the mirror and put on her mother's lipstick. She colored her cheeks from the little case of almost-used-up rouge her mother had left behind. One day she even went to school wearing a pair of Margaret's high heels. It was hard to run in them, so at recess she went barefooted like the poor kids. If her daddy actually noticed that his first grade daughter was gussied up like a streetwalker, he apparently saw no harm in it. When he joyfully told Emily that her mother and sisters were coming home with a new baby sister, Emily almost started crying.

While Emily had that happy memory of her brief time as an only child, Rebecca's memory of the same time was equally happy. Miss Mabel Glen, Miss Caroline, Miss Renee and Miss Lucille were waiting for her mama at the train station with all their kids. Everyone was so happy to see the Sobrals! And her mama was laughing and hugging all the ladies. In BelleBend her mama never laughed. It was just like Rebecca remembered it used to be in Bunkie, back before Dr. Monroe died. But it was better. They were company and special. They stayed at Miss Caroline's, and Mr. Ernest even let Rebecca and Tommy watch the toy train go round and round and blow its whistle. Sally took care of Kate and carried her everywhere; she would hardly put her down. Maybe the Robacheaux's maid was especially glad to see Kate because of her baby doll curls or because she held on to Sally so tight. *Jus like a lil monkey!* The mothers talked together and laughed so much. Tommy and Rebecca played cowboys and Indians, using brooms for horses. They were almost exactly the same age. The best thing was that Tommy had a wagon and he pulled Rebecca around the streets of Bunkie in the wagon because he was a boy.

One day Miss Mabel Glen brought a chocolate cake over to the Robacheauxs. While the ladies were visiting together in Miss Caroline's living room, Tommy pushed a chair up to the cake on the kitchen counter. As the two of them stood on the chair, he and Rebecca took turns licking the frosting off the cake. At first the mothers were mad, but then they laughed and laughed. They said Tommy and Rebecca looked like Sally and Maybelle. It made a good story. Whenever Rebecca thought about the time they went back to Bunkie so Elizabeth could be born, she tasted chocolate.

Margaret had no doubt that her fourth baby would be a girl. She was so resigned to the fact that she could hardly remember why she had ever wanted a little boy. She had already selected Elizabeth, after Elizabeth Barrett Browning, as the name for the new baby. "*If we cared for any meadows, it was merely/To drop down in them and sleep.*"

Elizabeth was a peaceful baby, completely unlike Kate who had seemed to never sleep, who always needed attention. Now two-year-old Kate tenaciously shadowed behind her mother. If Margaret stepped back too suddenly, more often than not, she'd knock little

Kate over, or trample her bare toes. Rebecca, on the other hand, kept an eye on her mother and also kept her distance. She was quiet and watchful. When Emily was not at school, she was down the road helping a neighbor girl take care of her horse, Blaze; horses were all Emily thought or talked about. She had very little interest in her younger sisters, so her mother was surprised one afternoon to find her kneeling on the big bed where Margaret had left the baby.

"It's not really soft," Emily looked up as her mother walked into the room.

"What? What's not soft?" Elizabeth was fussing. Margaret slipped her finger into the diaper to feel if it needed to be changed.

"The soft spot." Emily hopped off the bed and headed out of the bedroom, almost bumping into Kate. "I pushed on it and it's not soft like it's supposed to be." Emily sounded disillusioned, just as she'd been when the BelleBend fairy turned out to be a boat.

The afternoons when Emily was at school and Tee had left for Miss Elaine's, were endless. Rebecca and Kate were supposed to take naps, but they were never sleepy. Time stuck, the way that dragonflies got fastened to asphalt, their gauze wings unable to lift them from the sticky tar. Their mother rested from one to three and the two girls could imagine nothing more terrible than disturbing her. She had once told Rebecca that, even if the house caught on fire, she and Kate were to get the baby and go outside and not let the door slam. Waking Margaret Sobral from a nap was the same thing as jumping on top of her bed and stabbing her in the face with the ice pick Tee used to chip out the top freezer when she defrosted the Frigidaire. The two little girls lived in an agonized fear of floorboard crack noise or that Snowball, the dog that lived under their house, would bark. Kate spent much of those afternoon hours sitting on the floor with her head leaned against her mother's bedroom door, listening for the first signs of Margaret rising. Rebecca knelt on a chair in the living room and watched the cars pass on the River Road, or sat and carefully turned the pages of A Child's Garden of Verse, trying to remember the poems that went with the pictures. Baby Elizabeth was the quietest of all; she always slept the entire two hours.

"I'm not going to do it, Matthew. I feel like a sideshow freak around those people. Especially the Elks Club people."

"It's our first New Year's in BelleBend," Matthew pleaded. "I won't ever ask you again. You have my word, Margaret, just this once. The entire school board will be there and ---"

"And their gossipy wives."

She had relented and now was sitting alone at a small table, watching Matthew across the room as he enthralled a group of nodding men with one of his long-winded stories. Margaret tapped a foot to the music: *Aba daba daba daba daba daba dab Said the chimpie to the monk. Baba daba daba daba daba daba dab Said the monkey to the chimp.* She felt invisible and surprisingly relaxed, enjoying the music and being away from her kids, out on the town as 1951 became 1952.

"I hear you're a real snob." A woman with shoulder length honey-colored hair dropped into the chair next to Margaret. Jean Letter was the wife of the president of the bank where the Sobrals had their endangered checking account.

"And I hear you're 'almost as rude as a Yankee,'" Margaret retorted, in a heavy drawl.

"A fate worse than death. Bad manners." Jean shook a Camel out of her pack. "The only thing even more dire might be to have lived your entire life in BelleBend, Louisiana."

"Apparently, you too, are *not from here*," Margaret laughed.

"I am not. Though I have to say I'm not a Yankee either and, unlike what I hear about you, I do drink," she said, signaling to a waiter. "I drink a great deal. But I've also been known to read a book."

"Gone with The Wind, no doubt."

"Of course. Twice. But I've read some James Joyce, Virginia Wolfe and a smattering of Hemingway. Last year I actually proposed forming a reading group to the Ladies of the Elks. One of them counter proposed that, rather than books in general, we read the New Testament." Jean put down her unlit cigarette and, for a second, folded her hands in mock prayer. Then she shook out a second cigarette for Margaret. "Rosemary Dimm suggested we share opinions on the latest issue of Ladies Home Journal." She lit the two cigarettes with a small mother-of-pearl lighter. "BelleBend can make you question how women ever got the vote."

"The vote? Woman have the vote?" Margaret laughed again. "Whatever for?"

The last day of 1951 was the beginning of an almost fifteen-year-long-friendship. The two couples—Jean and Sam, Margaret and Matthew--socialized several times a week. Sam Letter jovially hounded and harassed Matthew about his frayed finances; confessed himself shamelessly enamored with Margaret's good looks and sharp wit, and ostentatiously declared Matthew unworthy of such a woman. Matthew and Jean shared a love for maps, martinis, Civil War history, and ignoring Sam Letter. Margaret and Jean saw one another almost every day and created a chatty and satiric refuge from their Deep South small town isolation. Both women were gifted mimics and amused one another doing impressions of BelleBend's characters and gossips. Their bond endured through the chaos of the Sobrals' houseful of growing daughters and Matthew's bounced checks, Jean's drinking binges and Sam's parsimonies. The friendship between Margaret and Jean managed to survive everything but the Civil Rights movement.

Packing Up—1980

"Remember when we would answer the phone and the person on the other end would say, 'Who is this?' and Mama would ---"

"Mama insisted we respond with, '*To whom do you wish to speak*?'" Kate interrupts Rebecca. "But instead of saying "Hello," which is standard throughout the western world, the person on the other end of the phone would really say, 'Who dis?' Not actually 'who *is* this.' Skipping the whole verb thing."

"But, the point is," Rebecca raises her voice. "The point is ---"

"But 'dis' does contain a verb. It's like 'tis' for Shakespeare. *Tis nobler in the mind to suffer the slings and arrows…* As in *who this is* answering the phone at the Sobral house?" I say. "'Dis.'"

"Stop interrupting!" Rebecca slams the cardboard top shut. "The point is how it was mortifying, we would just cringe to have to say, 'T*o whom do you wish to speak?*' to people who didn't have any idea of what in the hell we were saying."

"Some of them knew." Elizabeth reopens the box. "I had friends, who knew better, calling our house and saying 'Who dis?' just to hear 'T*o whom do you wish to speak*?' They thought it was hilarious."

The four of us are in our parents' bedroom, emptying the dressers, deciding what we will pass on to Goodwill or friends, and what we will keep. Elizabeth returns to France in two days. Our jobs and our children are all calling for us. When we complete sorting and giving away boxes and packing a moving truck, our orphan hood will be tangible, our *home* gone. My sisters and I will each be *nobody's child*. And we will be through with BelleBend.

In the story, *home* is monumental for the Sobral sisters. Their parents had left their respective homes, apparently without regret or a second thought. Their father had gone off to join a religious order, seemingly, without even looking over his shoulder. Though the South would always call him, ground him, there was no specific place, no nostalgia for parents made remote by death. In the story it is God and Margaret, not necessarily in that order who created *home* for Matthew. This story begins with their mother's break from her past, Margaret's determination to never go back the way she had come. Her parents, who were distant by virtue of their remoteness, their inability to express affection--if indeed, they fostered any--had no hold on her. There was probably no place on earth that their mother truly considered *home*. But, to the end of their days --or their story--home would always be that house on the River Road, the Mecca the four sisters venerated and forever aimed toward.

"I always wanted to be like them. Besides wanting a horse with all my heart and soul, I also wanted to talk and be just like someone from BelleBend," I say. "I wanted to fit in."

"You did not. You just wanted to drive Mama crazy." Rebecca shakes her dark cap of hair. "Look at your friends who stayed here. You wanted to be like them?"

"Ginny and Carmen are married to the first, and only, boy either of them ever kissed. I married a sophisticated older man, and felt sorry for my unworldly friends. Now they feel sorry for me. And I can see why. Their circle is small, but tight and secure. Unbroken. Their children--"

"'*Will the circle be unbroken, bye and bye Lord bye and bye*,'' Kate and Elizabeth break, almost simultaneously, into twangy song. "*There's a better place awaiting in the sky Lord in the sky*."

"Don't give away Mama's jewelry box." I reach into the carton and pull out a dark green leather box, pointedly ignoring my singing sisters. "I don't really have one. I'll pack this in my suitcase."

"*I was standing by the window on a cold and cloudy day …*"

After she died, we divided the few bits of our mother's jewelry, each of us taking a turn to choose, until the green box was empty. We drew straws for who got first selection, and mine was the shortest straw.

"Well, there's always a first time," Rebecca had said on the night of jewelry distribution.

"Meaning?"

"Meaning, you have always gotten first pick."

"First born, first pick," I had answered, keeping it light. "The natural order."

"Leaving slim pickings for the rest of us," Elizabeth said offhandedly. "I got the longest straw. Now this is what I call unusual."

"Not really," Kate had said. "You were Mama's favorite. Who wouldn't have chosen that straw?" She spoke wistfully, with no note of envy or resentment in her voice.

As a child, Kate had never learned to gage mother. She wanted to be with her so desperately that she could not do that one thing our mother asked of her. She could not leave our mother alone. She clung to her skirts, following her around, crawled behind the sofa to spy on her. It drove Mama crazy and made her mean. She'd close Kate up in a closet or lock her out of the house. She cursed at Kate in front of company, and would even hide in her bedroom, desperate to get away from her third born.

With Kate on Mama's trail, fastened to her like a tar baby, Rebecca wisely became the remote child. She hung up her own clothes, didn't leave them on the floor for the help to pick up, like the rest of us did. She made good grades, and never got into trouble at school. She sat quietly at the dining room table doing her homework every night. Our mother was always her focus, but Rebecca eased, unobtrusively, through the family dramas.

I was out of the house as much as possible. I wandered the riverside, with whatever family dog had not been run over on the River Road or murdered by the neighborhood's pair of Great Dane assassins. I stalked strange horses in distant pastures and read books about horses. I spent long hours in the school library and hung out in Daddy's office until he drove home at the end of the workday.

Only Elizabeth was able to maneuver our mother. Even as a toddler, she stayed clear of Mama's mood downswings and kept her company on the upswings. With no more incoming babies, it seemed our mother was finally able to enjoy a small child; settle in calmly with her lastborn. Elizabeth was Margaret Sobral's light at the end of the tunnel and surely Mama's favorite. We admired her for it. Rebecca, Kate and I were like ranch hands watching the last cowboy sit the saddle as the bronco stopped bucking.

"Really, Emily?" Rebecca says, closing the lid of the cardboard carton again. "You really want that banged up jewelry box? I wish I'd known that. I never can think what to get you for Christmas."

"Because I need everything?"

"Why the hell don't you collect alimony, Emily?"

"For the same reason you don't, Kate."

"But I'm supporting myself."

"Me too."

"Right. Minimum wage and take out boxes from the restaurant."

"Speaking of restaurants," says Elizabeth, our event planner. "It's time to clean up."

Sam Letter is taking us to dinner tonight. Daddy always joked about how Sam would rather run over his own hand with a car, than use it to pick up a check. But, momentously, Mr. Sam is taking the Sobral daughters out to The Steak and Ale Restaurant. He misses our father, they have been good friends in the years since Miss Jean died. But it will be our mother Sam will want to talk about.

I carry the green jewelry box to the bedroom I share with Rebecca and place it carefully on top of my suitcase.

Chapter 9

BelleBend—1952-1953

THAT SPRING THE principal's daughter was given the title role in BelleBend Elementary School's operetta, The Runaway Fairy.

"Matthew, you tell Mrs. Maduse that it is not fair for your daughter to get the lead in the play. In fact, it's more than unfair, it's very wrong. Tell her to cast some poor little girl from the country, who needs the attention." Margaret and Matthew were in the kitchen having a last cigarette before bed. "More attention is about the last thing Emily needs."

Matthew had bathed the three older girls and read to them. They were tucked into their beds; Elizabeth was already sound asleep in the crib beside Kate's bed in the back bedroom, her empty baby bottle clutched to her chest.

"This time it has nothing to do with me. Honestly." Matthew leaned over to light his wife's cigarette. "I walk by the first grade classroom almost every day. Emily is at least a head shorter than any of the other kids. What is that called? "He lit his own cigarette, and then remembered the phrase. "'Type casting.' She's the smallest kid in the entire school."

"So she got the lead in the school play because she's a dwarf?"

"Margaret!" Matthew laughed. "This is The Runaway Fairy, not Billy Goat Gruff."

Rebecca had to cover her mouth with her pillow to keep from laughing out loud when she heard her daddy laugh. She and Emily shared the bedroom next to the kitchen and were listening, intently, to their parents' conversation. Emily kicked her sister under the covers.

"Besides, she can't sing."

"How do you know that? I mean, you can't sing, and I can't, but ---"

"Our diminutive daughter got the lead in the school play so the elementary school teachers could curry favor with you. Admit it, Matthew." She took a drag of her cigarette and held in the smoke, her voice husky. "I was the smallest in my class for my first two years of school. My little brother too." She exhaled. "I know the faculty thinks I don't feed Emily. Jean told me that Rosemary Dimm told her that it is common knowledge that our children are close to starving due to the fact that I am a Yankee who does not know how to cook."

"Well, if you fed Emily properly, they wouldn't have anyone to play the fairy. They'd have to get themselves an entirely different operetta." Matthew smiled and reached to take Margaret's hand.

"Well, I won't make her costume." Margaret stood up and stubbed her cigarette out in the small glass ashtray. "I won't." She realized that Matthew would not talk to the teachers.

While to all appearances it seemed that her husband was blindly eager to do her every bidding, she knew that when he set his mind to something there was nothing Margaret could say to dissuade him. Emily would be the star of the show. The principal's wife would stay outside the fray, her sense of justice betrayed.

"Are we really starving? Rebecca whispered in her sister's ear.

"No," Emily whispered back. "The little pagan babies in China are starving. We're Americans."

Emily became a reader, teaching herself to read as she struggled to memorize the pages of the script about a little fairy who ran away from the forest because no one believed she was real. The night of the show, Emily did not miss a single line. Her dramatic portrayal was rote; all of her lines were delivered in the same singsong drone. Though she was, indeed, the smallest child on the stage, a visually believable fairy, Emily was most definitely not an actress. Her performance would have been a complete mortification to Matthew, were it not for his daughter's singing. Her beautifully rendered solo compensated for Emily's terrible acting: "If you believe in fairies," she sang in a strong clear voice. "Fairies will believe in you."

"Matthew, she is six years old. It is ridiculous to have her take singing lessons."

"And you can't afford it," Jean Letter pointed out, gingerly reaching thumb and forefinger to pull the olive from her empty martini glass.

"Shirley Temple was a lot younger than six when she broke into the movies," Matthew joked, anticipating the rise he would get from his wife. "Emily is just as cute."

"Shirley Temple! Jesus Christ, Matthew. You said yourself that, except for that song, she was a disaster! How in hell ---"

"I heard that Emily did the whole play like one of those little ducks you wind up with a key. The audience kept waiting for her to wind down and stop quacking." Jean handed her empty glass across the coffee table to Matthew. "Sounds more like the village idiot, than a fairy of the forest."

"It is true that her performance lacked a certain animation." Matthew plucked the glass from her hand and headed to the kitchen to mix a third martini for Jean. "But, she also sang like an angel. She really did."

"Matthew, it's singing lessons for Emily or new sandals for her and her sisters." Margaret called after him. "We can't afford both." She turned back to Jean and shook her head.

"Ducks, fairies, angels," Jean laughed and reached for her Camels. "At least he's keeping to the wing theme."

That summer was a bare-footed one for the Sobral girls. Emily took singing lessons for the next four or five months, and then refused to continue. An entire month to learn "Bye Bye Blackbird?" She didn't want to be a singer, she wanted to find a wild horse and tame it and ride it to Texas or California.

Polio! It was everywhere. It lurked in the colored people's water fountains. It grabbed hold of children who wouldn't take afternoon naps. It was in the cracks of the leather seats at The Grand Theatre. Rebecca waited for it to get her. She couldn't decide which would be better: braces on her legs and the cute crutches with the metal bracelets. Or an iron lung. After Emily fell asleep, Rebecca would pull her sister's share of the bed sheet loose and then tuck the sheet tightly around herself. She would press her legs together and squeeze her arms against her sides. *Oh, Rebecca, you will never be able to run and play like the other children.* She imagined her mother sitting by her iron lung day and night. *No more Easter dresses. No more hopscotch. I will open books over your head and turn the pages so you can see the pictures. And I will hold grape popsicles up to your pitiful lips.* Rebecca could bring herself to tears imagining her broken-hearted mother caring for her second daughter, the pitiful and noble child forever imprisoned in a giant metal tube.

Every weekday morning of the summer Matthew dropped his three oldest daughters off at the town pool at 8:30. Grover the lifeguard gave a half hour of swim lessons before the pool opened. He taught children between the ages of four and ten. Kate wasn't yet three, but Margaret needed the peace and quiet, so Kate went to the town pool too and sat on the warming concrete and watched the swimming lessons. Little boys and little girls lined up on the pool's shallow end, hopping from foot to foot in the chilly water. But it was only the little girls who Grover lifted and suspended, balanced on his forearm, to demonstrate proper stroke technique. His big hand opened over a small chest, the little girl's legs forked at Grover's biceps, he'd glide her through the water.

"Push your arm all the way back, now scoop the water behind you and turn your head sideways and breathe." The other children watched, teeth chattering, as Grover glided the little girl through the chlorinated water. "Other arm now, and kick kick kick."

"Like this? Like this Mr. Grover?" An eager little boy might ask, hopping dangerously into the deepening slant of the pool, spinning his arms like a weather vane in a tornado, slipping under the surface, swallowing water, chocking. Grover kept his eyes on the slippery little girl he was teaching to swim. An older boy, or maybe two of them, would grab the foolish eager one and pull him back into the shallows. The boys learned what they could from watching Grover's swimming demonstrations, listening to his pointers. Just like Kate, who watched the lessons from the poolside, her little pipe stem legs folded under her. "Kick kick kick," she chanted quietly. "Kick kick kick."

When the lifeguard blew his whistle to say the pool was open, Kate would climb down the ladder and walk on her tippy-toes to keep her chin above water. Sometimes Rebecca would hold her hand and help Kate float. You were supposed to get out of the pool and go inside when you had to go to the bathroom. But Kate didn't think anyone did that.

Grover seldom lifeguarded from the tall lifeguard chair. He preferred to watch over the swimmers from inside the pool, neck deep in water, leaning on the pool's edge. It was his habit to hold a little girl, her feet suspended, her back against his front. It was as though the little girl were lifeguarding too. He kept his big hand pressed against her belly, pulling her close and safe against his front. Grover's favorite junior lifeguards were usually six or seven year olds and remained his favorite for two or three days, sometimes as long as a week. He was democratic with his favoritism; he never chose one girl for too long. Emily did cannonball jumps near him, trying to get Grover to pick her as a favorite.

When he finally did, it was really boring. She wanted to show him how good she was getting at swimming. She wanted to talk, but he said, "Shssh," when she tried to say something. They had to hold still and quiet, watching for drowning people, while he pulled her tight and loose and then tight again with his hand low on her stomach. Emily ended up being glad that she was only Grover's favorite for one afternoon.

There was hardly a girl in BelleBend who had not had a brief reign as Grover's favorite. Kate was six the year Grover lost his job. That was all that happened to him. He was fired as lifeguard, after a decade of fondling little girls. He spent his remaining summers outside the hurricane fence that surrounded the town pool. His big hands wound through the wire diamonds as he longingly watched all the little girls splashing in and out of the water. Had it been little boys he fondled, Grover surely would have gone to prison. Such were the times.

Matthew picked up his three older daughters at noon, when the pool closed, and returned them at three when it re-opened. In between they ate lunch and then sloughed through the two hours of their mother's rest time. Sometimes Emily let Rebecca and Kate follow her and Snowball over the levee to explore the ponds between the levee and the mighty Mississippi. Once they caught a small green turtle, and built a cage for it out of pulled-up grass, but it escaped. They would throw sticks at the water moccasins shimming through the water, and make mud pies from the dark claylike mud on the pond edges. They liked to clap their hands to startle the big sunning turtles into clamoring off their logs and into the turgid water. But most afternoons, while their mother rested and their baby sister slept, Emily read books she had brought home from her daddy's library. The neighbor with the horse had moved away and Emily was left to only read about horses. While their older sister read and reread her small stack of books, Rebecca and Kate were abandoned to smother quietly under the hot still blanket of boredom that covered them until it was time to go back to the town pool.

"Can I go to the train station, Daddy? Please," Emily begged.

"Us too. We want to go," Rebecca said, grabbing hold of Kate's little hand.

John Monroe was coming from Bunkie to stay with the Sobrals. He didn't have a daddy, so Matthew would be his daddy for a week.

"'*At the beach, at the beach, at Pontchartrain Beach. You'll have fun, you'll have fun every day of the week*!" On the way to the train station the little girls sang the commercial they'd heard so many times on the radio. "*You'll love the thrilling rides, laugh till you split your sides, at Pontchartrain Beach*!'"

Matthew planned to take a day off to drive John and the girls to Pontchartrain Beach, which was a beach with real salt water, like an ocean, and also an amusement park with rides, near the city of New Orleans. On another day he would take the children into Baton Rouge, to the State Capital, and show them the bullet holes, next to the brass elevator door, from when Huey P. Long was shot dead. With fatherless John Monroe coming to visit, the slow summer was suddenly in motion, like a chained dog set loose.

Their mother was so happy to see the boy from Bunkie that she *hugged* him. Her daughters watched, amazed. Their daddy hugged them and the ladies from Bunkie hugged them. Not one of the girls could remember ever seeing Margaret Sobral hug a child.

On the second day John was on the River Road, he and Emily had made a plan. They would pack some supplies and walk along the levee looking for likely spots where there might be a cave along the river. John had just finished reading Tom Sawyer and knew for a fact that caves abounded along the Mississippi.

As soon as he heard Mr. Sobral leave the house for morning Mass, John untangled himself from the sheets on the living room sofa and tiptoed to the bedroom beside the kitchen.

"It's time, Emily," he whispered.

"Time for what?" Rebecca bolted straight upright.

"Nothing, Rebecca. Go back to sleep." Emily rose up on an elbow.

"Don't say 'nothing'," Rebecca raised her voice. "Something's going on and you want to leave me out!"

"Sshh. You're gonna wake up Kate."

"Well, tell me," Rebecca lowered her voice.

"We're going to discover a cave," John said quietly. "It'll be hard work. Probably too much walking for you." He needed a haircut, his blond hair was full of cowlicks.

"It won't be. I'm a good walker. As good as Emily." She folded her hands and rose up on her knees, a supplicant.

"No you're ---"

"OK, but no chickening out and wanting to turn back," John whispered. "It might take ten miles, or something."

"John, Rebecca is too little." Emily tried to state her case against her copycat sister, but John was already heading back to the living room to get dressed.

The three children had just placed a mayonnaise jar of water and a half loaf of Little Miss Sunbeam bread into a grocery bag when Kate tiptoed into the kitchen.

"Where ya'll going?" She rubbed her eyes with her small fists.

"Spider hunting," said Emily, hastily.

"Spiders?" Kate took a step back. "You looking for spiders?"

"We're going ---"

"I told John how afraid you are of spiders and he suggested we try to catch them all." Emily interrupted John. "To protect you. We have a jar to put them in." Emily pointed to the grocery bag. "We're going to catch every one we see."

"You are?" Kate was awe-stricken.

"Especially the big ones," Rebecca added.

"Then we'll pour gasoline over them and set them on fire and burn them to a crisp."

"Burn them dead?"

"Kate, it would be a big help to us if you could tell your parents that we'll be home in time for supper." John rolled up the top of the bag and tucked it under his arm. "Tell them not to worry."

Kate nodded, proud to be trusted.

The three children crossed the River Road and climbed up the levee, their bare feet and legs drenched with dew from the thick clover that grew knee high over the levee. Snowball followed them, leaping to make his way over the tall grass. When they got to the top, John looked purposefully both ways. BelleBend was upriver to their left and the unknown countryside downriver to their right. Across the road baby Elizabeth and her mother were still sound asleep. Kate was waiting in the kitchen, ready to tell her daddy the important spider news when he arrived home from church to make her mama's coffee.

"We're off," John said purposefully, switching the bag to his other arm.

Rebecca looked back at the white house under the pecan trees with a touch of homesickness. Emily made a show of walking fast, then trotting like a horse. No matter how far they walked, she would not get tired.

Soon the dew evaporated and the top of the levee became dusty, dust caked to mud between their damp toes. They walked in single file, John in the middle. Whenever they saw something promising, an area behind the levee that wasn't covered by a pond, they'd descend to explore. When they were sure there wasn't a hidden cave entrance they'd climb back up the steep sloop. It got hotter and hotter. They rationed the mayonnaise jar of water, carefully passing it around and taking small sips. Snowball turned around and headed home.

"Let's play circus." Rebecca hopped onto the top of the black irrigation pipe that crossed the levee from the river and ran under the River Road, then spilt out into a ditch that irrigated the far-off rice fields.

"We don't have time," Emily protested.

But John had put down the bag and was following behind Rebecca, his arms outstretched for balance, as they walked down the sun-warm pipe, carefully placing one foot in front of the other. Emily followed them, lifting her feet extra high.

"I think it's past lunch," Rebecca said, as they headed downriver again.

"And no breakfast," John said. "We should have thought of that."

They walked behind the levee to sit out of the sun in the shade of a wide-branched tree to eat their lunch.

"Let's save some for later." Rebecca held up the mostly empty bread bag.

"Let's eat it all now," Emily countered.

"No. Rebecca's right. After we find the cave, it'll take us a long while to get back. We'll need supplies."

"And our water's almost gone." Rebecca added.

They were walking more slowly. They had walked miles. The July sun pressed against their heads like a hot iron. The three went down the backside of the levee and waded into a muddy pond; lay back in the shallows to cool off their heads.

"I want to go home," Rebecca insisted; as they started walking up the levee, brown water streaming from their clothes. "It's too far."

"See! I told you." Emily said.

"We have to keep going," John said. His pale hair was darkened by pond water and mud, his hot face flushed.

Rebecca stayed behind John, with her head lowered, so he couldn't see that she was crying a little bit. They were all walking really slowly. They stopped noticing places down the levee that might have caves. Their clothes were drying off.

"We should maybe turn back before we miss supper," said John.

"And give up?" Emily asked, hopefully.

"And give up," he agreed.

"There's no more water," Rebecca pointed out. "We could die from thirst."

When the three exhausted children stumbled into the house, Tee was mopping the front hall.

"Tee, how come you're still here?"

"'Still here, Emily, at ten o'clock?' What you talking about? I don't go to Miss Elaine's for two more hours." She gave the mop a vigorous squeeze. "Ya'll track that mud on my clean floor, I'm gone be smacking me some little white be-hinds." Tee sloshed a puddle of gray water over the floor.

On Sunday morning Margaret got up early and began cooking, employing the skills and recipes she'd learned from Rose and Irma back in Bayou Goula. While Matthew and the children were at church, she fried chicken and made cold slaw and deviled eggs spiced with finely chopped sweet pickles. The day before, Tee had squeezed a sack full of lemons for lemonade while Margaret had baked a large pound cake. She packed plates and cups into a carton and buffered them with folded napkins

After Mass, Matthew drove John, Emily, Rebecca and Kate to the icehouse. He lowered the watermelon onto John's open arms.

"That's right, hold it like a little baby," Matthew encouraged the boy from Bunkie.

"At least this watermelon doesn't wiggle all over the place," the boy joked. "Like Elizabeth."

"Or drool slimy spit on your arm," Emily added.

"What does slimy mean?" No one answered Kate.

"If you swallow a seed, a watermelon will grow in your stomach," said Rebecca. "It kills you."

"What's slimy?"

"Careful now, son," Matthew held the door open to a freezer almost as big as the Sobrals' entire house. Great blocks of ice were stacked around the room like crystal stairways. Mr. LeBlanc, an old bent-over man in overalls, took the watermelon from John and tenderly slid it into an opening between the stacks of ice. Mr. LeBlanc had been a young man working at the icehouse back when Matthew's father had owned it. The two men went outside to smoke cigarettes and talk about the olden days while the melon cooled. The four children stayed in the icy room, for as long as they could stand it, playing North Pole.

Kate was waiting on the front porch when the car from Bunkie pulled into their driveway. They were here to take John Monroe back to his own house; but first there would be a picnic and swimming. The Robacheaux children started jumping out of the car before it had even stopped all the way. Then Miss Mabel Glen, Miss Caroline and Mr. Ernest opened the front doors and got out. Mr. Earnest threw his cigar down in the driveway and stomped on it.

"They're here, they're here!" Rebecca shouted from the living room.

Kate could hear her parents calling out to the Bunkie people and coming to the front of the house from the kitchen. Nobody saw her on the porch. All the kids and the grown-ups were so glad to be out of the car that they hurried past her and into the shadowy house. John Monroe and Emily were hiding under the house. Kate had followed them there. They said not to tell; they made her promise. Kate wanted to be in the living room with all the company, but she was shy. She balanced on one foot in the doorway, with her hands behind her back, listening to all the shouting and laughing, trying to tell the voices apart.

"You have grown so much, Kate," said Miss Mabel Glen, turning away from the noisy grownups and kids. "Look at these curls." She ruffled Kate's hair. "And your enormous brown eyes."

Kate swallowed hard, took a deep breath, and then said, "John and Emily are under the house." But Miss Mabel Glen didn't hear her. She had already returned to the living room and was talking to Kate's daddy.

All the kids piled into Mr. Ernest's car. The other grownups, the baby, the ice chests, and the baskets of food were in the Sobral car for the drive down the River Road.

"Pointe Jardin was so beautiful and unusual that the Army Corps extended the levee around it." Matthew explained to the Bunkie company. "The pond starts somewhere in those cypress woods back there." The two cars had driven over the levee and parked by a large bright bowl of water. "It's spring fed, which is rare enough around here, but look at all that sand." He pointed to the edge of the pond and to a high dune of sand that lay between the pond and the river. "No explanation for clean sand being so near to the muddy Mississippi. Or why the spring floods don't carry it away."

"Oh my, an isolated paradise." Mable Glen walked to the water's edge with baby Elizabeth balanced on her hip. "Eden. It feels like--"

"Don't none of ya'll bite into no apple now."

"Oh, Ernest!" Caroline slapped his arm, laughing. "The things you think of."

"Who would ever choose an apple over watermelon?" Matthew said.

"I doubt the Garden of Eden was this hot." Margaret headed toward the shade of a wide-branched oak tree festooned with hanging swaths of gray. She carried a basket of fried chicken and had a large tablecloth folded over her arm. A broad skirt of soft iridescent green moss encircled the base of the tree.

"Well, the watermelon and the beer are cold," said Matthew. "Come on, Ernest, we have ice chests to carry."

The pond water was cool under the July midday sun, sweet with the honeyed wood scent of cypress, and copper-colored like a pale shade of beer bottle glass. The older children were already splashing toward a half-submerged boat, climbing up its sides and diving off. Emily could hardly believe it when she clamored onto the boat ahead of John. She was faster and stronger than a boy!

"Tarzan!" she shouted, pounding her fists against her skinny chest before she jumped. Emily decided to be a boy. You could go to the bathroom without taking your panties down, and boys weren't afraid. She held her breath and swam under water, with her eyes open, almost to the farthest side of the pond. Did the other kids see how far she was swimming?

After lunch, when the older kids were so grumpy about having to stay out of the water because of cramps, Rebecca and Tommy Robacheaux went exploring. They couldn't swim anyway, so they didn't care about having to stay out of the pond. A narrow stream flowed from the pond between the big sand hills and toward the river. They could see swaying grass in the water and small green speckled fish with pink bellies. Tommy and Rebecca planned that they would each catch a fish and take it home as a pet. The two four-year-olds followed the rippling current, running in and out of the shallows with cupped hands, almost catching them, but then the fish were too fast and slippery. Suddenly they were at the banks of the river and forgot all about the pretty fish. A boat bigger than a house was going by on the gleaming spread of muddy water.

"Hey, hey! Hello!" Tommy jumped up and down waving. The boat belched a long loud horn sound. "They see us, Rebecca! They see us."

"Hello. Hello, we have watermelon!" she shouted, trying to be heard over the roar of the big boat's engines. The horn blew again.

The two children ran along the riverside, waving and jumping as the boat passed by, casting a big shadow over them. Then waves began crashing on the mud clay banks and it was fun. Tommy and Rebecca ran and slid on the suddenly wet and shiny mud; they fell and spun around on their bottoms and laughed at how hard it was to stand back up.

"Ice! We're ice-skating," Tommy shouted.

"We are!" Rebecca wasn't sure what ice-skating was, but it was fun to slip and fall and try to get up, and slip some more. Then she was in water over her knees and then her shoulders; the waves got higher and she couldn't touch bottom and began to spin around and around like the ride at Pontchartrain Beach.

"Get out, Rebecca!"

"I can't…." Water filled her mouth and she started coughing, still spinning in the brown water.

Tommy grabbed for her arms, but his hands were slick with mud and he kept losing his grip. Just when it felt like her head was going to go under the water and she wouldn't be able to see Tommy at all, Rebecca reached out and clamped hold of one of his legs with both of her hands; she pushed her feet beneath her as hard as she could while Tommy took small steps backwards, jamming his heels down to grip into the slippery mud, pulling her from the funnel of spinning water.

"Look at ya'll." Miss Caroline was disgusted. "Covered with mud. Ya'll go wash off in that water right this minute, before it sets in your swimming suits. I ought to spank the both of you!" She turned to the group lounging in the shade. "Those two get in more trouble, I swear. No telling what they'll do next."

"It's got to be Tommy's influence," Matthew laughed. "At home, butter wouldn't melt in Rebecca's solemn little mouth." He took a deep sip of his cold Jax beer and offered a small sip to Elizabeth, who was pulling herself up on her daddy's lap.

"Look at this sweet cotton top." Mabel Glen slid her hands under Elizabeth's arms, taking her from Matthew and lifting her overhead. "I thought my Diane was blonde! Nothing like your Elizabeth."

The baby laughed and reached for Mabel Glen's face with her small dimpled hands.

"Margaret looks like a swan," Miss Caroline said.

"Ester Williams, I swear." Mr. Ernest said. "Better!"

"Who knew that Margaret was such a great swimmer?"

"That's not swimming, Caroline, that's gliding." Miss Mabel Glen rose up on her knees, lifting the baby with her. "The water is hardly disturbed."

"*Kick, kick, kick,*" Kate whispered. Her mother was far off in the water, swimming toward the trees. "*Kick, kick, kick.*"

She looked over at her daddy. He was standing with his back leaned against the tree. His face looked different, surprised and proud and close to sad. His eyes watched Kate's mama as she got smaller and smaller. Her daddy couldn't take his eyes off her. Looking at him, seeing that he had tears in his eyes, Kate understood that her mother was swimming away. She wouldn't be coming back. She was leaving them all behind. She would swim through the trees and disappear, as if she'd never been here at all. As if none of them had.

"Mama!" Kate screamed and started crying so hard that Miss Caroline ran over and picked her up as fast as she could.

"Your mama is just fine, honey. She's a wonderful swimmer."

Kate couldn't catch her breath. She knew that only babies cry, but she just could not stop. She clamped her arms and legs tightly around Miss Caroline because she was crying so hard that she could not see and she was shaking and Kate needed to hold onto something.

On some summer evenings as the sun dipped and diminished into the far off glitter of rice fields and the chorus of frogs began to clamor in the levee ponds, a thin dark complexioned man would slowly peddle his bicycle down the River Road, ringing the bell on his handle bars with his thumb. A big brightly colored box was braced on the front wheel of his bike.

"Popsicle Man! Popsicle Man!" The first of the girls to hear the bell would call out.

The girls were not allowed popsicles every time the Popsicle Man came down the River Road, but sometimes they were. On those delicious popsicle nights, Emily, Rebecca and Kate sat out on the front steps in their underpants, each holding a popsicle half. As soon as their mother peeled back the white paper and divided them, the popsicles began to melt. Matthew and Margaret would settle behind the girls, sitting in the swing on the screened porch, sharing the fourth half with the baby. The little girls tried to make their treats last as long as possible, without wasting even a drop of the rapidly melting flavored ice. They licked at their knuckles and wrists, closed their lips over the final nub. When the last shred of ice was gone, they chewed on the wooden sticks. Fireflies began rising from the grass, the sky scattered stars above the levee, and the pecan trees disappeared into shadows. If only the night could be held off and the hard chore of summer sleep postponed:

"Get off my side, Rebecca!"

"I'm not on your side." Rebecca pressed her back against Emily.

"Off! It's too hot."

Whine, whine, whine, whine….

They slapped at the mosquito, or the mosquitoes, hovering at their ears. Emily and Rebecca had already peeled off their clammy nightgowns; their sheets were damp with sweat, tangled with little girl sleeplessness. *Whine, whine, whine….* No matter how many times they slammed their palms against their ears, the whining would not stop. They pulled the sheet over their heads until the heat was unbearable and kicked it off; then the mosquitoes were back. They'd been just outside the sheet, waiting: *Whine, whine, whine….*

"You are too on my side!"

"You're gonna wake up Mama," Rebecca warned.

Whine, whine, whine….

And so the summer passed in the aqua sparkle of chlorine, the plodding of still and thick afternoons, the rising haze of twilight fireflies. There were watermelon trips to the icehouse, and the sweetness of popsicle nights. Once they all went to the drive-in movies and saw The Wizard of Oz on the big screen suspended above the field of parked cars. Matthew's driver's side window was half open, with the sound box hooked over the glass. Elizabeth fell deeply asleep on the front seat between her parents before Dorothy had even met the Tin Man. Oblivious to the whining darts of mosquitoes, the colored waiters weaving among the cars, and the scent of popcorn and hot dogs, the three little girls leaned against the front seat entranced and transported. The Emerald City rose up frosty green and gigantic over the muggy Louisiana sky. *"There's no place like home. There's no place like home."*

School started and Emily was in the second grade. She was by far the best reader in her class. When it was her turn to read out loud, she read as fast as she could to impress her new teacher. The other children struggled, tying to urge words from letters in a school system that didn't teach phonics, while Emily read like a speeding train that could hardly be stopped. Sometimes Miss Hanson had her read to the class at story time.

Elizabeth had learned to walk and now began to trail after Rebecca and Kate. Sometimes they would run from her and other times they played "Mama and Daddy" and made Elizabeth be their baby. She did what her older sisters told her to do so she wouldn't be left alone with Tee; Rebecca and Kate were more fun. Even the time they pretended to be cooking dinner and offered her dirt to eat, she ate it; eating dirt was better than having no one to play with.

One weekday morning Margaret sat at the kitchen table reading poetry to her three youngest daughters while Tee washed the breakfast dishes. "*It was many and many a year ago in a kingdom by the sea, there lived a maiden we all knew by the name of Annabel Lee/ She was fair ---*"

"A maiden like Tee?" Kate interrupted. "Oww," she said when Rebecca kicked her ankle.

Margaret lowered the book. "A maiden is a girl, a lady, who isn't married yet."

"Also a princess."

"This look like a princess over here wiping bacon grease off you stove?"

"Why a princess, Rebecca?" Margaret put the open book on the table.

"Because…." she paused. Maybe she had said too much and her mother would stop reading. "Because of, of the *kingdom*?" Instead her mother laughed! Rebecca had made her mother laugh.

"In lots of places kingdoms are just another word for a kind of country or a state." Margaret shifted little Elizabeth to her other knee and reached over to ruffle Rebecca's cap of dark hair. "If we had a monarchy here, you would say the 'Kingdom of Louisiana,' for instance. Instead of--"

"Which Louisiana pretty much was when Huey Long was governor." Jean Letter walked into the kitchen. The girls hadn't heard her coming. Miss Jean came over for coffee with their mother almost every morning. "A kingdom ruled by a crooked, but benevolent, despot." Now the girls would be sent outside to play. Rebecca and Kate would have to take care of Elizabeth. It was ironing day for Tee.

"As in All the King's Men." Margaret lifted Elizabeth off her lap and stood her on the floor. "You're right, of course. But I was reading Edgar Allen Poe to the girls, not Robert Penn Warren."

"And you'd never want your three-year-old to confuse the two."

"I be thinking along that same line," Tee said as she turned on the heat under the coffee pot. "A shame to mix them babies up on what wrote what."

Sugar cane season arrived and big trucks roared down the River Road, their tires low under the weight of heaped up stacks of cut cane. Green-topped stalks fell from the overloaded trucks and the little girls would run out into the road to claim them; Brownie, the new puppy, leaping at their feet. Tee peeled away the tough outer husk and cut the cane into foot long chunks for them. They chewed the fresh stalks of sugarcane into fibrous pulp; their chins and fists sticky with their own candied treats harvested from the River Road. Autumn was the syrupy scorched smell of smoke from the sugar refineries, and the green sweet scent of crushed sugar cane on the roads; it was hurricane warnings, and dense river fogs where the boats along the Mississippi sounded their lost soul horns. When the little girls woke in the night to the long low moans from the river, they knew that the coming morning would be a foggy one. The autumn winds pelted the tin roof of their house and filled their yard with ripe pecans. Before Mass, Matthew would wake Emily and Rebecca in the shadowy predawn to have them clear the driveway of nuts so that he could back the car out and get to church without crushing the pecan crop.

"Imagine your grandparents up North getting these," he told the girls, as he loaded a big cardboard box with the nuts and taped it shut. "This many pecans would cost a fortune in Wisconsin. And they're free here." He lifted the box to show how heavy it was. "My Aunt Lulu always said Louisiana was God's masterpiece."

"Did you ask her why God didn't put any apples in his masterpiece?"

"Hell, Margaret, who'd want a damned apple when he could have pecans?"

"Or watermelon," said little Kate who remembered just about everything she ever overheard.

Winter came to BelleBend in fits and starts, barefoot days interspersed with days so cold and raw that getting out of bed was an act of bravery. The gas heaters flickering full and blue-flamed were woefully insufficient warmth for the airy high ceilings of the old house on the River Road. On the mornings after a frost the little girls woke up thrilled with the white-rimed windows; they scratched pictures on the icy panes with their fingernails. The chilly air would be flavored with the scent of hot cocoa and cinnamon toast. Margaret always made cocoa and cinnamon toast when the weather snapped into sudden cold.

The four little girls would sit at the kitchen table, holding onto their empty cups, while their mother gave the final stir to her special cocoa recipe and cheerfully recited one of the many sad poems she knew by heart:

> *"....as he was dreaming an angel song awakened the Little Boy Blue. / The years are many, the years are long, but the little toy friends are true/ And they wonder as waiting the long years through in the dust of the little chair, what has become of their Little Boy Blue since he kissed them and put them there?"*

By the time the foamy cocoa was cool enough to drink, Margaret's daughters would all be weeping, united in their sorrow for the little dead boy and his loyal toys.

On Christmas Eve, Matthew would counter with the story of "The Little Match Girl." Santa Claus was forgotten as his daughters cuddled on the sofa by the Christmas tree listening to their father tell the story of the tiny pathetic orphan who tried to earn her living by selling matches on Christmas Eve. "*Matches for tell, matches for tell,*" Matthew would lisp in the voice of a starving child. His daughters sobbing as the story went on to describe the small orphan burning her very last match for warmth, and then freezing-to-death in the alley of a city that did not care. The sad poems and stories forever tenderized the hearts of the four little girls.

Margaret always said that spring in Louisiana was too brief to actually be called a season. There would be a riotous bloom of gaudy flowers, and their heady scents, fresh buckets of strawberries for sale along the back roads, and snake-entwined bushes thick with blackberries behind the levee. Then spring was just about over. It was time to brace for the heat. Yet, on the River Road spring also meant the St. Amico parade: people walking barefooted to the big church in BelleBend to celebrate the Italian saint who had appeared two and a half miles downriver and performed a miracle. Everyone lined up along the River Road to watch the devout followers of the saint go by on their long walk. It took eight people to carry the statue of St. Amico and there was always a brass band and an American flag and a big cross in the parade. Some people in the parade would be saying the rosary, others would be dancing a little bit, saying hello to people they knew.

And then there was Easter when the girls and their mother got new outfits, and when the Easter Bunny came: Emily and Rebecca sat on the foot of their bed counting jellybeans in reverent silence. They each had twelve. Also nested in the shiny paper grass were two bright yellow marshmallow rabbits and two pink ones each, and a scattering of small foil covered eggs. Best and most amazing of all, a tall dark chocolate rabbit sat in the center of each Easter basket. It had bright yellow eyes and a pink bow tie. It was too beautiful to eat!

"Rebecca, the newspaper said that some chocolate rabbits have been poisoned by the Communists."

"Rabbits like these rabbits?"

Emily nodded solemnly. "I think exactly like these."

"What can we do?" Rebecca regretfully pushed away from her basket.

"I'm your big sister. I'll test your rabbit for you. I'll take a little bite of the ears."

"You will?" Rebecca could hardly believe it.

Emily nodded again. The ears were solid chocolate, the best part of the whole rabbit.

"Suppose you die?"

"That's better than you dying," Emily said nobly. She bit the top half off the thick pair of ears. It was up to the oldest child to be the most brave. She chewed thoughtfully, while Rebecca held her breath, waiting for her big sister to keel over. "The ears aren't poisoned."

"You sure?" She inched closer to her basket.

"But maybe the Communist were trying to trick us. Maybe the ears are OK, but what about the rabbit's head?"

Emily gradually ate all of Rebecca's chocolate rabbit, from ears to toes, while her younger sister watched her anxiously, wishing she were as brave as Emily.

The big Easter dinner--baked ham, potato salad, sweet peas, and pineapple-upside-down cake--was followed by Easter afternoon anxiety, the egg hunt:

"Kate, look in that bush." Matthew pointed. "Do you see what I see? Bright pink."

Kate shook her head and hooked the big toe of her right foot against the back of her left ankle. She knew that if she headed toward the pink egg, Rebecca or Emily would run ahead of her and grab it. Kate saw a yellow egg and another pink one tucked in the roots of a pecan tree. She was powerless in the frenzy of the hunt. Even Elizabeth had found an Easter egg. Thrilled with her find, her baby sister sat right down on the lawn and tried to bite into it. Groucho, who had been circling the yard in confusion, pushed his big head into Elizabeth's lap. Margaret ran across the yard and reached for the red egg as the shell shattered between Elizabeth's baby teeth. Groucho sat back on his haunches, wagging his tail and waiting for a bite of egg.

Emily saw Rebecca trying to reach a yellow egg that was tucked in the braided fork of a honey suckle vine and stretched over her sister's head for it. Neither of the girls was tall enough.

"Matthew, what in the hell were you thinking?" Margaret asked, plucking eggshell from Elizabeth's tongue, as she watched her two oldest daughters frantically jumping, each determined to be the one to reach the Tantalus egg.

Groucho snatched the egg from Margaret's hand. Matthew slipped three eggs into Kate's basket.

Emily would rediscover her own chocolate rabbit later that summer. She had hidden it on a closet shelf where it partially melted and then produced a gray green mold. The bunny had grown its own fur; Emily's clever trick had backfired. While she knew that she was being punished for eating Rebecca's rabbit, Emily also felt the disgusting moldy mound of former chocolate was glaring proof that it didn't pay to save things for later: *Eat ye rabbit while ye may.*

That year Emily and Rebecca began getting a weekly allowance of ten cents. Every Saturday morning, right after Matthew gravely handed them each two nickels, they would walk the mile into town and go to the big counter at Talabani's Bar and Grocery. Emily would get a nickel Coke and a bag of potato chips. Rebecca would get a glass of water with a straw.

One Friday morning Tee did not show up for work. Margaret had just begun washing the breakfast dishes when Matthew called to tell her that Tee had been killed. He said, his voice shaking, that Tee and her cousin Del had been coming back from a movie at the colored movie theater when Tee stepped into the road and was struck by a hit and run driver.

On that Saturday morning, Del--a small wiry woman dressed in a faded shirt, men's trousers, suspenders, and a pair of worn down work boots--arrived at Sobrals. Matthew and Margaret were smoking cigarettes and drinking coffee at the kitchen table. Emily and Rebecca had walked to town to spend Emily's allowance and Kate was supposed to be watching Elizabeth outside. Kate was worried because her mother had been crying at breakfast. She left her baby sister and shadowed Del down the driveway across the porch, through the back door and into the kitchen.

"Tee say you a good man, Mr. Matthew. I come ax you to talk to them peoples. Make them do what right." She frantically wiped her palms on the sides of her stained trousers. Del and Tee had shared a little house back-of-town for as long as anyone could remember.

"Are you a man?" Kate asked.

"Ain't nobody gone try to fine that white man," Delia sobbed.

Matthew handed her his handkerchief, sadly nodding his head in agreement.

"I talked with the sheriff twice, Del. He said we needed a witness, a ---"

"I seen it, Mr. Matthew," she looked up from wiping her eyes. "A dark blue Ford. White man driving. I seen it. Hit her with that car and kept on. Come fast and left fast. I right there. Two steps back a Tee. I seen it."

"He said a '*reliable* witness,' Del." Margaret angrily stubbed her cigarette into the ashtray. "He meant a *white* witness," her voice broke. Overwhelmed with equal measures of anger and grief, she could hardly speak. "That Neanderthal said 'colored people couldn't tell white people apart, just like all colored people look alike to white people.' Only---" she took a deep breath and glanced at Matthew for verification. "Only that piece of ignorant garbage mouth probably didn't use the word *colored*."

"Del, are you?" Kate insisted. "Are you a man, or a girl?"

"Kate, get out of this kitchen right this god damned minute!" Margaret snapped.

"But, Mama, I just---"

Margaret grabbed Kate's skinny little arm hard and pushed her toward the back porch.

"I right there, screaming out for somebody to help us. Earnest Hawkes come running. He call the ambulance and it don't come, it don't come." Delilah tried to catch her breath. "Time that ambulance come she be gone. Tee all I got in this world and she gone." Del covered her face with her hands and howled into the handkerchief.

Kate leaned anxiously in the doorway between the porch and kitchen, bewildered to see a grown man crying like a girl, trying to understand that Tee wouldn't be back. What did that mean? How could she not come back? With everyone so sad, maybe she would. Maybe Tee would come back once she knew how sad her being gone made everybody. Kate rubbed her arm where her mother had grabbed her.

"I talked to Leroy at the funeral home, Del," Matthew raised his voice, hoping the distraught woman could hear him. He patted her clumsily on the back. "We will pay all the expenses. Miss Sobral, the girls, and I will be at the funeral. You come on back to town with me and we'll go pick out a nice coffin. Something Tee would like."

"Tee all I got," Del moaned and lowered herself down to her heels, rocking back and forth on the kitchen floor, holding onto her ribs. Then she began shouting, "All I got. All I got!"

Kate covered her ears and ran across the porch and out the door. She would go find her big sisters. They would know what to do.

Packing Up—1980

"We should have given Daddy's suits to Del," Rebecca says, reaching for a fried oyster.

"Christ. Where've you been?" Elizabeth shakes the packet of ketchup back and forth and then tears at the corner with her teeth. "Del died the year before I graduated from BHS."

"No! I didn't know that. I thought Mama and Daddy still had her over here every year for Thanksgiving Dinner."

"There you go, Rebecca, constantly romanticizing Margaret and Matthew. Daddy carried a plate to her house on most Thanksgivings," says Kate. "Besides, Del would have been swallowed up in Daddy's suits. Our father was not a large man, but Del was smaller still."

"And not a man," I point out, biting off a chunk of shrimp.

For our last night in BelleBend we picked up orders of fried shrimp and oysters from the First and Last Chance Restaurant, the irony not escaping us. Now we are sitting on the floor of what was once our dining room, eating our Last Supper from take-out boxes, drinking red wine and lukewarm white straight from the bottles. The glasses and tableware have all been packed away.

"How did Del die?"

"The Holy Savior Parish disease of choice. They don't call our homeland the 'Cancer Corridor' for nothing."

"It kills me to see that enormous fertilizer plant sprawled out like The Death Star in Star Trek." I say, holding a shrimp tail between forefinger and thumb. "Right across the River Road from Pointe Jardin."

"Killing is the right word." Kate takes the ketchup away from Elizabeth. "Most of the dead people we know from here—and there are way too many dead for us to know at our tender ages—who were not brought down by smoking, as our mother was, were probably killed by breathing."

"Right," I say, wiping my fingers on my jeans so I can pull a Salem Light from my pack.

"Star Wars. "Rebecca is still holding the same oyster, mid-air. She has always been a slow eater. "The Death Star was in Star Wars, Emily, not Star Trek."

"Remember Pointe Jardin? Remember how beautiful it was?" I light my cigarette with Kate's Bic. "The cypress forest? The pond? I drove over the levee there a couple years ago," I say, and exhale a long stream of smoke. "There was not a living tree around. Big metal structures crossing the road and levee from the river to the fertilizer mother ship, cracked gray mud, abandoned machine parts." I raise the bottle of red. "A dump."

"Well, one's a movie and one's a T.V. show." Kate says. "Emily was talking about the T.V. show."

"There was no Death Star in the damned T.V. show!" Now Rebecca is talking with a mouthful of oyster, sending out a fine spray of fried batter. "The Death Star was in the *movie*."

"I doubt that you ever even watched Star Trek, Rebecca." Kate sips blithely from the bottle of white.

"Like it really ---"

"Our last night in our ancestral home and we're arguing about idiotic science fiction shows? I want to talk about *them*," Elizabeth says.

"Darth Vader and Captain Kirk?"

"Fuck you, Emily. I want to talk about the fact that Mama and Daddy didn't ever have Del come to our house for dinner. Sit down at our table."

"We didn't really know Del, Elizabeth, we just felt sorry for her," I say.

"But I'll bet it was Mama who remembered to fix up the Thanksgiving plate," Rebecca says, obliviously veering from Elizabeth's intended topic of racial politics. "Daddy was the front man, which is why everyone thought he was a saint." Rebecca is holding her second oyster, while Kate and Elizabeth continue to dig away at the diminishing pile of fried seafood. "Not that he wasn't a good man. But he was the one who invited people we hardly knew over for dinner. Mama was the one who had to figure out what to cook, how to come up with the loaves and fishes when he arrived home with unannounced dinner guests."

"And Daddy who ---"

"Well, until Babette showed up to cook for us." Now Kate wants to talk about her great culinary mentor. Shortly after Mama took over as editor at the BelleBend newspaper, Babette turned up at our front door and announced that she would be our cook. That very over-weight, fifty-year-old woman had been cooking for white families since she was eleven years old. She claimed her beloved favorite saint--St. Jude--had instructed her to come cook for us. Every weekday, for more than ten years, Babette fixed an elaborate midday meal for a wealthy BelleBend matron and then caught a ride down the River Road to prepare our evening meal. A decade of fabulous suppers, all made possible by St. Jude, the patron saint of 'The

Impossible.' Babette hated the South and eventually left BelleBend for the bright lights of New York, or rather her daughter's Harlem apartment. The daughter who got away.

"And Daddy, who invited *white* people over for dinner," Elizabeth insists. "Never any black people."

"Are you calling our daddy a racist?" I reach for a shrimp with my free hand.

"You know what I mean about Daddy always being the good guy and Mama having to play the heavy," Rebecca plunges onward. "Remember it was Daddy who offered to pay for Tee's funeral and ---"

"In installments to those blood suckers," says Elizabeth.

"And Mama, who spent uncounted sleepless nights trying to figure out how to pay bills and cover rent while keeping up the payments to Christy's Funeral Home," Rebecca continued.

"Babette literally *could* multiply the loaves and fishes," Kate shakes her head at the memory. "The meals she made from nothing, amazing meals."

"A white-owned black people's funeral home, where the prices were maybe double…."

So the sisters reminisce, interrupt, and argue away their last night in the house where they were raised. The ghosts of their parents could be just around the corner in the empty kitchen, sharing a last cigarette before eternity, while their daughters construct and deconstruct a past that would keep its teeth forever fastened to their ankles. All of them stumbling forward as hard as they could, while the past tenaciously held onto them.

"Daddy was a humanist, Elizabeth, not an activist. Considering that he was also a product of his upbringing, the Old South and all that shit," I say. "He did pretty damned good. It would have confused him no end to join a dinner party with black people at the table, when all he'd ever seen was black people *serving* the table. But don't you know he would have been courteous, mannerly to a fault?" I drop my cigarette into an empty wine bottle.

"How can you say he wasn't an activist? Daddy was the one who broke that picket line when those red necks across the river surrounded the high school after the order to integrate the schools came down!" Kate says.

"With his gun," I add, which makes us all laugh.

Our father was superintendent of schools for Holy Savior Parish when someone called to tell him that there was a crowd encircling Carville High School across the river, not letting anyone in. Our father was as fearful of integration as anyone, but it was the law, and it was the right thing to do. He drove over to the Letter's house and borrowed Mr. Sam's hunting rifle. No one was closing any schools on his watch.

"Remember Mr. Sam put the rifle into the trunk of our car and Daddy drove off like John Wayne to confront the marauding hordes?" Elizabeth reaches over for my cigarettes. "With an unloaded gun."

We all laugh again. We know this story so well. One night, when I was stoned, I had acted out an entire make believe scenario of Matthew Sobral driving up to the angry mob, carefully parking the car and then asking one of the rednecks to help him to open the car trunk. After that I had our father asking the enraged bigot to please lend him some bullets, and then to please show him how to load the gun, and then asking how to aim it, and so forth. I had milked the story, making us of all laugh so hard.

In reality, our father had driven up to the school grounds and the sight of that gentle man with gray streaked hair getting out of his car, all dressed up in a nice suit and tie, with a determined expression on his face, had been enough to disperse the crowd. The schools of Holy Savior Parish re-opened the next day as desegregated institutions.

"Mama was the one all gung ho for integration," I say. "But she would never have confronted that crowd."

Before Elizabeth, Kate and I polished off the entire pile of seafood, I had put aside three shrimp and two oysters, for slow-grazing Rebecca. She gradually nibbles at her small pile of leftovers. Meanwhile, all four of us drink three bottles of wine and open another. We finish that one too.

"Moving truck at dawn." Elizabeth stands and stretches, raising the fourth empty bottle over her head.

We clean up our picnic, jamming the boxes from the First and Last Chance and the empty wine bottles into a small garbage bag. Then we straggle off to our respective bedrooms. While Rebecca is in the bathroom tediously engaged in her unending teeth flossing routine, I wait for my turn at the sink and reorganize my suitcase. On whim, I open our mother's old green jewelry box and push my fingers over the frayed satin lining. There is something tucked away beneath it. I gingerly lift the loosened back of the lining and pull out a small folded square of paper.

Chapter 10

BelleBend-1953-1957

REBECCA STARTED SCHOOL quietly and unobtrusively. Still, there were those on the playground who taunted, "You think you're so smart, just because you're the principal's daughter." Little Rebecca kept insisting, "No I'm not. No I don't."

On the second day of school, Emily was out on the playground and heard Jeanie Hood—whose older sister, Brenda, was in third grade with Emily—teasing Rebecca. "You think you're so smart. You think you're so smart!" Rebecca had her head lowered, her bangs and straight hair obscuring her face. Emily knew that her sister was trying hard not to cry, trying to pretend she didn't care. It made Emily want to cry. It was all Brenda Hood's fault! How else would Jeanie even know Rebecca's daddy was principal if Brenda hadn't told her? Emily and Brenda had been enemies ever since last year when Brenda announced to the entire second grade class that Emily Sobral didn't have a mother. She said that—about Emily not having a mother--because Margaret Sobral had never once set foot in BelleBend Elementary School. Yesterday Emily had tried to talk her mother into at least coming for the first day of school to help set up Rebecca and Emily's desks, like all the other in-town mothers did. Emily's mother had said she'd 'rather chew glass than spend an hour with the two-faced faculty and other assorted BelleBend gossips.' Emily wasn't quite sure what a faculty was, but she was very sure that she couldn't change her mother's mind.

"Brenda Hood, get off that god damned swing!" Emily stood, with her legs spread and her hands on her hips, facing the girl on the swing.

"Make me." The redheaded third grader was dressed in brand new patent leather shoes and sky blue socks that perfectly matched the trim on her yellow dress and the sky-blue bow in her hair. "It's not your swing and I'm going to tell Miss Bunn that you were cussing." Brenda Hood thought she was Queen of the World.

"You go tell your sister to stop picking on my sister Rebecca or I'll punch you in the stomach."

"Make me."

By that time other kids on the playground had begun to surround the two girls. Out of the corner of her eye Emily could see Rebecca sneaking back inside the school building. Emily did exactly what Huck Finn would have done in her place: Emily made a fist and hit Brenda Hood so hard that she fell backwards off the swing and started bawling like a baby.

"Julia Bunn said Emily was 'cursing like a sailor.' She brought her up to my office in a cloud of righteous indignation. When I told Miss Bunn that I couldn't imagine where Emily had heard curse words, our daughter looked at me like I was Peter denying Jesus."

Matthew shook his head, smiling ruefully. "Margaret, you really need to watch your language around the children."

Rebecca and Kate were sitting on the back porch, their backs leaned against the wall to the kitchen, listening. Emily was in trouble and was hiding back of the levee with their latest dog, Twinkle. She was in trouble because of Rebecca, so Rebecca felt protective of her big sister. She needed to know what was going on. She had sneaked onto the porch and found Kate already eavesdropping.

"This isn't funny, Matthew." Margaret turned from the stove, where she was thickening a cheese sauce to pour over thin-sliced potatoes.

"I surely know it's not funny. But, still, if you had seen the look on Emily's face."

"The swearing aside, hitting another child is serious business."

"You don't need to tell me, I was horrified. In a hundred years, I couldn't imagine Emily hitting someone. To make matters worse, Elwood Hood is on the school board. It was his daughter Emily punched. The phone is going to start ringing at any minute. I ---"

"Emily has got to go to the Catholic School now. Surely you realize this? The nuns ought to be able to do something with our irascible daughter. Your hen house faculty certainly never will. We should have ---"

"Think about it, Margaret, how will it look for the principal of the public school to have a daughter over at the convent?"

"Well, you're the god damned Catholic, Matthew. You go to Mass every single day. It's not like you're a rabbi sending your daughter off to make her First Communion." Margaret poured more milk into the sauce and adjusted the burner. "Rebecca will be the sacrificial lamb. She can stay on at your school; she surely won't be making waves."

"What are waves?" Kate asked Rebecca.

"Well, you're right. I know you are. It's not the first time Emily's gotten in trouble and been marched up to my office." Matthew folded his arms and leaned back against the Frigidaire. "I'll call Sister Marie tomorrow."

"Trouble," Rebecca whispered, pressing her forefinger to her lips, urging Kate to be quiet.

"No, please call her now. Let's do this 'under cover of night.' That way you can take Emily over to St. Catherine's before school starts in the morning."

So, to Rebecca's great heartache -- after just two days -- she was never again in the same school as Emily, who had bravely defended Rebecca in front of all the kids at BelleBend Elementary. Even though Emily mostly ignored her at home, now Rebecca knew that she was really important to Emily, like Emily had always been to her.

Rebecca and Kate remained crouching near the kitchen doorway until their mother slid the potato casserole into the oven and their father went to the living room to use the phone. Then the two little girls quietly slipped off the porch and went outside where Elizabeth was sitting on the grass, patiently waiting. Rebecca had promised her baby sister a long piggyback ride in exchange for Elizabeth staying by herself in the backyard and not *making waves.*

The summer after Emily had learned to read, she read all the books in BelleBend Elementary's small library. By the beginning of third grade she had consumed every non-boring book in her daddy's high school library. Emily couldn't get enough of reading; she felt like her eyes were little starving bird mouths open wide for words, instead of worms. Then on a Thursday in October—the sugar cane trucks rattling by on the River Road—Emily arrived home from school to a stack of books she had never before read: Anne of Green Gables, Great Expectations, a Trixie Belden mystery and--the best book of all--The Black Stallion. It had always been her dream to find a wild stallion that would trust only her and let only Emily ride it. The Black Stallion was just exactly like that; The Black only allowed Alex to get near him. There was no horse in the world as fast as The Black. Alex, who was about Emily's age, rode him in races after he had tamed the beautiful, huge wild horse.

Every Thursday there would be a new stack of books waiting for Emily. They were from her mother; her mother had picked them out especially for her. Emily couldn't get over that. Thursday was the most special day of the entire week, better than Saturday.

"Miss Jean, what's a psychiatrist?"

"Kate, out of the living room, right now! Go find your sisters. They don't hang around like little Nazi spies. They find--"

"I was just asking ---"

"God damned it!" Margaret stood up and Kate began backing toward the hallway.

"Wait, Margaret. Why don't you answer her?" Jean Letter was amused. "It's a good question."

"Don't encourage her."

"Go on, really. I'm not kidding." Jean placed her cigarette in the ashtray, crossed her arms and leaned back, tilting her head to show how interested she was. "This I want to hear."

"You really want me explaining Freud and Jung to a four-year-old?"

"Not before you explain them to me, I wouldn't," Jean laughed. "Just answer her simple question. Tell Kate what a psychiatrist is."

"Remember the Wizard of Oz, Kate?" Margaret said. Jean laughed again.

"The movie with the mosquitoes?"

"Not the movie, but the man behind the curtain in the movie. The man who gave Dorothy her sparkling red shoes."

"Actually, Margaret, Glenda the good witch gives her those shoes."

Almost every time Jean and Margaret exited on the east bank ramp of the early morning ferry, they would sing, "*We're off to see the wizard, the wonderful….*" It was their joke as they set out on the almost two hour drive to New Orleans. While Jean had her appointment with Dr. Reese, Margaret walked over to the New Orleans Public library and wandered blissfully among the shelves looking for books she had recently seen reviewed in The New Yorker. She would check out a couple novels for herself and four or five books for Emily; maybe one of the Pooh books to read to the little girls; occasionally she would get a book by Winston Churchill, or Bruce Catton for Matthew.

Margaret met Jean by the car to unload her pile of books and then the two of them went to Maison Blanche, the most elegant department store on Canal Avenue, to look at the latest clothes fashions and housewares. Afterwards, Jean would treat them to a wonderful ladies lunch in the elegant Maison Blanche dining room: chicken or Waldorf salad and delicate crust-less sandwiches; Jean would have a Manhattan cocktail and Margaret a tall glass of pink lemonade with a mint garnish. After a dessert of Napoleon pastries and chocolate mousse, they would get the car from the parking garage and make the long drive back to BelleBend. Jean Letter's struggle to come to terms with her miserable childhood was Margaret's gateway out of backwards BelleBend and into the urbane sophistication of glamorous New Orleans.

"When do you get your red shoes, Miss Jean?"

"Go outside right this god damned minute, Kate. Now!"

"*I wandered lonely as a cloud---*" Rebecca couldn't remember the rest of the poem that her mother sometimes recited. Stars and flowers and the Milky Way were all in the poem, she was sure of that. She was lying on her back on the levee looking at the sky and the clouds. A cloud by itself was lonely, but most of the time there were other clouds around.

Rebecca would be lonely without her sisters. If they were gone, she would wander the whole world looking for them. She would go to London where the bridge was always falling down, and she would ride a fine horse to Banbury Cross. Even if she had rings on all her fingers, she would still be so lonely. If you had bells on your toes, how could you walk? What would it be like to not have sisters?

Rebecca and Kate and Elizabeth always had tea parties under the house. They would pick fig leaves and set them around on an upside down cardboard box. '*Pass the tea, please*' one of them would say, and then they lifted their leaves and pretended to take sips. Elizabeth could play tea party for hours, she loved playing ladies. Kate would start building things out of sticks, or would practice holding her eyes open without blinking, but she always stayed close to Rebecca and Elizabeth. And what about Emily? Rebecca would not be able to get to sleep if she didn't hear Emily breathing beside her in the bed. She never fell asleep until after her big sister did.

And what about the moon, she wondered. Even if a cow did jump over the moon, then what would happen? Would it fall out of the sky? How did the cow get there? Maybe it got up to the moon by jumping on clouds.

Thinking about the moon made her notice that it was starting to get dark. Rebecca would be missing supper and her mama would be mad. Her daddy would be worried sick. She got up and ran down the levee, across the road, up the stairs, through the front door and down the hall to the kitchen. Everyone was already at the table. Didn't they notice that she wasn't? Would they have gone on and eaten without her? Rebecca slipped between her chair and the table, quietly sitting down without moving her chair.

"Where've you been sweetheart?

"I was wondering ---"

"Emily, get your elbows off the table!"

Rebecca had meant to say to her daddy that she'd been *wandering*, not wondering. She could imagine telling her family that she'd been to London and the moon and to Banbury Cross. *How did you get to all those places, Rebecca?* They would ask. *Why were you wandering?* Everyone would be quiet and listen while she told them about the lonely cloud from the poem.

"I didn't know it was suppertime. I ---"

"Elizabeth, use your fork!"

"Rebecca honey, you worry too much," her daddy said. "Life isn't as serious as you make it out to be."

"Wandering. I was wandering like a cloud."

"Rebecca, please take a pork chop and pass the platter on to Kate," her mama said. "You always slow things down. The food is getting cold."

Virginia Palermo said there was no Santa Claus. She said that parents were Santa. Emily definitely did not believe her. But she had to prove it. She looked in every closet in the house. She looked under her parents' bed. If her mama and daddy were really Santa Claus, where were the toys? There was only one other place to look. Her parents and Miss Jean were smoking cigarettes in the kitchen, her little sisters were under the house. The coast was clear. Emily opened her daddy's dresser drawer and took out the car keys. If there were no such thing as Santa Claus, the toys would be hidden in the trunk of the car.

"Kate, do you have something to tell us?"

"What, Daddy?" Kate was kneeling on a chair by the table watching as Margaret rolled out pie dough on the kitchen counter. "Tell you what?" she turned to face him, her light brown eyes wide with curiosity.

"About the car keys."

"What about the car keys, Matthew?" Margaret wiped her hands on her apron.

"Look at this." Matthew held up the key chain to show that the end of one of the keys was broken. "I had a hell of a time trying to get it out of the lock in the trunk. I went looking for the keys and they weren't in my dresser drawer. I found them, with the driver's key bent in the trunk lock." He tossed the set of keys on the table.

"Kate!"

"Mama, I didn't take the keys. I didn't." She got down from the chair and stood next to it, holding onto the seat. "I didn't."

"Kate, honey, when your mother's flour sifter was missing, who had it?"

"Me, Daddy, I was fixing it!"

"There's nothing she doesn't fiddle with. I turn my back for a minute and she's some place where she shouldn't be meddling. Honestly." Margaret sat and folded her hands together on the table, making a case for Kate's incorrigibility. "A coat hanger bent so badly it can't be used. Remember when she tied the pot lid to the back of the tricycle? Who else would do such a thing?"

"I didn't take the keys. I did not." The little girl shook her curly head empathically. "I didn't, I didn't."

"We need you to tell the truth, Kate." Matthew picked his daughter up and put her on his lap. "I have another key. We can still drive the car. It was wrong to take the keys. But now just tell the truth. Lying is the worst wrong. If you tell lies, sweetheart, who can trust you?"

"I am not. I am not telling a lie!"

Who else would have done such a thing? Only Kate. Matthew could not abide lying. It was usually Margaret who put Kate in the laundry closet, but if she did not tell the truth, this time it would be Matthew putting her there.

"You get one more chance to tell the truth, Kate, or, I'm sorry honey, we'll have to punish you."

"I didn't I didn't!" Kate started crying.

Emily had been exploring behind the levee with Twinkle, so it wasn't until supper that she heard about Kate being in trouble. Kate was at the supper table, hic-cupping because she had been crying so hard. She was holding her fork in her little hand, but not eating because she could hardly catch her breath. It was too late to tell. Kate had already been punished. What was the point of two people getting punished for one broken key? And, besides, Emily didn't want anyone to know about the Santa Claus problem. Not her sisters, not her parents. How could she tell that she had tried to open the car trunk without telling why? If she could have saved Kate, if she had been around before Kate got punished, Emily would have told the truth. She was pretty sure she would have.

That night Emily couldn't get to sleep. Rebecca complained about it because she couldn't fall asleep until Emily did. Emily stared at the ceiling, trying to figure out a nice thing she could do for Kate and trying to lift the heavy feeling off her chest. Maybe she would tell Sister Helen what she had done at school on Monday? Sister Helen knew everything. Then Emily remembered that she would be making her First Communion and her First Confession right after Christmas. This sin against her little sister was her greatest sin and she would tell it and it would be forgiven by God Himself. Finally Emily could fall asleep.

When Kate started school—her wild curls tamed into tight French braids by Margaret—Elizabeth was left alone on the River Road. During the mornings she tagged after Loretta and sometimes Loretta let her help mop or sweep. Occasionally, if she weren't visiting with Miss Jean, Elizabeth's mother would read to her. But most of the time Elizabeth was alone. The afternoons, while her mother napped, were the worst.

On the second week after Kate started school, Elizabeth set off, barefooted, down the sidewalk that followed the River Road with Spotty following her. She passed the Jambras' house, but didn't stop. Two old sisters lived with their two old brothers in the little house with 'no running water' next door to the Sobrals. The Jambras got their water from a cistern that collected rainwater and they did their bathroom business in an outhouse that you could sometimes smell from the Sobrals' back yard. The sisters were nice, but the brothers were scary and didn't speak English. Next door to what her daddy called 'the Jambras' genuine Acadian cottage' was a white house with a wide front porch. Little Miss Dugas lived there with her husband and no children; her large sister-in-law, Big Miss Dugas, lived with her family three doors further up the River Road. Elizabeth climbed the gray wooden steps, walked across the porch and knocked on the gray front door. Little Miss Dugas opened the front door almost immediately. Spotty sat down on the bottom step.

"Elizabeth? Is that right?" Elizabeth nodded. "You're the last one, aren't you?"

"Do you want to play?" The barefooted little girl looked shyly down at a pair of very small feet in pretty pink high heels.

"Play what?"

"I don't know," Elizabeth shrugged, her white blonde hair barely touching her raised shoulder. "What do you like to play?"

"Paper dolls?" Little Miss Dugas suggested, as she stepped back to open the door wider.

"OK."

Elizabeth walked into the fanciest living room she had ever seen. The windows had ruffled curtains that looked more like fog, or clouds, than cloth. There were bookshelves filled with tiny china animals. A beautiful tea set was all by itself on a small round table. There was a television set, just like the one at Miss Jean and Mr. Sam's house, facing a purple sofa with little tablecloths on the arms. She followed Little Miss Dugas into a sparkling clean kitchen with yellow wallpaper and a big round white table in the center of the room, surrounded by white chairs with yellow seat cushions.

"You sit at the table, Elizabeth and I'll get us some vanilla wafers and some milk."

To Elizabeth's great wonderment, Little Miss Dugas poured their milk into real teacups with saucers. The cookies were on little matching plates.

"Where are your paper dolls?"

"We'll make them," she said, raising her little finger as she took a sip of milk. "As soon as we finish our tea."

Little Miss Dugas carried in magazines with pictures of movie stars, and other magazines with pictures of clothes and stacked them on the table. She let Elizabeth pick out the biggest pictures of the prettiest ladies and then she carefully cut those pictures out of the magazines. She outlined them on cardboard, cut the cardboard, and then let Elizabeth help glue the magazine ladies to the cardboard ladies. It took three more afternoons to find paper clothes to fit all the dolls they had made.

Sometimes they played paper dolls, sometimes they played hide n' seek, and sometimes they played cards. Since Elizabeth had no idea of how to read numbers, Little Miss Dugas would play both of their card hands. Most of the time Elizabeth won. The child-sized adult let the little girl take home pairs of high-heeled shoes that she didn't want anymore. There were enough small hand-me-down shoes for Elizabeth, Kate and Rebecca to play ladies to their hearts' content.

Little Miss Dugas didn't always answer the door when Elizabeth knocked. She explained to the little girl that 'she had headaches during her monthlies and took to her bed.' Those were endless days for Elizabeth. She would play tea party under the house pretending that Kate and Rebecca were at the cardboard box table. She would even talk to them. She talked quietly so her mother wouldn't wake up and have a fit. She walked up and down the sidewalk, trailed by Spotty, almost all the way to town, hoping someone along the River Road might invite her in for cookies. One day a horse ran past her on the asphalt. The clop of its hooves had startled her, and then it was gone. She imagined telling Emily about it, and imagined her big sister asking Elizabeth to help her catch the horse. She hopped up and down the concrete front steps of her house, glancing down the River Road, waiting for the school bus to bring her sisters home.

The summer Emily was ten—a few days after John Monroe's yearly visit --she woke up in the middle of the night unable to move her legs. Her back hurt and she tried to call for her parents but her voice was stuck in her throat, a dry wad that wouldn't loosen. Emily started crying without making a sound. She remembered the time she broke the key and Kate got punished for it. She thought about poor Spotty getting run over, and about how sad it was that Emily had never had a horse of her own. Now it was all too late. Her back hurt so much, her ears were gurgling with tears and she couldn't make a sound.

"Emily, you pooped!" Rebecca threw back the covers and scrambled out of bed. She turned on the light. "Emily, you're crying and you pooped all over the bed. "What's wrong?"

Miss Jean came over to watch the three younger girls, even though she didn't know anything about children. Matthew carried Emily to the car in his arms and settled her into the back seat with a pillow under her head. He started the motor while Margaret was still getting into the car. They were driving to Our Lady of The Lake hospital in Baton Rouge. Matthew had called Dr. Laseigne and the doctor said that he would meet them there. It was the same hospital where Emily had been born.

Matthew drove as fast as he could. It was too early for the ferry to be running so they had to drive all the way to the Baton Rouge Bridge; thirty miles through a string of small towns, instead of taking the straight shot Airline Highway on the east bank. He ran all the red lights, speeding though the sleeping river towns.

"Faster, Matthew," Margaret was afraid to turn around, she dreading looking into the back seat and seeing her daughter dead. She began crying, trying her best not to sob out loud in case Emily might still be alive and would be frightened by hearing her mother cry. "Hurry, hurry. Jesus, hurry."

"It's going to be all right, Margaret." The expression on Matthew's face was terrible, not hopeful. "Our little girl will be just fine." The needle on the dashboard showed that he was driving seventy miles an hour along the curvy roads. Matthew had never driven so fast. The green and white Chevy was an arrow pointed at salvation.

"If it's not polio...." Margaret sobbed. "If it's not polio and if she's going to be all right, I'll go back to the church. I will, Matthew, I swear I will." Margaret twisted around and leaned toward the back seat, frantically placing her hand on her daughter's hot forehead. "I swear," she said, as though Emily's head were a bible.

It wasn't polio; it was an infected kidney. Emily stayed in the Baton Rouge hospital for three days. She had hoped she would stay longer and that she would at least need crutches. Within a week—to her great regret—things went back to normal. Except that her mother went to her first confession in years and began attending Sunday Mass. When school started, the nuns told Emily that she had been an Instrument of God and, possibly, even the recipient of a miracle.

Emily entered a very religious phase, pious in her specialness. She walked alone on the levee --as slowly as a bride--whispering prayers and imagining a shimmering glow encircling her head. Whenever she found a four-leaf-clover, or caught sight of the first star, she would press her hands against her heart and fervently wish that the Blessed Mother would appear to her like she had to Bernadette. Emily asked the parish priest to bless a mayonnaise jar of water so that she could have her very own Holy Water at home. Emily imagined digging her eyeballs out for Jesus, just like St. Lucy had.

"I think every night after supper our whole family should kneel down in the living room and say the rosary together. We could ---"

"For Christ's sake, Emily. Enough is a goddamned enough!" Her mother pushed her chair away for the table and reached for her Chesterfields. "Finish your meatloaf."

"*Mole face, Mole face.*" Elizabeth couldn't take it anymore. She was running away and never coming back. Her sisters, especially Kate, called her that all the time: *Mole face.* She had a small dark speck on her left cheekbone. Little Miss Dugas said her sisters were just jealous, jealous of Elizabeth's pale blue eyes and white blonde hair. Elizabeth knew her sisters weren't jealous. They were too pretty and smart to be jealous. And they didn't have moles.

"Movie stars paint moles on their faces exactly where you have one naturally," Little Miss Dugas said. "They call it a 'beauty mark.' Every time your sisters start singing their mean little chant think that they are saying 'beauty mark, beauty mark,' instead of 'mole face.' Think of it that way."

But Elizabeth couldn't. Other people told her nice things: 'Look at that beautiful hair, those eyes.' 'What a pretty little girl you are.' But no one in her house ever said anything nice to Elizabeth. Not one nice thing. Ever. She was running away and would never come back. Even if they begged her to, she wouldn't.

At Christmas Miss Jean and Mr. Sam had given her a bright pink suitcase for her doll clothes. Elizabeth carefully pulled out all the doll clothes, almost crying to think no one would ever dress her dolls again. It was like "Little Boy Blue." Her doll clothes would 'wonder the long years through….' She put her smallest doll, all of her under panties, and a roll of toilet paper into the suitcase. She was never coming back.

When Elizabeth was nowhere to be found at suppertime, Matthew went driving slowly down the River Road, looking to the left at the levee and over to the right at the sparse scattering of houses and pastures. Then he sighted the little pink suitcase. Elizabeth had apparently walked almost three miles, barefooted, before stopping to rest in an open field. Matthew parked the car, crossed the ditch, and walked into the field. He looked down at his sleeping daughter in her faded yellow sun suit and smiled, *what a beauty you are, and as headstrong as your mother*, he thought. Elizabeth's pale floss of hair was fanned out over an iridescent patch of green clover, her cheeks were flushed from the sun, and she was clutching the handle of her little pink suitcase. Matthew gently loosened her fingers, tucked the suitcase under his arm and carefully lifted his sleeping youngest daughter.

Rebecca, Kate and Elizabeth were the 'little girls,' and then there was Emily, who read all the time or wandered behind the levee in a life separate from her sisters. But the four Sobral girls finally came together as a unit in late 1956 when Elvis Presley hit the headlines. It was a covert union.

"How ridiculous." Their mother would point to pictures in the newspaper of girls going crazy over Elvis. "Mindless." She turned the radio to another station whenever one of his songs played.

"Just what people used to say about Frank Sinatra."

"Matthew, that's like comparing a good novel to a comic book."

One thing the four Sobral girls had always held in common was an awe of their mother as the arbitrator of taste. She told them that pink and red clashed and they pitied anyone ignorant enough to wear those colors together. She said it was bad manners to touch your hair in public, to snap chewing gum, to point with your forefinger, and to say 'who is this' when you answered the phone. 'People in the North were smarter than people in the South,' and 'children were to be seen and not heard.' Her daughters knew all those things to be unquestionably true.

Elvis was a conundrum. Emily loved him, and Rebecca thought she might love him too. Kate and Elizabeth listened to their older sisters talking and realized that Elvis Presley was both very important, and a secret. If their mother ever found out that any of them cared at all about Elvis, it would be like a slap in her face. Little Miss Dugas gave Elizabeth well-thumbed movie magazines filled with pictures of Elvis, which Elizabeth presented to Emily like a sacred offering. The four girls constantly leafed through the magazines and kept them hidden in the big cardboard box under the house. If their mother ever found the magazines, she would think her daughters were worse than girls who wore pink and red together, that they were as ignorant as southern people who pointed with their forefingers. The cardboard box under the house became the Sobral daughters' opium den.

Miss Jean and Mr. Sam gave the girls a record player for Christmas. As a joke, Miss Jean also gave them an Elvis Presley record. "Hound Dog" was on one side of the record and "Don't Be Cruel" was on the other. The girls could hardly believe they owned their very own Elvis record. In front of their parents, they pretended to much prefer the other two records the Letters had given them with their record player: Gene Autry singing "Rusty was a Rocking Horse" and Burl Ives singing "Polly Wolly Doodle." Though she would never tell her sisters, Kate really did prefer the rocking horse song because it told a story and had a happy ending. At first no one paid attention to Rusty because he was just a rocking horse, but then in the end he caught a bank robber and was a hero.

Emily and Rebecca made up an Elvis act. They would put "Hound Dog" on the record player and Emily would move her lips to the song, holding an invisible guitar, sticking her hips all over the place and twisting one foot up on its toes. Rebecca would sit in a chair and scream and almost faint every time Emily did the thing with her foot. At the end of the song Rebecca would fall out of her chair and Kate and Elizabeth would furiously clap their hands. To the great amazement of the girls, their parents thought the act was funny and even asked Emily and Rebecca to perform it for Miss Jean and Mr. Sam.

Under the house, their Elvis magazines spread carefully on the box top—cute little Floppy dozing at their feet--the girls speculated about Emily and Rebecca performing their act on the Ed Sullivan Show. They had never seen the Ed Sullivan Show, but there was a lot about it in the magazines and their parents watched it at the Letter's house. The two oldest Sobral girls would be on television and they would meet Elvis and be famous in BelleBend. When their mother saw how polite Elvis Presley was, she'd change her mind about him. The whole family would go to see Love Me Tender together, the six of them sitting in the front row of the Grand Theatre--because they actually knew Elvis in person.

Chapter 11

Packing Up—1980

"WHO CAN REMEMBER the names of all our dogs?" I ask.

It isn't quite daylight. Elizabeth, Kate and I are leaned against the kitchen counter sipping from lukewarm cans of Coke. The coffee pot was packed away with the pots and pans. Rebecca is sitting on her suitcase in the middle of the empty floor, her hands folded on her lap. It looks like she is waiting for a bus. It is unspoken that in this last hour or so we will avoid talking about our parents. I also certainly don't want to dwell on the small square of paper I found last night. I slipped it back under the lining of the green jewelry box, wishing I hadn't seen it. So, when no one speaks up, I say:

"Really. In order. Name our dogs."

"The first one I remember is Snowball," says Rebecca, without much enthusiasm. "The janitor at Daddy's school gave ---"

"Mr. Dill?" Kate interrupts.

"Yes, Kate, Mr. Dill. The janitor. That's what I said."

"The only dog that was ever really mine was Floppy," sighs Elizabeth. "My very own Cocker Spaniel that Little Miss Dugas gave me for my fifth birthday."

"And that Patches and Nig tore apart right in front of you," I say, referring to the neighborhood assassins. Nig, the older Great Dane, would pin down the victim while Patches viciously ripped the dog or kitten or pet bunny rabbit to pieces. "I felt so sorry for you, Elizabeth. No one should have seen that, especially a five-year-old."

"It was pouring rain and we all watched, screaming, from the front porch while those two monsters tore that bouncy little puppy to pieces," says Kate. "It was already too late when we saw them."

"In the sunshine with slingshots and stones, we couldn't have stopped them." I shudder, shaking my head against the memory.

"I always wanted to find out who in the neighborhood finally poisoned that dastardly duo," says Elizabeth. "I wish that I could have done something really nice for them. Like mow their lawn for a year. Or baked them a six layer cake."

"After Snowball, there was Brownie who got run over," Rebecca continues. "Then Groucho, who kept catching the ferry and crossing the river until Daddy got tired of going to pick him up and gave him to a family on the east bank."

"Wonder what the east bank had that we didn't?"

"I don't know, Elizabeth. Maybe people over there let their dogs into the house," I say. "We had plenty of dogs, but never a house dog."

"Except Twiggy," says Kate.

"Twiggy was different," I pause. "Anyway, all the rest were yard dogs, left on their own in rain, heat, cold, and hurricanes."

"They were under-the-house-dogs." Kate corrects me.

"Then there was Twinkle, followed by Spotty, both of them hit by cars on the River Road. After them, Hilda, who arrived here long enough to birth and wean a litter of ten pups before she moved on." Rebecca puts out her hand for my Coke. "We found homes for all of the puppies, but two. I don't remember their names. Maybe because Patches and Nig slaughtered them both before they were full grown." She takes a sip, grimaces, and hands the Coke back to me.

"Mutt and Jeff," I say, putting the can down and reaching for my cigarettes. "I think Mutt was a female."

"Jenny, who died of distemper three weeks after we got her," Rebecca is determined.

"Can you imagine having a dog for just three weeks in this day and age?" asks Kate. "We've had Kemah since before Emma was born."

"I almost forgot Koto. She was still little enough for Loretta to accidently fold up into the hideaway bed." Rebecca stands and stretches. "Squashed her dead."

"Pets were temporary, like loose baby teeth," I say.

"Only Twiggy lasted. She was half grown when I left for LSU, and…." Elizabeth doesn't finish.

We are all silent, remembering our father reeling around the front yard. *"My wife loved that little dog. My wife loved that little dog."* He said over and over to the kind stranger who had stopped his car to carry that scruffy little body from the side of the road and place it carefully onto the front lawn. *"My wife loved that little dog. My wife loved that little dog."* Rebecca and I were frozen in the driveway, still holding the bags of groceries we'd been unloading when cheerful little Twiggy ran out of the house to welcome us. In her excitement, she got too close to the River Road and a speeding Plymouth Barracuda.

We buried Twiggy in the back yard beside the others. Then we four stood together encircling, but not quite touching, our pale, shaken father. Not a one of us wanted to go into the house to tell our dying mother that her beloved dog had preceded her in death.

"Should we have called Mistretta's Gas and Electric?" Elizabeth breaks the silence. "To have the gas turned off?"

"I turned it off."

"The whole line, Kate, or the stove?"

"At the source, Elizabeth. Under the house." Kate tosses her Coke can into the open trash bag.

"How do you know that stuff?" Rebecca asks.

"It's not like I didn't spend most of my childhood playing under the house."

"We all did," I say. "I can't tell a gas line from a garden hose. You sure didn't get your mechanical aptitude from Daddy. I swear the man couldn't change a light bulb."

"Not that he didn't try," says Elizabeth." But then, after he twisted it in too crooked to get it out of the socket, he'd have to call Mr. Dill to come over. He thought Mr. Dill was a genius."

"Maybe the catastrophe of Daddy's repair attempts explains why every time a light bulb burned out Mama would have a minor nervous breakdown," Kate says. "It wasn't a darkened room, it was *the night at the end of the tunnel*." She covers her head with her arms, exaggerating our mother's complete panic over a burned out light bulb, a dripping faucet, or a stuck window.

"The end of the world," Rebecca intones like Orson Wells.

We can't help ourselves. We are talking about them again.

"The simplest mechanical things completely thrilled and mystified Daddy. Remember when we got the Oldsmobile and he just couldn't get over the automatic blinkers? No more sticking your arm out the window to indicate a turn." I imitate our father behind the steering wheel. "Daddy thought it was magic, the way you pushed the little shift up and the blinker went clicking to the right, pushed it down, and damned if it didn't go left!" My sisters are nodding their heads, laughing.

"'And the damnest thing, girls,'" Rebecca deepens her voice, imitating our father. "'The damnest thing is that the blinker shuts off after you make your turn. Now how ---'"

"'Now how does it know?'" Kate interrupts.

"Remember the time Mr. Dill came over to fix the porch screen Groucho had ripped out?" I ask. "Daddy made us all stand around and watch, like it was the moon landing, or something."

"But there wasn't a historical date in Western Civilization he didn't know." Rebecca pulls a cigarette from my pack. "Or a line of Shakespeare that Daddy couldn't place."

"He just never knew which way to turn a faucet to stop the water." Kate's voice is sorrowful.

A horn sounds in the driveway. The moving truck is here. This is it. The end.

BelleBend—1958-1968

The year after Elizabeth started school, the editor of the BelleBend Bugle died of a sudden heart attack. The very conservative publisher brought Margaret Sobral in as temporary editor, a position she held until her own death twenty-three years later. The publisher's policy was to avidly avoid controversy. So, though Margaret was at the helm during years of profound social change in BelleBend, there was never a mention of racial tension or U.S. foreign policy in the town's weekly newspaper. When the public school integrated it was a page three story, while the entire front page of that issue was devoted to the remodeling at the National Food Store. The dull articles about school board meetings, stray livestock, family reunions, house break-ins, and minor lawsuits were impeccably written.

Aside from an upward swing in grammar, punctuation, style, sentence structure and layout, there was little perceptible change at the BelleBend Bugle. The change for the Sobral household was profound. Margaret was often out late at night reporting on various civic meetings, but she no longer ever seemed tired. It was the end of dull silent summer afternoon hours when the swimming pool was closed. Their mother was 'at work.' The girls had friends over; they walked at will down the hall, slammed doors, and talked on the phone. A barking dog was just a barking dog, not machine gun fire, or an ice pick to Margaret Sobral's heart. During the school year their mother left the house when the girls did in the morning and returned home after them. She arrived home with stories to tell. Her tirades disappeared almost completely. The Sobral girls had a transformed mother. Their evening meals were also transformed: gumbos, oyster patties in rich dark sauce, rabbit stewed in wine, shrimp remoulade.

Babette Johnson was a legendary cook. She had occasionally come to the Sobrals to prepare a special meal when the Bunkie people or Margaret's brother from up North visited. Three days after Margaret became editor of the BelleBend Bugle, Babette became the Sobrals' cook.

"Mr. Matthew I don't want for you to pay me. St. Jude sent me here. You my Act of Mercy, with Miss Margaret off working. You just got to learn how to make groceries at The National." Babette lowered her considerable bulk into a kitchen chair. "Those people see you coming a mile away and convince you to collect up the soft potatoes, the pork getting stiff on the edges. I seen you in the store. And it worries me."

"I could go with him," Kate offered. From the front porch she had watched Babette's skinny little son-in-law pull into the driveway; she had followed Babette into the kitchen.

"Of course we'll pay you Babette."

"Then it be a job, Mr. Matthew, not no Act of Mercy. You just learn to make groceries. Let this one here help you." She pointed a thick calloused finger at Kate.

Matthew never did pay Babette. At the end of each week, he pulled a varying number of bills from his wallet when he dropped her off at her house. *For St. Jude* or *for playing Bingo,* he'd say. It left both Matthew and Babette with their pride. And Matthew eventually learned how to 'make groceries.'

White middle class southern married women did not have jobs. Margaret working at the newspaper could have been humiliating for Matthew. After an initial, and completely useless objection, Matthew got used to the idea and took great pride in his wife's career. He had fallen in love with Margaret because she was like no other woman he had ever met. When he proposed to her she was a newspaperwoman. Life was funny. Here she was, a newspaperwoman again. Sometimes he joined Margaret for her coffee break at the Letter's big stucco house, two blocks from the newspaper office. Margaret would regale Matthew and Jean with the paper's unpublished stories: callers trying to get their family feuds into the Bugle as news, the mayor's horrendous grammar and hysterical malapropisms, a fist fight at the police board meeting. Every day, at noon, Matthew dropped lunch off for Margaret and then went back to his office at the high school. Margaret ate alone at her desk, reading copy, running a soft red pencil through staff mistakes. The paper had part-time writers for the sports and society pages. Margaret wrote the carefully tempered editorials, occasionally slipping in an actual opinion. Her column was called "Belle Views."

"Emily and daddy fight all the time," Rebecca told her friend Patty. The two girls were sitting on the levee braiding clover flowers into a long rope.

"About what," asked Patty.

"Oh about lipstick and going out with her friends instead of staying home with us. She wanted to see Blue Denim with all of her heart and soul and Daddy wouldn't let her, and ---"

"But *we* saw Blue Denim!"

"Yeah, well I spent that night at your house and nobody ever told *me* not to see the movie." Rebecca pinched a clover flower stalk off at its root and handed it to Patty. "I mean Blue Denim was about all Emily talked about. She kept bringing it up and our parents kept saying she couldn't go. I just didn't mention it. Emily says she hates our daddy. When she talks to her friends she calls him, 'My Old Man.'"

"He is a little bit old," Patty said apologetically.

"Well she doesn't mean old like fifty years old, she means it like a beatnik or a rebel without a cause. Except Emily says she does have a cause and it's freedom. Her friends get to shave their legs and wear lipstick and ride in cars with the tenth-grade boys." Rebecca stood up holding the braid of flowers to show that it was taller than she was. "She should just wait to put the lipstick on until after she's out of the house."

"All the girls in eighth grade shave their legs."

"Mama says Emily doesn't need to because she doesn't have any hair on her legs. She also says Daddy doesn't understand teenagers because he never got to be one." She tied the braid into one big circle. "I think Mama was a teenager like Emily. That she had a lot of friends and she also didn't want to ever stay home with her parents."

"Emily is pretty popular." Patty took the circle of flowers and looped it twice around Rebecca's shoulders. "But you have friends, Rebecca. You have me and Sarah and Rosanna."

"Mama calls the four of us 'The Ghosts.'"

"Is she afraid of us?"

"Ha! The opposite. It's because we aren't noisy like Emily's gang. We don't do interesting things like swimming in the river naked and building big bonfires behind the levee. When Emily's friends are in the house, they fill it with laughing and joking, arguing, each of them louder than the next. That's why it seems the four of us pass though as quiet as ghosts. One time Emily's gang accidently caught the whole levee on fire. The fire department came, and everything." Rebecca un-looped the braid, doubled it, and wound it around Patty's neck like a Hawaiian necklace. "Emily is always in trouble for making bad grades, which drives my parents crazy. They yell at her and take away her allowance. But then they don't ever say anything about my straight A's."

"We should figure out some kind of commotion to create."

"I've thought of that. Sometimes I study my big sister and try to figure out how to be like her. But it's hopeless; we are night and day. "Rebecca lifted the braid of clover flowers, then pressed her back against Patty's and put the circle around both of their necks. "I love being with Emily and being with my family. When we're all together it…." Rebecca paused, thinking how to describe her feelings. "It just seems safe. I guess I don't understand how come Emily would rather be any place but home. She says our house is a prison."

When her mama or Miss Jean would ask Babette how to make something, Kate noticed that Babette never did tell them the whole recipe. She would always forget to mention one or two things. Miss Jean said nothing she tried turned out like Babette's dishes. Kate watched everything Babette did. She trailed behind her at the stove, across the kitchen to the table, and then back again to the stove. Babette didn't mind, she didn't think Kate was in her way. Babette hummed to herself and Kate watched how she pressed her palm against the top of the big knife when she cut onions in a blur of speed. Kate watched Babette take leftover boiled crawfish one-by-one and snap off their heads and scoop the insides out into a bowl. She put the empty heads to one side and then pinched the sweet meat from the crawfish tails. Kate would help her do that, pinch the tails. Babette took the bowl with all the goo from the heads and heated it up; she stirred in onions, peppers, garlic and then added flour, stirring and humming. Kate's daddy said 'The gods in heaven would come down to earth to eat Babette's crawfish bisque.' Kate would imagine all those men in short skirts and sandals sitting at the Sobrals' kitchen table.

Babette's favorite time of day was when Kate's mama got home, and before her daddy drove Babette home. It was Kate's favorite time too. The two ladies—one thin and pale and smoking one cigarette after another, the other bigger and more dark than the lady on the side of the syrup bottle—drank coffee and talked about what they'd read in the Times Picayune that day. They were both most interested in silver rights, so Kate was too.

One Sunday the Sobral family went to visit an old cousin of Matthew's who lived near New Orleans. Emily hadn't wanted to go, she kept arguing for staying home so she was the last one in the backseat and had to sit in the middle with her feet on the hump.

"Elizabeth, if you sit with your feet on the hump, it feels like the roller coaster at Pontchartrain Beach."

"No it doesn't. I always sit there." Elizabeth scrunched closer to Kate.

Two hours in the car! Emily tried to look out the window but her eyes couldn't keep up with the tall swamp trees lining the Airline Highway. She would focus on one, but then the next one caught her eye. It made her dizzy and her stomach lurched. She needed to gag and yawn at the same time.

"Look, look at all the turtles!" Kate loved trips. Even a trip to the National Food store still excited her. The watery swamp they could see on the left side of the car was filled with water lilies, turtles, and long-legged white birds, so much to see.

"Eight on one log, I counted them, "Rebecca said. "You saw them first, Kate, but then I counted them. And the next log had ten turtles!"

"I already counted them. Eight."

"You didn't see the one with ten. I did."

"Mama, Kate's squashing me."

"I'm not, Elizabeth, you're squashing me."

"I can't even move my arm."

"That's because ---"

"God damn it to hell, you stop fighting back there or I am jumping out of this goddamned car!"

"But look at Elizabeth, Mama. She really ---"

"I mean it!"

The trees went by in a blurry whiz, the back of Emily's throat watered and she clutched her stomach. If she asked her daddy to stop the car, her mother would have a fit. If she vomited all over the car, her mother would have a bigger fit. Emily closed her eyes so she wouldn't be forced to watch the trees weave by. She took deep breaths and thought about her friends all getting together at Susan Inness's house to listen to her new Bobby Darin and Paul Anka records. "Put Your Head on My Shoulder" was Emily's favorite song and she could have been listening to it the whole afternoon. And drinking Cokes. Susan's mother always let them have as many icy little bottles of Coke as they wanted.

The day at cousin Lee's house was even more boring than Emily had thought it would be. After Sunday dinner none of the adults moved from the table. They sat around talking about BelleBend in the olden days and family trees. It was boring, boring, boring. Emily's sisters had lingered around the table hanging on every word, like they were listening to Dragnet or The Lone Ranger instead of four adults saying just about the same thing over and over. Emily had walked outside on the flat straight street lined with brick houses, thinking that maybe she might see a boy, or some kind of teenager. Someone she could tell her friends about. But the street was empty under the press of late afternoon sun.

It was getting dark by the time the family packed back into the car. Emily was in first and got the window seat behind her mother. They were less than an hour back on the highway when there was a loud boom, the car jerked while her father clutched the steering wheel trying to keep control.

"Oh shit, Matthew! We're wrecking! Oh my god, the kids…."

Kate started crying.

"Calm down, Margaret." He guided the bumping car off the highway onto the medium ground. "It's just a flat. It's OK, honey."

"We'll never get home. Matthew, you can't change a tire. You can't even change a goddamned light bulb! We'll still be here, stuck here, all night, we'll ---"

"Margaret, people are good." He reached across the seat and tried to pat her shoulder. "I'll stand by the highway and someone will stop and help us. This is Louisiana." He opened the car door. "People help one another down here."

When her father had been standing on the side of the highway waving his hand for over ten minutes, Emily's mother sent her out to stand beside him. She got out of the car, tightened her ponytail, smoothed down her white skirt and walked along the roadside to join her father. The next car down the highway stopped immediately. An approaching car, brakes screeching, crashed into the stopping car. Emily and her father watched, horrified, as the two cars collided in a shatter of steel and breaking glass and slid off the highway. The first car stopped several feet from them. The second car pushed into the Sobrals' car, which spun in a half circle and then settled into a dead stop.

"No, no, no!" Emily grabbed her father's arm and they ran together toward the car holding their family. That short distance felt like the longest run of Emily's life, her legs had no bones; it was only her hand on her father's arm, his hand pressed over hers, that kept her going forward. Through the open back window they could see her sisters huddled together; Rebecca was in the middle with her arms around Elizabeth and Kate. Apparently, none of them had been hurt. Emily couldn't see her mother. She wasn't in the car. Her mother was missing! She was gone.

"Mama!" she shrieked.

Her sisters started calling out for their mother, their voices wailing above the sound of slowing and passing traffic, car horns blowing. "Mama! Mama!"

"Margaret, Margaret...." Her father opened the driver's side door and crawled over the front seat. He reached down and pulled up his wife from the floor of the car where she was huddled with her eyes squeezed shut.

"I thought, I thought…." Her voice was quivering. "I thought you and Emily had been…. I thought the car hit you!" She covered her mouth with both hands; her eyes were still closed.

The police came and an ambulance. Cars all up and down the Airline Highway stopped to watch the commotion. A wrecker arrived on the scene and the driver changed the flat tire. He told them that the Sobral car could still be driven. They could go home, and that the only problem was that the passenger side door wouldn't open. That could be repaired in BelleBend. One of the other two cars had to be towed. The ambulance made a big U-turn on the medium ground and headed back empty. No one had been seriously hurt.

In the middle of the night, long after they had gotten home and everyone was asleep, Emily woke herself up screaming, "Together! All of us together, together!" She shouted from a nightmare where she had lost her family.

The summer she was eleven, while her sisters were scattered around the town pool playing in the water with their friends, Kate sat on the side of the pool by the new high dive and watched a boy from her daddy's high school go off the diving board. Each time before he dove he would announce—to no one in particular— "Swan dive." "Jack knife." "Triple."

Swan dive. Jack knife. Triple. Kate watched the teenager spread his arms like an airplane and then slip, headfirst, into the water at the very last second. "Swan dive," she whispered. After the boy went away, Kate climbed the ladder and walked to the end of the diving board. When she jumped, she didn't lift high enough, she could tell.

So she stopped herself from going off and walked back to the beginning of the diving board; she got a running start and bounced on the end of the board as hard as she could. Kate rose into the air and spread out her arms; then she lowered her head and put her hands together like a prayer, arched her back, kept her ankles together and slipped into the water. When she opened her eyes among a million tiny bubbles, Kate thought, *Swan dive.*

She was an eleven-year-old girl flying alone over the chlorinated waters of the BelleBend town pool. Twelve years before Title Nine, mandating equal school sports activities for girls became law, Kate's spectacular dives went unnoticed.

One afternoon Elizabeth got home from school and her sisters weren't around. She could play ladies and no one would make fun of her. Kate said that fourth grade was too old to 'play ladies,' but Elizabeth knew she was wrong. It was a perfect time. Little Miss Dugas' high heels fit her exactly. It wasn't even like she was playing ladies. It was like she really was one!

Elizabeth went into the closet she shared with Kate and pulled out a purple sequined dress from a box of Little Miss Dugas' hand-me-downs. She put on the dress and a pair of white patent leather high heels and clattered into her parents' room to use her mother's lipstick and rouge. There was a long mirror in their bedroom where she could see herself. She would pretend that she was Eva Marie Saint in North By Northwest, a mysterious blonde alone with Cary Grant.

"You are safe from the spies with me. I love you," she declared to the mirror. "Come my darling. Kiss me, kiss me...." It didn't feel right to wrap her own arms around her own shoulders. Elizabeth embraced the bedpost. That felt better, it felt good. She began to whisper and sway. "You are the only one for me, I love you, I love you." She pulled closer to the post. "We can run away together. We ---"

"For Christ's sake, Elizabeth, what in the hell are you doing?"

Her daddy was standing in the doorway of the bedroom shaking his head. Then he turned around and walked out. Elizabeth was confused. She always played with her mother's lipstick. Her mama got mad about it, but not her daddy. Sometimes he said, 'You better wash your face before your mother gets home.' Why didn't he want her wearing lipstick now? Whatever the problem was, it ruined her nice time. Elizabeth felt stupid for playing ladies, ashamed. Kate was right.

The Sobrals had finally gotten a television; Matthew, Margaret, Emily and Rebecca sat on the folded up hide-away sofa, the two younger girls sat on the floor with Babette standing beside them. They were watching a late afternoon re-broadcast of that day's Presidential Inauguration. Matthew, who had already seen it live, saying, "I never thought I'd see this day. A Catholic in the white house!" Margaret trying to hush him, listening to every word the new president said.

"For man holds in his mortal hands the power to abolish all forms of human poverty and all forms of human life."

You hear that, girls? You understand what he is saying? The atom bomb, for—"

"Matthew!"

"If a free society cannot help the many who are poor, it cannot save the few who are rich."

"This is history, girls, right before your eyes. History. You'll tell your grand children about--"

"God damn it, Matthew. Shut up!"

"'Ask not what your country can do for you, ask what you can do....'"

The four girls were almost collectively holding their breaths. They believed their daddy. They knew they would always remember this: the old poet, the snow, the handsome new president. Watching all those people bundled up against the cold in Washington D.C. while John Kennedy put his hand on the Bible was like opening a window to a cool breeze on a stifling hot day.

Afterwards Margaret and Babette had coffee together at the kitchen table. "That Mamie look like a ole prune," Babette scrunched up her face, and made her wide mouth small and shriveled, her voice shrunken and squeaky like a cartoon. She was an excellent mimic and constantly amused Margaret with her renditions of various BelleBend characters, especially the school board wives. "Them little wienie curls, that chicken butt mouth."

"Shame on you, Babette." Margaret laughed.

"And there be Jackie like she walk off the cover of a fashion magazine," she said in her normal voice. "A field scarecrow and a china doll, them two." Babette heaped three teaspoons of sugar into her coffee. "Then our new president with his thick pretty hair standing by bald ole Mister 'I Like Ike.'"

"That's not fair, Babette," Margaret laughed, shaking her head at the same time. "Remember that bald man won the war, and

Mamie didn't have Jackie's advantages. 'It's not how you look, it's what you do.'"

"'Pretty is as pretty does. '" Babette countered.

"Kennedy surely gave a great speech, stirring." Margaret wanted to steer the conversation to more substance. "I don't think FDR could've topped it."

"Nothing's never gonna be the same. This a new day, Miss Margaret. A brand new day. For colored and white alike."

"This country needs a new day, Babette. If Kennedy governs half as well as he speaks, then you're right and there's hope for us all." Margaret stood to get the coffee pot and pour more coffee. The two women would raise their cups, like a toast between teetotalers.

Just about every important thing that happened to teenagers in BelleBend happened in the summer at the Wednesday Night Dance in the VFW Hall. For the past two years Rebecca had been in the car when her daddy went to pick Emily up at ten O'clock. There were always teenagers smoking on the front steps and on the hoods of cars to escape the heat of the dance hall. You could hear music way out on the street and through the open double door see dancers spinning around, the flared skirts of the girls whirling above their legs. Emily had told Rebecca that for the slow songs like "In The Still of The Night " or "Let It Be Me," the couples danced close together: the girl with her fingers entwined around the back of the boy's neck; the boy with his hands clasped low on the girl's back. Emily and Rebecca had practiced dancing that way until Rebecca was sure she could do it. Her sister had said that the couples going steady stared into one other's eyes and hardly moved their feet at all. When the song ended, they always stayed on the dance floor kissing until a fast song, like "Poison Ivy" or "Hit the Road Jack" started. Teenagers met and fell in love forever at the Wednesday Night Dance. Now Rebecca was finally old enough to go.

School had ended for the year on Friday and tonight was the first dance of the summer. Rebecca, Sarah, Rosanna and Patty had called each other about a hundred times in the last two days. They had helped one another pick out outfits, traded clothes and mixed and matched. The first one there would wait for the others by the front steps of the VFW Hall. Rebecca would have been very nervous if Emily hadn't already been going to the Wednesday Night Dances for two years, and if her big sister wasn't about the most popular girl in tenth grade. Emily would look out for Rebecca and her friends.

Rebecca had brushed her teeth for a long time and was standing in front of the bathroom mirror, practicing her smile, when Emily walked in.

"You know that I'm spending the night at Virginia's after the dance, right?" Emily asked. Rebecca nodded into the mirror, keeping the same smile. "Well, my gang is going out to The Club tonight. Virginia's parents don't care. Jimmy Clanton is playing."

"Wait a minute! You said you were going to the Wednesday Night Dance." Rebecca turned from the mirror. "I thought the best thing about summer was the--

"Usually that's true, Rebecca. But this is different. Special. And it just happens to be on a Wednesday. You know Mama and Daddy won't let me go to The Club until I'm maybe forty years old. But it's *Jimmy Clanton.* 'Just A Dream' has been my favorite song since the first time I ever heard it." Emily stepped around her sister to stare at herself in the mirror. She licked her forefinger and pushed at the arch in her left eyebrow. "Everybody's going. This could be the most important night of my life. *Jimmy Clanton*."

Emily put her arm around her sister's shoulder and pulled her close, so that the two sisters were staring together into the mirror: Rebecca with her dark shiny Buster Brown and Emily with her pale shoulder length pageboy. Looking at her sister's face, Rebecca could see how serious the situation was.

"Suppose Mama and Daddy find out?"

"But they won't, if you tell them you saw me at the dance. You're a great story teller, you're always making up stories for Kate and Elizabeth." Emily stood behind Rebecca and ran her fingers up the back of her sister's head, fluffing out her silky hair. "Just make up some story, maybe about Virginia and me dancing with boys from across the river. Or something that sounds like we were there."

Rebecca and her friends stood in a small clump in the hot, smoky room. Even though it was packed with teenagers, you could just feel Emily's gang missing: about eight tenth grade girls and most of the twelfth-grade boys. Everybody knew them and not having the senior boys there made it seem like a dance for kids. Rebecca had always imagined The Wednesday Night Dance to be like the song "Behind the Green Door." It didn't seem as if anyone was having the 'hot jazz' kind of fun Rebecca had expected. A ninth-grade boy asked Patty to dance to "There's A Moon Out Tonight." After that one song he walked her back to her friends and never returned. The four girls stood together pretending they were having a wonderful time and weren't interested in anything else but just talking to one another. They went out to wait for Patty's daddy long before the ten O'clock pick up time.

"Ya'll all want Slow Gin Fizzes?" Joseph Sedonea asked Emily and her friends. "The waiter will bring them to our table." The Club was a real nightclub with a bar in front room and a dance floor and tables surrounding the stage where the band was already playing in back. Emily didn't like Slow Gin Fizzes but kept hoping she'd develop a taste for the sticky pink drink. She and her friends always got them at the First and Last Chance on Friday nights. You parked in the back of "The Chance" and honked your car horn and a colored man in a white apron came and took your order. The Club was different, the colored waiters wore jackets and there were lots of people Emily didn't know, some of them seemed to be the same ages as her parents. In fact, as Andrew Capone pulled out a chair for her to sit down, Emily could have sworn she'd seen a man who worked at Mr. Sam's bank.

"*..., all our plans and all our schemes, how could I think you'd be mine---*" Andrew sang into her ear as they danced. Emily hadn't come all the way out to The Club and lied to her parents so she could hear Andrew's voice blocking out Jimmy Clanton's. He was getting her hair wet and making her ear hot and damp. She tried to pull her head back and look over toward the stage, but Andrew turned her around on the dance floor and kept singing in her ear. "*Just a dream I dream in vain, with you I'd only live in pain.*" Emily imagined stomping on Andrew's foot with her high heel. She imagined Jimmy Clanton jumping off the stage and taking her in his arms. She thought how amazed her friends would be, and how Jimmy's band would try to keep the beat while their lead singer danced with a mysterious girl they didn't know. "*Just a dream, just a dream....*" Now Emily just wanted the song to end so she wouldn't have to keep dancing with Andrew, and before he completely ruined her hairdo.

Virginia's parents hadn't minded that the girls got in after midnight. In fact, they hadn't even left the front porch light on. Now Virginia was sound asleep and Emily was lying on her back staring at the ceiling. She had raised her grades to keep her parents happy and had fought hard for a midnight curfew, which they'd given her because she was 'trustworthy.' Suppose the man from the bank told Mr. Sam that he'd seen Emily at the club? What if The Club had burned down, like the Coconut Grove fire she had read about in Reader's Digest? Her parents would have gotten up in the morning without knowing their oldest daughter had burned to ashes. When she wasn't home by supper they would call Virginia's house and the phone would keep ringing. Her poor parents. Emily could hardly catch her breath worrying about them, about how innocent they were. She didn't deserve their trust. Shame sat on her chest like a refrigerator.

Emily was still awake at sunrise. She was restless and bored and anxious waiting for Virginia to get up. She couldn't concentrate at breakfast and she couldn't concentrate after breakfast listening to Virginia talk about how much she loved Buddy Davis and how he didn't know Virginia existed. "I saw him watching you last night," Emily assured her friend. "He's just shy." All she could really think about was how she had failed her parents. There was no way around it. She would have to confess, she needed to tell them—and surely tell them before they heard it from someone else—that she had not gone to the Wednesday Night Dance. She'd been at The Club with Andrew Capone slobbering in her ear. She would walk to the newspaper office and tell her mother.

While her daddy's secretary was on vacation, Rebecca had a job answering the phone at the high school office for twenty-five cents an hour, a dollar and fifty cents a day. Late on Thursday morning she answered the phone and it was her mother calling her daddy. Rebecca went back to re-reading Jane Eyre, her very favorite book. When she looked up her daddy was standing in the doorway of the reception room.

"Rebecca, what did you say about your sister at the dance last night?"

"What do you mean?" She felt suddenly chilly as though she and her daddy were walking together into the icehouse to retrieve a watermelon.

"What did you tell your mother and me about the dance when you got in last night?"

"That it was fun?" Rebecca closed her book without saving her place and held it against her chest.

"About Emily. About the tall boy from across the river wearing the blue shirt with red palm trees on it and white slacks with big cuffs who kept asking your sister to dance."

"Un-huh, but she.... But she wouldn't dance with him? That boy?"

"Emily just told your mother that she didn't go to the dance. "He folded his arms and leaned against the doorframe. "That she went to The Club instead."

"Well, that must have been after I saw her." *Emily told Mama and didn't tell me she was going to tell?* Rebecca couldn't believe it. "Maybe the boy with the palm tree shirt drove her over to The Club?" Rebecca offered. "Maybe that happened after we left?"

"Nope. She wasn't at the dance at all."

They were both punished for the duration of the summer. No Wednesday night dances, in fact no activities with their friends after five in the afternoon until school started. Forever more Emily and Rebecca referred to the summer of 1961 as 'The Summer of Our Discontent.'

"Daddy, it's not fair it's really not fair. The only thing Rebecca did wrong was what I asked her to do. *She* didn't go to The Club, I did! She was just doing what I asked, like a good sister. Why are you punishing her?" Emily clenched her fists so tightly and dug her fingernails into her palms so deeply that she guessed she was probably bleeding, maybe like the Stigmata. "*Please* don't punish Rebecca too!"

"The only thing worse than a cheat is a liar." Matthew was adamant.

"*'Duzzzzz your chewing gun lose it's flavor on the bedpost over night. If your ma tells you...*'" Margaret sang at the top of her voice, flipping the Saturday morning French toast at the same time. Lately she had replaced her occasional breakfast poetry recitation with foolish songs from the Top Ten Countdown. Matthew got a kick out of her singing at the top of her voice. It both delighted and frustrated her daughters.

Their uncle from up north had sent the girls a small pink transistor radio and they kept it playing most of the time they were in the house. They tried to get their mother to pay attention to important songs like "Running Bear," "Save The Last Dance for Me," and "Tell Laura I love Her." But she latched onto the foolish ones like "Purple People Eater," "You Talk Too Much," and the chewing gum song. She thought they were hilarious. The wonderful thing about their mother singing the silly songs was that it meant she was in a good mood and her good moods were contagious. Yet, they realized that something as simple as a spilled glass of milk could still send her into a rage of despair. Trying to balance the checkbook or someone tiptoeing to the bathroom in the middle of the night would sometimes make their mother cry out as though hot oil had been poured over her. If any of her daughters went to the bathroom after their mother was asleep, it surely had to be an emergency.

"'*Can you catch it on your tonsils and heave it left and right, does your chewing gum...*'"

It would be a good morning. The girls were all smiling, and keeping an eye on their milk glasses.

Her two powder blue Samsonite suitcases—a graduation gift from her parents-- were all ready to be put in the trunk of the car. It was barely daylight on Emily's last morning on the River Road. Virginia had given her an all-girl going away party the night before. Two days earlier Emily had gotten a frantic feeling about having to see *everyone* before she left and drove with her sisters all over BelleBend, waving out the car window at everyone she knew. Only three girls from her graduating class of twenty-four were going to college and Emily was the only one leaving Louisiana. It was as if she were going off forever; on their last night together she and her friends had rehashed memories like aging veterans of the foreign wars:

"Emily, remember the night at the drive-in movies when Ben Hur was playing and your had your first date with ---"

"And *last* date with date with Anthony Gimbroni," Emily interrupted her friend Susan.

"And, first kiss of all, he French kissed you and you jumped out of the Joseph's backseat and ran crying into the girl's bathroom," said Susan, rattling the ice in her bourbon and Coke.

"We all followed you," Virginia added. "We thought he had tried to 'feel you up.'"

"Not all of ya'll. Nancy Reynard pulled Anthony out of the backseat and was going to beat him up for violating me. Poor Anthony started crying."

"Well, we all thought he'd done something terrible to you." Karen picked up Susan's lighter.

"Ugh, that *was* terrible. The only reason I went to the drive-in with him in the first place was that I felt sorry for him. And then he had to go stick his tongue in my mouth!"

Virginia's rec room was dense with cigarette smoke. Everyone, but Betty LeBlanc, smoked. Virginia's mother had set the girls up with a fifth of bourbon, some Jax beers, a cooler full of Cokes and 7-ups and a big bucket of ice.

"Remember when KEX played "Sea Of Love" ten times straight and Joey Folse said he would lie down in the middle of Railroad Avenue if the disk jockey played it five more times?"

"And on the fifteenth time, he did!" Rose Marie laughed and tapped her cigarette ash into the overflowing ashtray.

"We were all standing in the middle of the avenue to block traffic and Joey was lying there in the street looking up at the sky and singing, *'Come with me, my love to the sea, the sea of love…'* Beth started the song and all of the girls joined in.

"I want to tell you how much I love you…."

"Emily, tell about the time you and Karen and me took off all our clothes to swim in that clear pond in the woods back of the cane fields."

"The place we called 'Paradise,'" Karen said wistfully. "Bulldozers ran over it last winter to make more room for growing cane. That place was so beautiful, cypress trees, honeysuckle vines, and that clean little pond. Way back, when they cleared the land, they kept those patches of forest and ponds for watering the mules. Now--"

"We were what, Virginia," interrupted Emily. "In ninth grade? Having so much fun swimming on a hot day in that cool water and we didn't hear or see the Boy Scout troop until we heard them running away."

"Those little shitheads had thrown all our clothes up in the trees around the pond," said Virginia.

"Every time I see a Boy Scout, I feel like sticking up my middle finger."

"Karen!"

"You try going home and explaining to your Mama why you don't have underpants."

They had talked and reminisced until the bourbon bottle was empty. Now Emily was sitting at the kitchen table with her sisters in her last hours on the River Road and had nothing to say. The four of them had spent the entire previous day together until she left for Virginia's house. They had all gotten up before the sun this morning. Emily expected to be excited and full of plans. But her only feeling was that she had made a big mistake. She looked at her three pretty little sisters wishing she could press pictures of them into her brain. They sat at the kitchen table, each in her own place, staring at Emily, waiting for a cue from her. Two pairs of solemn brown eyes, Rebecca and Kate; and light-eyed Elizabeth with her hopeful Petula Clark hairdo. When they were younger, Emily had ignored her little sisters. But they always paid attention to her and stood up for her. She needed to make up for being a bad big sister, but now there wasn't time.

"I wish we were the Lennon Sisters and instead of anyone going to college or school we could just sing on the Lawrence Welk Show," said Elizabeth mournfully.

"We'd stay in hotels and ring for room service," Rebecca picked up an imaginary phone. "'I'd like sirloin steak, a hot fudge sundae, and a root beer float.'"

"I want us just to stay here." Kate started crying.

"Together," Emily's voice broke, surprising her.

After her father left for Mass each morning, Kate got up, plugged in the iron, put a towel on her dresser and ironed her hair. She wanted it straight like Jackie Kennedy and Joan Baez. By the end of the day her curls usually broke through, especially on these humid September days. Thinking she might have a better chance at making friends where her father wasn't the principal, she asked to change schools at the end of eighth grade. She had already been at Catholic High for almost two weeks. Now she was sitting on the curb, waiting for her father to pick her up and pretending to be studying her history book so it wouldn't look like she was sitting alone with no one to talk to. She heard a motorcycle leaving the school parking lot. It was zooming in her direction; she pulled the book closer to her face.

The motorcycle stopped right next to her and the olive-skinned driver -- with a mass of dark hair as curly as Kate's -- put one booted foot on the curb and the other in the street. Kate had to look up. He said something she couldn't hear, so she shrugged. He turned off the motor.

"I said you're too pretty to be sitting all by yourself."

Kate wanted to throw down her books and run. Why would someone she had never even seen before want to be making fun of her? She shrugged again and looked down at her book. If she ran away, he could make more fun of her.

"We had that book when I was a freshman, I think in Colorado. But maybe it was Connecticut. I tend to confuse the C states."

"You don't remember where you lived?" That was the craziest thing she had ever heard. Maybe he was retarded.

"Not when I go to four or five different schools a year. My name is Roger, by the way. Fortunately I've gotten real good at introducing myself."

She knew who he was. She also knew that the girls called him 'The Leader,' like in the song, "The Leader of The Pack" about a boy from the wrong side of town who meets a girl at a candy store. Nobody new ever came to BelleBend. Much less a handsome boy who had lived around the world and had his own motorcycle. All the girls had crushes on him. Kate knew this because she heard them talking in the bathroom where she ate her lunch every day, too humiliated by her aloneness to sit in the school cafeteria. Kate would lock a bathroom stall and sit up on the toilet tank to eat her bag lunch, her feet on the lid so no one realized she was there. She knew a whole lot of what was going on at the Catholic School.

"Why so many schools? Are you a juvenile delinquent?'

"Never had time to work into it," he laughed. "You have a name?"

When Matthew drove up to the Catholic School, Kate was nowhere to be seen. He hoped she had gone off with some new girl friends; that the school change was finally working out. Instead Kate was speeding down the bayou road on the back of a motorcycle, her books tucked into the motorcycle's saddle bag, her arms squeezed tight around Roger Francisco's chest, her cheek leaned against his shoulder.

Roger became a fixture at the Sobrals. He went crazy over Babette's food and would go on and on about it being better than anything he'd eaten in all of France. Babette mainly loved him because he wasn't from the South. Rebecca and Elizabeth loved him because he taught them how to play poker. Roger, Kate and her sisters played poker for hours, using pecans as poker chips. Her sisters also loved him because now they didn't have to worry about Kate being by herself whenever they weren't with her. It freed them up to feel better about having fun with their own friends. Margaret and Matthew thought their daughter's boyfriend—the son of a surveyor for Gulf Oil-- was worldly, good-natured, and very temporary. They worried.

"It's too far down. You won't be able to hear it hit the water," Roger said, dropping a quarter over the railing.

"Next time let's bring something big and heavy. Like a can of red beans."

"Bet we still couldn't hear it." He put his arm around her and pulled her closer.

Roger and Kate were sitting on the edge of an unfinished bridge arched over the Mississippi. It had been erected four miles out of BelleBend as a political favor by Governor Jimmy Davis, and then abandoned when the funding ran dry. There were enormous barriers built on either end of what was known around Louisiana as *the bridge to nowhere.* Roger drove his motorcycle along the rutted dirt work road and was able to ease it between the barriers. He and Kate had picnics in the middle of the abandoned bridge. They had their first kiss there and on weekend evenings watched the sun set from there. Sometimes Kate brought the pink transistor radio out and they would dance on the bridge; it was just the two of them on the steel arch rising over the water with a view of miles of ripe sugar cane fields. Seen from so high, the fields might have been a rain forest. "That's really what the jungles of Brazil looked like from an airplane," Roger told her. "As far as the eye could see, green, green, green."

From the bridge they could also see Pointe Jardin nestled in a wide curve of the river and, when the light was just right, the pond glimmering like a solitaire diamond. "That's the only place Mama will swim." Kate pointed to the lit water. "She's the most beautiful swimmer I ever saw."

Roger taught her how to jitterbug and they spun around to the fast songs; they held one another and kissed to the slow ones, two curly-headed teenagers, suspended on a dance floor high above the Mississippi. Roger told her about his tumbleweed life, the places he'd lived and the people he most remembered from those places.

Kate regaled him with stories of BelleBend characters she had heard from her mother, and exaggerations of Sobral sister misadventures.

On school mornings he picked her up on his motorcycle and he drove her home in the afternoon; they sat together in the cafeteria for lunch. 'The Leader' and Kate Sobral were the shining couple of Catholic High School. But they didn't even notice.

Then, two weeks before Thanksgiving, Roger moved away. After he left, Kate couldn't eat or sleep. The only thing that interested her was the mail. Matthew stopped faithfully at the post office twice every day. Several times a week there would be a letter for Kate from San Diego. She didn't want to go to school, she stopped listening to the radio; every song reminded her of Roger, made her remember where they had heard it. Her school uniform began to hang loosely on her; Kate had dark circles under her eyes. And then something far more terrible than losing Roger happened.

"The President's been shot!" Emily was just leaving her dorm room when someone shouted. "The President's been shot!" *A Lincoln joke*? she thought. But the President really had been shot. He could die. It might have been the Russians. The girls from the dorm crowded into the snack room to watch the television for news. Three months later the snack room would be even more crowded as the girls packed in, pushing for a glimpse of the Beatles on the Ed Sullivan Show. But that early November afternoon many of Emily's college classmates were there stunned and quiet, staring at the T.V screen. The college's loudspeakers announced that classes were being held as usual. 'The President would want American students attending classes,' the announcement said. Emily walked to her chemistry class as though she were being led by her feet, that the real her had stayed behind in the snack room to keep watch on Kennedy, to keep him alive. She didn't believe the wounded president would want her listening to a lecture and taking notes about acid-based reactions. He would want her and the whole world to stop everything and pray for him. But Emily went to chemistry class and, by the time class was over, John Kennedy was dead. It was all over: toddlers playing hide-and-seek under the desk of the President of The United States, the glamorous receptions, the Civil Rights bill, all the promise of change and all the security of being an American. All of it was given over to the pomp and circumstances of a rider-less horse and a veiled widow flanked by the president's grieving brothers. The end.

Emily, like her father, had always looked on the 'bright side,' but despair settled over her that cold November day like a cowl she couldn't raise her head above. Since she had never felt despair before, she didn't recognize it. School was really over for her, though she kept attending. What else was she supposed to do? She stopped paying attention to much of anything. Nobody knew she was broken, not even Emily.

"What did Caroline and John-John get for Thanksgiving? "asked Tony Marcello. "A Jack-in-a-box! How do you tell a ---" Before Tony Marcello could finish his next joke the principal had him by the scuff of his neck. Matthew pushed the boy ahead of him down the hall and physically threw him out of the front door of BelleBend High School. The principal was much smaller than the hulking junior, but his anger made him mighty

"Matthew you can't expel someone for telling a horrible joke." Margaret had just gotten into the Oldsmobile on the Monday after Thanksgiving. "Haven't you heard of the First Amendment?" The car was parked in front of the newspaper office.

"I don't give a damn about the First Amendment. That little son-of-a-bitch can find another school!" Matthew turned the key and started the motor.

"'Gawd willing and the creek don't rise.' I swear that's what she said. Our First Lady!" Jean smashed her Camel out in the ashtray. "I mean the two of them ought to move into a log cabin and give the White House back to Jackie."

"Different styles for sure." Margaret pinched a flick of tobacco from her tongue with her thumb and ring finger. "Kennedy had to cover his bases by bringing Johnson onto his ticket. He couldn't have been elected without him."

"So that justifies leaving us with those hillbillies?"

"That hillbilly got the Civil Rights Bill passed. It's doubtful that Kennedy could have."

Rebecca was reading over her journal at the dining room table, half listening to her mother and Miss Jean. She'd started writing a journal when Emily left for Ohio; it was something to do with her sleepless hours. So many thoughts and so many things to say to no one she could imagine listening. This was her third notebook in the six months since Emily left. It took Rebecca forever to get to sleep in the empty hide-away bed. She was embarrassed by her insomnia and kept it to herself.

"LBJ will find out that the repercussions are going to be worse than any cattle stampede he ever saw back in Texas."

"What do you mean?"

"Margaret, you're just naive if you think some little ole amendment is going to change a way of life. Let them try to start mixing the races. There will be blood in the streets."

"'Blood in the streets?' Now you're sounding like a backwoods preacher, Jean. You were talking about poor Lady Bird. Listen to you. And as far as ---"

"Jean! How about a martini?" Matthew slammed the front door behind himself. "There're glasses chilling in the freezer and just time to indulge before I drive Babette home."

"I'll do it, Daddy. Ya'll go on and relax, I'll bring the martinis out on a tray."

"That's my girl, Rebecca." Matthew walked over to the doorway and gave Rebecca a kiss on the top of her head. "See that Margaret, your fifteen-year-old ---"

"Sixteen, Daddy. I'm sixteen."

"Your sixteen-year-old daughter can make a martini and you can't."

"That is my deepest ambition for our daughters, Matthew. May they all become barmaids."

Rebecca was already walking back to the kitchen. It made her nervous when her mother and Miss Jean talked about integration. She was glad her father had come home. Kate was at the kitchen table eating a bowl of gumbo and Babette was at the stove stirring something in her beloved black iron pot. Babette had been trying to fatten Kate up. Rebecca's sister looked like a scarecrow.

"Kate, do you remember what Daddy told us about making a martini? I know it's two jiggers of one thing and a few drops of the other."

"Just dribble a tiny drip of vermouth on the side of the…. I'll do it." Kate stood.

"No mam!" Babette turned from the stove. "You keep your boney behind down on the chair until you finish that gumbo. You think I got nothing better to do then fix special food for you?"

"Where's Elizabeth?" Rebecca asked.

"At cheerleader practice." Kate rolled her eyes and plucked out a shrimp to eat with her fingers. "She's been trying to do a cartwheel for a month. Now they've worked out a routine where she stands in the middle with her arms extended overhead while the other cheerleaders do cartwheels all around her."

"What's the point?"

"Well I guess they want her to be a cheerleader bad enough that ---"

"Maybe she represent the goal post," Babette suggested.

Kate and Rebecca laughed.

"Now I'll be making them martinis so Mr. Matthew get me home on time. I got the Bingo tonight."

When Emily went to sign in for her first final exam, the proctor pulled her aside and explained she was ineligible. Her tuition had not been paid. Emily's eyelids felt gritty and she was groggy; her concerned friends had kept her up most of the night helping her memorize portions of the periodic table, explaining element interaction.

"So. . . . So what do I do," Emily asked. "Go back to the dorm and pack my suitcase?"

"Maybe it just slipped your father's mind." The young instructor was trying to be helpful. "You could always phone him and have him call the bursar's office, say the tuition is on the way and then your father could wire the money. That might work."

Rebecca was just pulling out her calculus binder when the classroom PA system announced that 'Rebecca Sobral was to report to the principal's office.'

It was close to the end of the month and Matthew had less than fifteen dollars in the household checking account. He and Rebecca drove together to the First National Bank and she withdrew five hundred dollars, almost all of her savings in an account she had proudly opened, with Mr. Sam's help, when she was eight years old. Seven years of saved allowances and babysitting money to pay for her older sister's second semester of college.

As it turned out, it was a complete waste of money. Emily could have gone ahead and not taken those exams, and done almost as well. In addition to losing her scholarship, she completely failed her only year of college; a year she had mostly wandered through in a fog. Depression had not yet entered the American consciousness, no help was on the way. Emily got a summer job at a lake resort hotel near the college. It paid almost nothing but offered room and board. She could postpone arriving home in disgrace.

Roger was coming to visit. He would sleep on the living room sofa, just as John Monroe had back in the summers he stayed with the Sobrals. Roger's family had recently moved to Houston; he was taking a bus to visit Kate. Once she had been sleepless at the loss of him, now she could hardly sleep for her happy anticipation. She went with her father to Baton Rouge to pick Roger up at the Greyhound station. He was the first person through the bus door. He looked heavier and his hair was cut close to his scalp, his curls were gone. He ran down the steps and lifted Kate in his arms, turning around and around, hugging her.

"Prettier than I remember. Oh little girl I missed you!"

Kate felt like she was someone in a romance movie and she also felt embarrassed that Roger didn't notice her father standing and watching him turn her around and around. She wanted to ask why he had cut his hair. She didn't know what else to say. It turned out that was all right because Roger had so much to say. He talked all the way to BelleBend, sitting in the front seat talking to her father about the oil business and gas millage and the rise in gas prices. Then he would turn towards the backseat to tell Kate about surfing, sleeping on the beach back in California, and his new car. His parents had actually put down roots; they were staying in Houston. Roger's last year of high school and he could finally try out for a football team.

When they got to the house on the River Road, Babette had made stuffed crabs, his favorite. Everyone was happy to see Roger. Kate had been so sad for so long and now Roger was here. After the dinner dishes were cleared, Elizabeth brought out a bowl of pecans and a deck of cards.

"All right, Mr. Nathan Detroit," said Elizabeth. "Luck is with the ladies!"

"'The oldest established permanent floating poker game in BelleBend,'" sang Rebecca, paraphrasing. Miss Jean and Mr. Sam had taken the girls to Baton Rouge that spring to see a touring company of Guys and Dolls, a show about gamblers and their girlfriends. Kate had bought a copy of the record, from the movie, with her own money.

"Count out the nuts," said Roger who had not seen the musical, or heard the songs but did remember pecans substituting for poker chips. "Deal the cards!" In between hands he told Kate's sisters about California, his favorite Beach Boy songs, and his new car.

"A motorcycle is a lot cooler than a car," Elizabeth commented.

"Than a Mustang? Are you kidding?"

Kate said nothing.

After the card game Kate and Roger went for a walk on the levee. A rare August breeze rustled the clover, bent the pond trees, and opened the sky to a spray of stars. They held hands and walked slowly along the crest of the levee. Kate had a difficult time concentrating on all Roger had to say. He was talking so much and nothing he said was very interesting to her.

"Kate, if I make the team, do you think your parents will let you come to the Homecoming game? My parents would write to them. I'd pay for your ticket."

When Kate didn't answer, Roger pulled her hand and turned her so that they could kiss. He tilted her face and kissed her forehead and then her lips. Kate had waited so long for this and all she could feel was his front teeth pressing her lips against her own teeth. One of them had forgotten how to kiss. Kate felt like she was pretending to be a girl kissing a boy, that she was an actress caught in the wrong play. Roger stepped back.

"Well, will you, Kate. Will you come to Houston?'

"Roger, I don't know. I just have a bad feeling about Texas."

"Bad feeling. What does that mean?"

"You know, after Dallas."

"Dallas?"

They continued kissing and holding one another. It seemed essential to Roger's visit.

"My parents won't really go to sleep until we're back inside." Kate said, turning toward the darkened house. "We don't want to worry them."

Roger took her hand; they hurried down the levee, across the River Road and into the house. Even though Kate was terrified that they'd wake her mother, she sat with Roger on the bedding arranged over the front room sofa and they kissed some more. He leaned her back and she let him touch her breasts. It wasn't wonderful or passionate. It made her feel like a milk cow, as though Roger was trying to urge forth something that her small breasts could not yield.

"I have to go to bed, Roger," she whispered. "My mother is the lightest sleeper in the world."

Later, Kate sat alone on the back steps of the porch smoking Rebecca's Kents. She heard the boards on the porch creak and braced herself to face Roger again. But it was her mother. Margaret Sobral, wide-awake at three in the morning, and tiptoeing; it was stranger than anything Kate could have imagined. Her mother acted like it was OK for Kate to be smoking, even though Rebecca had only just gotten permission.

"It isn't what you thought it would be, is it Kate?" Her mother sat on the step above her and leaned down, lifting Kate's cigarette, taking a puff and handing it back.

"He's completely different."

"Maybe you're the one who has changed."

"I just want him to go home. These are going to be the longest three days of my life."

"They will pass," her mother reached again for Kate's cigarette. "You don't think they will, but they will."

"He came all this way, Mama," she was almost crying. "He bought his ticket with his ---"

"Whatever you do, Kate. Don't feel sorry for him. Be kind, of course. But hold onto yourself. Don't let feeling sorry for him make you someone you're not. Or worse, make you tie your life up with Roger's. You are two different people, and you pretending otherwise, would eventually make you both miserable."

Kate could hardly believe that her mother was out sitting by her in the night and talking to her. Just talking to her. Just Kate. She tried to think of what to say next, what she could say that would make her mother stay. Her mother was already standing up.

"And you're too damned young to be smoking," she said, flicking Kate's cigarette over the railing. She walked back across the porch and into the kitchen, without tiptoeing.

That summer Elizabeth and the rest of the squad had gone to Cheerleader Camp. In BelleBend they were practically movie stars, but among the other groups from all over south Louisiana, they didn't even measure up to pep squad members. The best of them, Patty Munk, could do three or four cartwheels in a row. And that was only sometimes. The BHS cheerleaders looked like water boys next to the high-energy squads from other places. There were girls at that camp who could go from a dead stop to a double somersault, four cheerleaders at a time, passing one another without colliding in mid-air.

"They should have joined the damned circus," Theresa Mistretta had said, watching the whirling dervish of pony-tailed blondes.

"If one of them misses and lands on her head, she'll be paralyzed for life." Peggy Jofferon said hopefully.

"We just need to work harder," Elizabeth had said, trying to keep up everyone's spirits. Elizabeth had been a cheerleader for over two years, working very hard, and still could not execute even one crisp cartwheel. None of the BHS cheerleaders knew a thing about football.

When football season started again and they watched the cheerleaders from the other teams, they realized that those girls consistently outshone the BHS cheerleaders by a mile. Elizabeth and her friends were determined to bring more glory to their team and their town. They studied the opposition and--besides the high jinks and impossible body moves-- they noticed that, when the other team won, their cheerleaders dashed onto the football field after the game, leaping about, hugging the players, and being generally perky and very cute. Tonight BelleBend High was winning; Elizabeth and her cheerleading friends had practiced different leaps manifesting thrilled joy, the euphoria of victory. Elizabeth's boyfriend, Pat, was team captain. She planned to pull off his helmet and kiss him on the lips while the crowd in the stands was still on its feet cheering.

"Is it time? Is it time?" Peggy was shifting from foot to foot, anxious.

"Not yet."

The home crowd in the stands stood up, roaring.

"Now! "Theresa shouted.

The BHS cheerleaders held hands and ran onto the field. They were excited, peppy and heady with victory. They surrounded their team players, jumping up and down, clapping their hands, tossing their ponytails.

"Good game, Pat!" Elizabeth yelled, pulling at her boyfriend's helmet.

"What the hell are you doing?"

"Good game! Good game! Yea!"

"The game's not over Elizabeth! Ya'll lost your minds?"

"What so interesting about a colored man being treated bad?" Babette put her coffee cup down and picked up her fork. "Is it that the man is colored or that the man is really a white man and ain't that a shame he had hisself such a hard time?" She scooped the whipped cream off the top of her second piece of Margaret's superb chocolate cream pie.

"So you weren't crazy about the book?"

"You want a interesting book?" Babette spoke through the whipped cream, swallowed, and wiped her mouth with the back of her hand. "White Like Me. How that be for the name of a book about a colored living good as a white man?" Margaret had given Babette a copy of Black Like Me for her birthday and now Babette was delivering her critique. "Come to think of it. Maybe that what Dr. King and all them talking about. They talking about colored ought to get to live like white. All us passing for white."

"OK, OK," Margaret pushed her empty saucer away and picked up her Chesterfields. "I should have given you The Fire Next Time."

"I read that already, Miss Margaret. My daughter give it to me for Christmas. She say everybody she know in New York done read it. None of us need no white man telling us ---"

"Mama, the forms for University of Wisconsin are still sitting on daddy's desk. Neither of you signed them." Rebecca walked into the kitchen and pulled a chair up next to Babette. "I got all the information and typed in all the blanks, all you have ---"

"Number one, you interrupted a conversation, Rebecca. Number two, we never said we'd sign anything for you to go anywhere but LSU. I thought we'd made that clear. After Emily's fiasco ---"

"But I'm not Emily. Mama!" Rebecca slammed her palm down on the kitchen table. "I make straight A's. I always have, I ---"

"We don't have the money and that's that."

"You don't have the *money*?" Rebecca was incredulous. "I did have the money, I've been saving for . . ." She didn't finish her sentence.

It was too ironic, too unfair. All she could accomplish by pointing out the obvious was to make her mother feel badly. Rebecca realized that there was no money for her college. If she were honest with herself she knew that she had never actually expected there would be. She had just hoped that with the two scholarships she'd located and the savings she had pulled together in the year and a half since she loaned her father five hundred dollars, he might be able to make up the small difference. But of course he couldn't.

Rebecca knew that her face looked calm; that all the rage and frustration she felt was bottled inside with all the other waves she had never made. She would sit at the table and let her mother get back to her conversation with Babette. Rebecca, as a rule, seldom interrupted.

"This some great pie here, Rebecca."

"It's too close to suppertime, now." Margaret took one last drag on her cigarette before she put it out. "The pie is for dessert."

Rebecca ended up going to LSU for a year, working as a part time secretary on campus and saving enough money to supplement her scholarships and get herself into the University of Wisconsin the following year. The low flame of suppressed fury over the injustice of her lost savings would glow on forever.

In March of 1966 Emily called long distance from Jackson Mississippi where she had been sharing an apartment with Virginia, and working as a bank teller. Kate answered the phone.

"Emily? Hi!" Long distance calls were rare and Kate was surprised to hear her sister's voice. "You doing OK, Emily?"

"I'm great. I'm really happy. Really."

"That's good, because ---"

"Kate, honey, go get Mama and Daddy. And ask Daddy to get on the phone first."

When Matthew took the phone receiver, with Margaret standing beside him, Emily's boyfriend, Stan Hubbard, asked Matthew for his daughter's hand in marriage. Stan had just been appointed vice-president of a new branch of the bank opening near Charlotte, North Carolina. He wanted Emily to move there with him, as his wife. They were in a hurry. He had to start his new job in less than a month.

Later that night Kate sat at the dressing table in their room while Elizabeth stood behind her setting Kate's hair on big rollers.

"I cannot wait to tell my friends." Elizabeth flattened a small mass of curls over the pink plastic. "This is so romantic!"

"What is so romantic, Elizabeth? Bank teller marries banker." Kate handed her sister two bobby pins. "Not exactly Tristan and Isolde."

"You don't think Stan's handsome?"

"I think Emily is beautiful. The two times we met him I have to say Stan reminded me of, of…. of a robot, or a windup toy soldier."

"Maybe he's like you, Kate. Maybe he's really shy and masks it by acting aloof." Elizabeth pulled a thick strand of hair between her fingers.

"I think he thinks he's too good for us country people."

"That's what people say about you."

"He's nothing like me and nothing like us." Kate fumbled for another bobby pin. "Poor Emily."

"'Poor Emily?' Mama and Daddy don't need to worry about her anymore. She's taken care of. She's going to be married to a good-looking man with a good job. She's safe."

"'Happily ever after?' Huh, Elizabeth?" Kate fastened the pin around a curl that Elizabeth had missed. "And they say you're the smartest girl in your class. God help the dumb ones."

That summer the priest at the black church asked Kate and Elizabeth if they would tutor a group of black children in preparation for school integration. The Bishop had closed down BelleBend's small black Catholic school in an effort to help force the mandated integration. The first afternoon the Sobral girls arrived at the abandoned school there were only six children in a classroom where they'd expected at least twenty.

Elizabeth looked down at the list of students that Father Hopper had given her. "I don't see the point of calling roll. Why don't ya'll just tell me your names?"

All six of the children were shy, intimidated by the white teenagers, especially the tall blonde one. There were some whispered mumbles.

"Kids, you're gonna have talk louder or we're never going to get around to telling you about Plymouth Rock and George Washington." Kate sat on the edge of the scarred teacher's desk. "Looks like you're the only fourth graders from St. Catherine's who think you'll need American history for fifth grade."

"Back a the fields," a little boy mumbled, looking down at his feet, pulling on his own shirttail.

"What are you saying Malcolm?" Elizabeth asked. "That is your name, right?" She put her hand on his shoulder, she didn't want him to be frightened and she didn't want to misunderstand his husky whisper. "Malcolm?"

"No bus go back a the fields. It summer, mam."

It turned out that the six children who appeared for summer school were all able to walk to St. Catherine's. The rest of the children lived along graveled roads far out in the country, or in the 'quarters" set behind the sugar cane fields of the plantations surrounding BelleBend.

Kate and Elizabeth turned the Sobrals' Oldsmobile station wagon into a school bus. Every weekday for the last two weeks of

June and all of July, they would jam the three smallest children between them on the front seat and let the back seat and the rear of the station wagon be a free-for-all: eleven little black children squeezing in as best they could. Elizabeth drove and Kate worked the radio, trying to yell out a music education as the station wagon swerved from the glaring, dusty country roads onto the shaded streets of BelleBend.

"OK, OK, this is 'Penny Lane.' Listen, it's from the Beatles' very best---" Or, turning the radio even louder: "Aretha Franklin, hear that, kids? See she's spelling in the song? If ya'll'd listen ya'll could all learn how to spell 'respect.'"

But mostly it was chaos in the car, fun chaos, nine and ten-year-olds pushing the electric buttons making all four car windows go up and down, Kate yelling song lyrics and trying to be louder than the children; occasionally a child would reach the button for the windshield wipers and the wipers started swishing back and forth on a perfectly sunny day while the electric windows went up and down and Elizabeth tried to steer the big car without moving her elbows. It was a hilarious sight. Sometimes a couple of cars full of Elizabeth's friends would good-naturally follow behind the Oldsmobile station wagon, honking their horns and playing their own car radios loudly, waving out their open windows down the streets of BelleBend; teasing Elizabeth and Kate, while cheering them on. The cars would pull up to St. Catherine's like floats at the end of an unplanned parade.

On the second week of that August in 1967, Matthew and Elizabeth drove Kate to the Baton Rouge Greyhound station. She was taking a two and half day bus ride to Madison, Wisconsin. She would get a job on campus and share an apartment with Rebecca and two other roommates. Rebecca had been at the University of Wisconsin for almost a year. From her first day on campus she knew that she had finally found her place. She grew her shiny dark hair long, lost her virginity, pierced her ears and wore jangling big earrings. People noticed her; she was a presence. Rebecca was elected secretary for the campus chapter of Students for a Democratic Society. Her friends were campus leaders, people who stayed up all night talking ideas and revolution. Meanwhile, Kate had finished high school without a single plan for her own future. Madison fit Rebecca perfectly the way BelleBend never had, and everyone hoped it would fit Kate too.

On the last Tuesday morning in August, Matthew walked into Jean Letter's house for coffee and found her in the living room, rather than the kitchen.

"Where's Margaret? She running late?"

"I called and told her I wouldn't be here this morning." Jean was leaned in the doorway, her arms folded, a smoking Camel between her fingers. "I won't be here tomorrow either."

"You on your way out, Jean?" Matthew was concerned. Sometimes Jean left town and got herself a motel room and drank for two or three days. It had been a few years since that had happened. "Is something the ---"

"And I'd appreciate it, Matthew, if you wouldn't park your nigger mobile in front of my house."

Matthew took two steps back, inhaled deeply, turned and walked out of the dusky formal living room, down the wide hall and through the front door of the Letter's house. He would return nine years later to offer condolences to Sam the day after Jean Letter died of emphysema.

In the fall of 1967, the Sobrals' house became a center of teen activity. Elizabeth's crowd of friends took to gathering in the living room of the River Road house where they could smoke cigarettes and talk about integration, Freedom Riders, the draft, and the war in Viet Nam. Joan Baez, Bob Dylan and The Beatles blared out on the record player. A new boy in the junior class, Randolph, often brought over his guitar and they all joined in on songs like "We Shall Over Come," "Where Have All the Flowers Gone?" and "All You Need Is Love." They felt courageous and defiant and were positive that they would brave tear gas and fire hoses for their beliefs. Elizabeth's mother recommended books and articles for them to read, which made them feel smart and worldly, part of the great wave of change taking place in America. Her father served them beer and hi-balls. While none of the new black students at BHS ever joined the teenagers at the Sobrals' house, Elizabeth and her friends talked a lot about how to involve them. They made a point of hanging out with the black students in the school halls and sitting next to them in classes.

Work resumed on the abandoned bridge over the Mississippi; a new couple, the Higgins, had moved to BelleBend he was the engineer in charge of overseeing the final bridge construction. It turned out that Camille and Christopher Higgins were also circumspect civil right advocates and they too began attending the black church. They had a son, Randolph, who was Elizabeth's age and they had rented a house less than a half-mile down the River Road from the Sobrals. Camille Higgins applied for a job at the BelleBend Bugle; although there were no available positions at the paper, Margaret was able to assign an occasional article to her. The Higgins began stopping by the Sobral house several evenings a week. Both households watched Walter Cronkite every night and subscribed to The New Yorker. There were heated discussions around the kitchen table comparing points of view on the escalating war in Viet Nam. At first Matthew had been in favor of the war, but then he changed his mind after reading "The Village of Ben Suc," an eyewitness account of the senseless invasion and bombardment of a small village printed in The New Yorker. The writer of the article, Jonathan Schell, called the war "a bloody playground for our idealism and our cruelty."

"Americans. Americans soldiers treating people that way...." Matthew was stricken wordless at the thought. It was an entirely new way of thinking about his country.

"We've come a long way from handing out Hershey bars and oranges." Margaret closed the kitchen door against the commotion coming from the young people in the front of the house.

The four adults often talked far into the night. Margaret and Matthew had not kept such late hours since their Bunkie days. If Margaret missed her old friend Jean, she never mentioned it.

One rainy afternoon in the early spring of Elizabeth's last year of high school, she happened-- by some miracle-- to catch sight of a very small puppy swirling in a current of rainwater in a ditch along the side of the River Road.

"Stop the car, Randolph!" She was pulling off her boots and socks. "Stop it right now!" She rolled up her jeans, threw open the car door, stepped out into the pouring rain and waded down into the ditch.

The puppy was frantically paddling in the muddy rush of water, trying to keep its small head above water. It was raining so hard that Elizabeth could hardly see; she kept slipping in the thick mud of the ditch bottom as she reached for the puppy. Randolph was just getting out of the car to help as Elizabeth closed her hands over a shivering mass of wiry fur not much larger than her grasp. She cupped the quietly whining puppy against her chest, oblivious to the muddy water staining her peasant blouse.

"It's all right, little one. You're OK."

The puppy stopped whining, wagged its little bit of a tail and nuzzled against her wet blouse.

"Kind of looks like a rat." Randolph turned the car heater on high for the drive to Elizabeth's house. "A drowning rat," he laughed.

"Shame on you, Randolph." Elizabeth pulled the puppy higher and tucked it under her neck, trying to warm it with her skin.

Margaret and Matthew arrived home just as Elizabeth was getting out of Randolph's car. Margaret got a clean towel and put the pup on her lap to dry it. She carefully dabbed at the little face, rubbed the towel lightly over the wiry fur and let the puppy lick her face. Elizabeth was amazed, and would become even more amazed when that night her mother made a bed for the puppy beside her own bed.

"She is the skinniest little thing," Margaret patted the towel over the puppy's sunken belly.

"Like Twiggy," Elizabeth said, referring to a famous British model, who maybe weighed about eighty pounds with her clothes on.

From her very first night in the Sobral house, Twiggy became Margaret's dog. Elizabeth might have rescued the cheerful little puppy, but it slept on the floor by Margaret's side of the bed, followed Elizabeth's fast walking mother wherever she went in the house, and tenaciously waited by the front door for her whenever Margaret was away.

On April 6, the day after Martin Luther King was murdered, Elizabeth arrived home from a tumultuous day at school to find Babette sitting alone on the living room sofa. She was wearing her trademark white apron; her hands, with their thick calloused fingers, covered her face. Her shoulders were shaking; tears ran between her fingers and over the back of hands marked by a lifetime of stove scars. The sight of that grieving woman, sitting all alone, made Elizabeth start crying too. She pushed next to Babette and put her arm around the big woman's shuddering shoulders.

"Oh, I'm so sorry, so very sorry."

Babette pulled slightly away--avoiding Elizabeth, or making room for her--she took her hands from her face and wiped them on her apron.

"I feel a fool," she stopped to catch her breath. "I feel a fool for the hope I was feeling, Elizabeth." She shook her head slowly, forsaken. "I got to leave this place. I can't live here no more." She slapped her hands on her aproned knees. "No more!" she said, slapping her knees over and over. "No more! No more!"

Chapter 12

Leaving—1980

THE MOVING TRUCK rumbles out onto the River Road. It's just us again, the survivors. Our footsteps reverberate through the empty house. Not a house, really—a hull. Rebecca is ticking off the tasks on our list. They are all done. It is time to go, but we wander around, each of us lost in her own thoughts. I am still in last night, in the terrible moment where I read the note I found hidden beneath the satin lining of our mother's green jewelry box:

> *M,*
> *"If thou must love me, let it be for nought*
> *Except for love's sake only. Do not say,*
> *"I love her for her smile—her look—her way*
> *Of speaking gently, — "*
>
> *For love's sake only,*
> *David*

The paper had been torn from a physician's prescription pad; it was discolored with age, written by Dr. Monroe sometime before the birth of the youngest Sobral, the sister named after Elizabeth Barrett Browning. What good would ever come from telling her sisters what Emily had found, David Monroe long in his grave, and now their parents too? In this story there are no unshared secrets among them, no lover or romance for their mother, their father never betrayed; and, certainly, no half sister. Elizabeth would forever remain Matthew's youngest daughter. Their mother's great secret had been torn into infinitesimal bits and scattered like dandelion floss over the predawn darkness of the Sobral's abandoned backyard.

"We have to get to the airport," says Elizabeth, standing in the middle of the emptied living room, rattling the keys to the rental car, our tall blonde sister taking quiet control of this last transition.

In single file we follow the youngest of us out of our ancestral home, across the front porch and down the curved concrete steps for the last time. The ghosts of all the dogs of childhood rustle under the house, circle, turn noses to tail and settle down to be still forever. It is so quiet; nothing goes by on the early morning River Road. It is over.

It is over, all over, the late night soul settlings, the singing of the old songs, the making of our story. We survivors of our fierce created past leave our own childhoods for our childrens'. We have put away the bygone and never been, broken up the set and scattered all the pieces: Dirge drummers knelling fading rhythms; fluid tadpoles adrift in the silent forgetfulness of the womb (that only time alone with Mama). The midnight moans of train whistles echo across sugar cane fields and the mournful call of fog-bound riverboats forever intertwined with the sweet sleep breath of sisters. Sisters ready for the pandemonium of poems served up with breakfast, the tinkle clink of Sunday dinner goodtime platters, the competition for front seat victory rides to town.

Epilogue

THE SUN WAS easing behind the hills, cooling the air on the small stone balcony above the square; a light breeze had risen. The tall silver-haired man carried out a pale blue woolen blanket and tucked it around Margaret's legs. Then he stood behind her with his hands on her shoulders and they both gazed out over the sea. The calm surface of the water was a rippled sheet of copper in the fading light as the last one of the village's small fleet of fishing boats pulled into the stony harbor. Down on the square the butcher was rolling up his awning and the grocer carrying in a final crate of oranges. The air smelled of garlic and salt, warm bread and fish. Somewhere down one of the winding cobbled streets leading from the square a mother was calling for her children.

"I never tire of watching the day give way," she paused and then laughed ruefully. "Now it has become metaphor. Promise you'll come back, Bruce, "she looked up at him. "You'll come back to this cubbyhole of an apartment and sit here at the end of the day, and remember us both looking out over the sea in our most favorite place of all. I need to know that you won't be maudlin, or ---"

"Is it?"

"Is it what?"

"Our most favorite place?" He tucked a silver-threaded curl of light brown hair behind her ear and ran his forefinger lightly over the rim of her jaw. "Better than that place on stilts beside the waterfall in Bali? Or what about the Idaho house we rented two summers in-a-row?"

The butcher locked the door of his shop and pocketed his key. He was on his way to the tavern where he would meet up with the fishermen and play cards and drink wine until his wife arrived to fetch him home. The mother had begun calling again for her children; her far away voice was unhurried, and muffled by stone. A pair of frigates skimmed the shimmering surface of the sea.

"They were wonderful, all the places." Margaret pulled the blanket up to her neck. "Well, I might re-think Denmark."

"Or at least winter in Denmark." Bruce rubbed the back of her neck.

"But remember, afterwards, there was the amazing year we spent in Provence and the novel I wrote in that vineyard cottage, the ---"

"Oh that novel," he interrupted her. "There but For Fortune, which made you a National Book Award finalist." He jostled her shoulder, as if reminding Margaret of something she'd forgotten.

"Yet this quirky little village is where I hope you come every April when I am gone. Every April, Bruce, until you are too bent and cranky to travel. You sitting at our table near the fireplace in the corner at Serratino's, or down at the harbor arguing over the price of a pail of sardines."

They were silent for a while. He kept his hands on her shoulders. In the hills behind them a church bell leisurely chimed out the hour. As though the last knell were a signal, he stepped away to get the balcony's other chair. He pushed it close and then sat down next to her.

"If only we could have a handful more years, Meg. How could, say, two more have been too much to ask?" He lifted the blanket and then smoothed it over both of them. "Imagine being able to say we'd had forty years together? Forty. Rather than merely thirty-eight." He kept his hand on her narrow thigh on top of the soft cloth.

"Why not fifty?" She laughed.

"Because we aren't greedy, my darling." He leaned over and kissed the sharp ridge of her cheekbone. "We agreed, both of us. We talked to the doctors together, and then you made your choice. Now I am keeping my part of the bargain."

"And I have no regrets," she said, folding his hand between hers and looking out to the water where the last light had raised a pale green ribbon between the sky and the sea. "Really."

"Then I will also try to have none." He took a deep breath. "What about the other choices? "

"There were others? I can't remember."

"No permanent home? The choice to live rootless these last twenty years."

"And free. Gratefully free, thanks to you, free to do the only thing I'm any good at."

"With no children?"

"No tykes to leave behind to fuss over you in your dotage?"

"Seriously."

"Oh, Bruce, they would have been on their own, poor things, like little wild animals. Or worse. I would have tried to mother them and lost my mind not being able to write. I can't imagine the damage a depressed mother would have done. Making up stories is the only thing I'm fit for. You know how even you were gone to me when I was really working, lost in the writing."

"I managed."

"You more than managed," she laughed. "The question remains, would I have managed without you? My patron."

"We could have had someone take care of them."

"Of who? Our 'children?' What would have been the point of having children then? Besides we talked this all out long ago." She kissed his hand. "A mother having babies to have babies to have babies. The going-on of it."

"So, no regrets?"

"All the places we've seen together? The unimaginable things we've been able to do." She took his hand then and spread his fingers open over her chest. "Several lifetimes. We raced camels beside the pyramids."

"And rode elephants in Zambia."

"Remember the babies, how goofy they were with their droopy trunks, tripping over them; imitating the big elephants, flopping their flaccid trunks around the tall grasses, and ---"

"And then pulling hard," Bruce interrupted, laughing. "Staggering back and coming up with nothing. Their little trunks drooping underfoot like damp beach towels. "

"And it was also in Zambia where we swam in that calm river pool perched above Victoria Falls."

"We couldn't see one another for the mist."

"Couldn't hear one another for the roar."

"The three months we spent walking and paddling, China's Three Gorges, our sleeping bags spread out over ancient temple floors."

"The amazed Chinese lifting their children to see their first 'white people, *ghosts*.'" She lifted his hand and kissed his palm. "Our adventures, Bruce, all the people and all the places you've helped."

"And all the books you've written."

It was dark now. The butcher's wife had finally led her husband home. Someone at the tavern had turned on the ancient record player and a scratchy recording of Puccini was trailing out above the water, a soprano trilling "*Donde Lieta Usci*." The breeze over the sea had stilled, leaving a scatter of stars in its wake.

"So many lifetimes in just this one. And only one misunderstanding."

"My grandfather's ring---"

"This ring," she twisted the gold band on her left finger, leaned her head against his chest.

"An almost unimaginable life away from that very first time, Margaret. The scent of sweet olive over a southern lake in the long ago."

"A dream. It's all been a dream."

Near midnight on a spring night in 1981 two teenagers sneak out of a tall abandoned house on the River Road; they step gingerly over the rotting boards of the back porch stairs. Holding hands, they leave the house and run across the weed tattered back yard. They run toward the girl's small brick house in a subdivision located on the far edge of the field behind the old house. It is a clear night, with the moon three quarters full, so they have little trouble making their way over the rutted field. The abandoned house behind them has set high and empty on its brick pillars along the River Road--its dusty cracked windows staring blankly out at the levee--for as far back as anyone can remember. The teenagers hadn't been inside the house for very long, the rot and emptiness made them uneasy; they both imagined the sound of children's voices, a woman singing off key. They put their clothes back on quickly, and heedlessly left behind a glowing cigarette that the damp spring breeze now slides into a corner where pecan leaves have heaped beneath a broken window. The same breeze fans the singed leaves into slow flames that finger creep up the cracked dry walls and tap at the high ceiling. Then the fire inches through an arched doorway, gradually finding its appetite, and begins to scurry frantically over the empty rooms, biting at the wide wooden floor boards, elbowing its way through windows and toward the outside sky. By the time the fire trucks arrive it is too late, the house has collapsed onto itself; imploded into flames and sparks and a thundercloud of smoke. The old house is gone; one more post war relic of a dying town, an atavistic way of life, given over to ashes. So many of the old River Road houses have been lost to fire this way. By morning only the curved concrete steps of the house remain; sturdy and staunch they stand, a mute testimony to vanquished dreams and untold stories.

Acknowledgements

MY MOST PROFOUND appreciation goes to Lynn Hill who brought GONER back from the dead and then performed the hard, hard work of resuscitating the novel. I also owe deep thanks to Diane Goff and Mary North, gifted writing partners for four decades, and to my beloved Rick who has always bade me: *write from the heart.* Finally, with immeasurable gratitude to, and for, my children: Paul, Gretchen and Tod—the best story of all.

CPSIA information can be obtained
at www.ICGtesting.com
Printed in the USA
LVHW041604050919
630060LV00014B/737/P

9 780999 566800